Twilight's Brightest Star

THE WINDS OF CHANGE TRILOGY
BOOK THREE

RACHEL VALENCOURT

MARMONT PUBLISHING

Cover Design—Lilly Dormishev
Editors—Ann Leslie Tuttle, Jenna O'Malley, Jodi Fodor, Amanda Collier, Cindy Roper
Chapter Image—Tattoo Style Flower @ Freepik
Section Image—Goldenborder by yodafunkyo@Pixabay
Format Designer—Dawn Baca

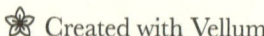 Created with Vellum

Blurb

Twilight's Brightest Star, the final chapter of the Winds of Change Trilogy, follows Starla Silverson from a small town in California to an epic global adventure, transforming her life in ways she never imagined.

After enduring the aftermath of her cousin's kidnapping and her parents' rocky reunion, Starla is determined to pursue her dreams. As a flight attendant, her job whisks her around the world, where she meets Sebastian Wylder, an enigmatic English rugby player. Their instant connection ignites a passionate romance, but old wounds resurface, challenging both their relationship and the future they have begun to build.

Years later, just when Starla believes she's found her happily ever after, a shocking secret turns her world upside down. With her mother by her side, she must confront the past and decide: will uncovering a long-buried truth bring the closure she's yearned for, or will it shatter the life she has fought so hard to create?

As secrets unravel, Starla's journey becomes a gripping exploration of love, family, and the unbreakable bonds that define us. This sweeping family saga blends heartache with hope, honoring the resilience of women across generations and leaving you questioning what it truly means to find peace and whether some truths are worth uncovering.

Dedicated to my incredible daughters,
who light up my world with endless hope.
May you move through life with strength,
chasing dreams as bright as the future you inspire.

Prologue

Starla
Forty Years Old

T he afternoon sun dipped toward the horizon, casting long golden shadows across the pavement. Amid the lively crowd of family and friends, I caught sight of Erin, weaving through the party with effortless grace, a steady beacon in the fading light.

She moved with the kind of confidence that only Erin could pull off, a blend of mystery and energy that seemed untouched by time. As she came closer, a rush of memories hit me: late nights, laughter, and all the wild plans we'd made. Erin was my oldest friend, the one who knew the dreams I'd barely admitted to myself. Standing there, she was like a piece of my past brought back to life, a reminder of the days before our paths had taken us in such different directions.

Lately, we hadn't seen each other as much as we did in our carefree youth. Yet somehow, we'd carved out spaces in our hearts for each other, picking up right where we left off every time, as if fate itself conspired to keep our bond alive. A smile tugged at my lips, rekindling memories of wild, unburdened adventures before careers and children took center stage. Her gaze met mine, a glass of wine dangling from her fingertips, and in that instant, the years between us dissolved.

"Starla, you look like you just stepped out of The Great Gatsby—if Gatsby decided to join a biker gang," Erin teased, her playful grin widening.

I chuckled, adjusting my burgundy blouse with its deep, billowing sleeves, channeling all that vintage glam. "I had these killer Art Deco shoes I was going to wear, but they were pinching my feet like crazy." I twirled, letting the light catch the buckles on my boots. "These were in the trunk—my trusty old standbys."

"Only you could pull that look off, just the right amount of rebellion and sass. And hey, they're probably better for dancing." Her eyes sparkled with amusement.

I giggled, clinking my glass against hers. "We may be getting older, but that doesn't mean we have to dress like it. We're still the Fly Girls, right?"

We used to call ourselves "The Fly Girls," a representation of our teenage dreams of becoming flight attendants and exploring far-off countries together. But that was a life-time ago. Tonight, as we gathered to celebrate Grandma Dawn's 90th birthday, laughter filled the air—a powerful reminder of the connections tying our families together.

Erin took a long sip of her rosé, her silver flapper dress sparkling with every move. The fringe swayed, accentuating her figure, while her bold red lipstick added a touch of movie star glamour.

It felt like no time had passed since we'd wandered the cobbled streets of Paris, filled with dreams and convinced that life was ours for the taking.

"This wine is incredible! Your winemaker really outdid himself," she said, flicking her hair over her shoulder as she scanned the crowd. "Where *is* that handsome hubby of yours?"

"He's been out of town at a winemaker's conference. He and Dad should be here any minute. The kids are over there singing karaoke with the cousins."

"It's great seeing everyone together. It feels like old times." She squeezed my hand, flashing that million-watt smile that always turned heads back in high school.

"It really does. Too bad Aunt Talie couldn't make it. She would've loved this."

Erin nodded, a shadow of sadness crossing her face. "Yes, she's enjoying life back on the reservation. She misses these gatherings but sends her love. Her doctor doesn't want her flying ever since they discovered that heart condition."

"I'm sorry to hear that. I hope she doesn't have any more problems with it. How old is she now?"

"No one really knows. Must be close to your grandma's age. Their generation is so secretive, and Gram Talie is keeping her lips sealed." Erin turned to me, curiosity glimmering in her deep brown eyes. "So, what's going on with you? You've got that look you have when you've got news."

I took a deep breath, anticipation pulsing within. "You know me too well. I *do* have something I want to tell you."

"Okay, spill it. I'm all ears."

Moments later, we found ourselves standing outside my SUV. I popped open the hatchback, revealing an old box, yellowed with age and smelling slightly musty.

"Does this look familiar?" I asked, my voice hardly a whisper as I gestured to the weathered box. I'd placed it in the trunk earlier and was excited to finally talk to someone about it.

Her eyes widened in recognition. "Is that the box my mom gave your grandma the day we moved to Harvard Street?"

"It sure is," I confirmed.

"What's in it?" Erin asked, her fingers fidgeting with the box's corner. "And why do *you* have it?"

I lifted the lid, revealing a jumble of old letters, journals, and photographs. "Remember that book Grandma Dawn always talked about writing? Well, I guess she thinks I'm an author now."

Erin's expression lit up with joy. "Oh, Star, it's going to

be incredible. I've always thought you should do more with your writing—I've read every one of your blog posts, you know. I'm *The Winemaker's Wife's* biggest fan." She held up my grandma's old WWII pin-up photo. "I wonder how many girls felt they had to do this type of photo, to keep the boys abroad happy? She sure was a beauty, though."

"She sure was. It's not so different from the girls today doing those boudoir shoots or posting their whole lives on Instagram."

"I suppose you're right. Now, tell me more about this book." Erin placed the old photograph back in the box.

"I guess I'm the new keeper of memories." I ran a hand through my honey-blonde hair.

Grandma Dawn's voice cut through the air, as if she were speaking into a karaoke microphone, interrupting our conversation with its commanding tone.

"We'd better get back to the party. Sounds like Gram is gearing up for her speech, and trust me, there'll be hell to pay if she notices we're missing." I clicked the alarm on my SUV.

The bustling chaos enveloped us again as Grandma Dawn, standing proudly at five-foot-two, commanded the backyard's attention. Her vibrant red hair was expertly styled into a high pile, and those large gray eyes sparkled warmly. Her welcoming smile lit up the space, and her distinctive Jensen nose—slightly oversized for her round face—only added to her charm. With a clear, raspy voice, she captivated the crowd, drawing them in with the promise of her words.

"If you could all lend me your ears for a moment," she called out, her voice husky and strong despite her ninety years. The backyard fell into an expectant hush.

"I want to thank everyone for being here tonight. Celebrating this milestone is quite the occasion, and there's nowhere else I'd rather be." She eyed the crowd. "Life is a marvelous party, and I am so blessed to have all of you as my guests. Here's to love, family, and another year of adventures."

With that, she raised her glass high, prompting a chorus of cheers and clinks as everyone joined her in a toast. Suddenly, Andrea, a bright-eyed girl with dark braids, tugged at Great-Grandma Dawn's hem.

"Will you tell everyone about when you met the president?" she asked, bouncing on her toes, her enthusiasm evident.

Grandma smiled broadly and gestured for the children to come closer. "Now *that* was a day to remember," she began, her voice brimming with affection as the crowd quieted. "The whole reservation was buzzing with anticipation. President Roosevelt and his wife were visiting, and oh, how we all spruced up. Mama curled my hair into ringlets, and I wore my Sunday best."

Even though I'd heard this story many times, I listened with rapt attention. Erin and I exchanged a glance, silently agreeing to cherish these moments.

"Before the president arrived, we had been preparing a time capsule to bury on the Makah Reservation, way up in Neah Bay. When no one was looking, I slipped in my favorite Raggedy Ann doll—my prized possession. I wanted the children of the future to see it when the time came to open the capsule," she continued.

Chuckles rippled through the crowd, and the children's eyes widened with delight.

As Grandma Dawn immersed herself in the memory of meeting such an influential figure, a profound realization washed over me. Her stories transcended mere recollections; they intertwined with the fabric of our family legacy, whispering of a belonging to something far grander than ourselves.

"Now, let's get this party started with some more dancing!" Grandma Dawn sat the mic back in its stand and motioned for everyone to join her on the makeshift dance floor.

I couldn't help but be swept up in the sentiment of Grandma Dawn's words. Her tales from her youth always sparked memories of my own childhood. One memory, in particular, came rushing back—the day Erin moved in. It set off a domino effect, knocking over the rest of our lives and shaping everything that followed.

"As if sensing my thoughts, Erin leaned in and said, 'Remember the day we moved in next door?'"

"How could I forget? We spent hours trying to build a tree house with scraps of wood and old moving boxes, only to end up on your porch swing, dreaming of traveling the world together."

Just the mention of that day pulled me back in time, wrapping me in a cocoon of nostalgia. Memories swirled around me, warm and inviting, as if the echoes of laughter and whispered dreams had never faded. It was a beautiful beginning, setting us on a path we'd walk together, filled with both the mundane and the extraordinary. Our bond forever woven into the fabric of time.

PART ONE
Starla Silverson

"Sometimes when you're growing up, everything around you seems so big and daunting. You feel like you'll never find your place in the world, but it's just part of the process of finding your own identity."

— *Markus Zusak, "The Book Thief"*

One Day

MONTCLAIR, CALIFORNIA

SUMMER, 1990

Starla Silverson
Thirteen Years Old

T he familiar scent of scones rising in the oven surrounded me, mingling with memories of countless mornings spent in this very spot. Grandma Dawn moved with her usual grace, hands dusted in flour as she carefully shaped each scone, her motions as practiced and gentle as a lullaby. In her kitchen, there was always something delightful baking—cookies, pies, or her legendary Pig 'n' Whistle cake—each treat a delicious testament to her boundless love.

"Are you sure Erin's even going to remember me?" I asked, leaning against the counter, as I fiddled with my turquoise bracelet. Grandma Dawn shot a knowing smile at me, her hands busy working the dough.

"How could she forget you? It's been a few years, but don't forget the connection you shared was special. Besides, you're unforgettable," she added with a wink.

Her words helped settle my nerves a bit. "I hope you're right. I don't wanna mess this up."

"You won't, lovebug. Let's get these scones next door."

I grabbed the basket, and together, we made our way over as a blue station wagon pulled up, trailer in tow. My heart thumped when it came to a stop. It felt strange to think my childhood friend would be living right next door.

As the car doors swung open, I spotted her right away—Erin Shaw. Those messy, dark curls, that same sparkle in her eyes. She was taller and a bit older, but it was definitely her. I swallowed hard, unsure of what to say.

"Welcome to the neighborhood," Grandma Dawn called, waving as we walked up. Erin's mom, Tammy, gave Grandma a tired but warm smile.

"Aunty Dawn! It's been too long," she said, pulling Grandma into a long hug. Then, she turned to me. "And look at you, Starla! You've grown so much. Do you remember Erin?"

Before I could respond, Erin stepped forward, her grin bright but tinged with the kind of awkwardness teenagers sometimes have when they haven't seen you in a while. "Hey, Starla. Of course, I remember you."

I let out a breath I didn't realize I was holding. "Welcome to the neighborhood. It's been, like, forever." I glanced at the movers behind them. "You guys must be exhausted and hungry. We brought scones."

"Freshly baked scones, with clotted cream and apricot preserves from my garden," Grandma chimed in, handing over the basket we carefully arranged.

Erin's mom smiled. "Oh, thank you. Mom always said you loved to bake. Would you like to come in for a bit? We could use a break." She looked back at the movers, who were unloading boxes.

We followed them inside, and soon enough, Erin and I were left alone, awkwardly hovering in the kitchen while the women caught up.

"So," I said, slipping my hands into my pockets, "feel like checking out the backyard?"

Erin looked down, scuffing her shoe on the floor. "Yeah, sure. Anything to get away from all these boxes."

Outside, the backyard looked wild and overgrown, like it hadn't been touched in years. The perfect escape. We wandered to a rusty set of monkey bars that had seen better days.

"You ever sit on top of these?" I asked, pointing at the bars.

Erin's eyes lit up. "All the time at my old place. You want to?"

"Why not?"

We climbed up, our hands gripping the cool metal as we hauled ourselves to the top. Perched up there, everything felt different, like the rest of the world was far away with the two of us looking down on it.

Sitting cross-legged on the bars, I glanced over at Erin. "Remember when we used to climb these things and pretend they were castles?"

Erin laughed, a little breathless. "We sure had wild imaginations back then. It feels like forever ago."

I leaned back, propping my elbows on the bars behind me. "I guess things change. How're you liking California so far?"

Erin looked out across the yard, her smile fading slightly. "This is the last place I thought I'd end up. I had to leave all my friends behind in Washington."

I glanced at her, feeling a pang of sympathy. "That sounds rough, but I'm glad you're here. You already have one friend. Me!"

She smiled a little lighter this time. "You're probably right. At least I'll know one person at school on Monday."

We sat there in silence for a bit, the breeze gently rustling the leaves of the pepper tree nearby.

"So, what's been going on with you?" Erin asked, breaking the quiet.

"Not much. School, family stuff, trying to figure out life, I guess." I paused. "What about you?"

She sighed. "It's been weird. Everything's changed so much. My parents splitting up, moving here."

I nodded as the weight of her words settled between us. "That's a lot."

Erin laughed softly, the sound hollow. "That's one way to put it."

We stayed on top of the monkey bars a while longer, talking about everything and nothing, relating to each other in the way children from broken homes often do.

"Are you girls all right out there?" Erin's mom shouted from the kitchen window. "Do you want to come in for some scones?"

"We'll be right in, Mom," Erin called back.

We climbed down from the old monkey bars when the roar of an airplane caught our attention. We both turned, gazing up through the branches of the old oak tree at the jet slicing across the sky, leaving a thin trail of white behind it.

"Where do you think they're going?" Erin asked, her voice soft but curious, as her eyes tracked the fading jet stream. Her face had a distant look again, like she was imagining herself up there.

"Probably Ontario Airport. It's close by," I said, squinting up at the shrinking plane. "I bet they're coming in from somewhere amazing. Europe, maybe? I wonder what it's like to see the world from way up there, looking down on everything. I bet the people inside don't even think about how small it all looks." My words faded as the thought of escaping washed over me, carrying me far beyond the ground beneath my feet.

Erin sighed. "I've never even been on a plane."

"I went once," I said, trying not to sound like a showoff. "Mom took me to Reno for one of Dad's motocross competitions. I don't remember it much, but I do remember the flight attendant was so glamorous. She took me up to the cockpit to meet the captain. She even told me about her job, and how when she was little there weren't a lot of career opportunities for young women to travel."

Erin's eyes widened, like I thought they would. "What? That's so cool! Did she have a uniform and everything?"

"Yep. Navy blue with stripes on the sleeves. She had this little scarf tied around her neck, too, like the kind you see in those old movies. I remember feeling important. I was just a little kid." I laughed at myself. "I guess everyone remembers their first trip on a plane."

Erin's gaze stayed fixed on the sky, her voice quieter. "That sounds like the best thing ever. Traveling all over the world, seeing different places. You think I could do something like that?"

"Why not?" I said, my excitement building. "We could *both* be flight attendants! Travel for free, meet famous people, see everything. I can see us jet-setting across the world."

Her face lit up like a light bulb. She laughed, a little too loud, but it felt good. "Yes. We'd meet celebrities, maybe even fall in love with one. Can you imagine?"

"Yeah, mom wants me to be an author. But becoming a flight attendant? That sounds even better. I've always wanted to see Big Ben. Maybe, I could write books about our adventures."

"Big Ben?" Erin tilted her head, a half-smile forming. "What's that?"

"That huge clock tower in London. You've seen *Peter Pan*, right?"

"Of course. Grandma Talie sewed me a dress just like Wendy Darling. I wonder what happened to it." She laughed, but I could see a flicker of something behind her eyes, the kind of longing that comes with outgrowing things, people, and places.

My stomach growled, loud enough to break the silence. "Let's go inside and get some scones. I'm starving," Erin suggested, grinning.

"You're going to love these. They are a hundred-year-old recipe from my English great grandma. Wait until you try our Pig 'n' Whistle. It's divine."

"Wait—why is it called that? Is there pork in it or something?"

My laughter turned into a snort, and then I froze, mortified. Erin stared at me for a second before bursting into laughter.

"Did you just—snort?" she gasped between giggles, and soon we were both doubled over, laughing so hard we could barely breathe. My face burned, but I didn't care. Our hysterical laughter made me feel like we were little kids again. Maybe things hadn't changed so much after all.

"Nobody knows how it got the name, but there's no pork or meat in it. Don't worry," I reassured her.

A few moments later, we gathered around the kitchen

table, the scent of freshly warmed scones wafting through the air, warm and inviting. The buttery aroma mixed with the sweet notes of sultanas and raisins, creating a cozy embrace.

Tammy had heated the scones in her oven, and they looked perfect on the fancy plates she set out. I watched Erin pick out the raisins, one by one, and a twinge of disappointment crept over me.

"You don't like raisins?" I asked, hoping for a different answer. She shrugged. "Not really. Sorry, the rest of it's great, though."

I bit my lip, feeling a bit silly for getting so worked up. I hated thinking we'd gone through all that effort only for Erin not to enjoy them. "Next time, we'll use a different ingredient—maybe blueberries or cranberries, whatever you like."

"Don't stress it," Erin said. "It's the thought that counts. I love the apricot jam. That more than makes up for the raisins."

I smiled, feeling a little better as we finished eating, licking the last sticky crumbs from our fingers. The comfort of the moment filled the room, but a heavy atmosphere followed when Erin's mom made an announcement.

"I've got something for you in the car," she said to Grandma Dawn, getting up quickly. A few moments later, she returned with a weathered box in her hands and placed it on the table. "Mom wanted you to have this." She set it in front of Grandma Dawn.

The room seemed to be still for a moment, and her smile faltered a bit before she nodded.

"Thank you, Tammy," Grandma said, her voice thick with something I couldn't place. "I'll look through it. Later tonight."

Erin and I exchanged glances, curiosity sparking between us. I asked, "Can we see what's inside?"

Grandma shook her head, her grip on the box tightened. "Not now, lovebug. I need to look through it first. Even us old ladies like to have our secrets."

The mood shifted, the air thickening with a tension that left me feeling confused. It was like something important hovered beneath the surface, a truth, waiting to break free but trapped in silence.

"Why don't you girls clear the dishes?" Grandma said, her voice gentler, but her eyes stayed on that box. "Tammy has had a long drive today."

"Yes, ma'am," Erin and I mumbled together, but we both knew the real conversation happened without us.

As we washed up, Erin leaned in, her voice barely a whisper. "I wonder what's in that box."

"Me, too," I whispered back, my eyes flicking over to Grandma, who was deep in conversation with Tammy, her hands resting protectively on the box.

The hours slipped by and we soon found ourselves on the porch swing. The air cooler, the sky a soft pink as the sun dipped lower.

"I'm glad you're here," Erin said, her words barely

audible over the gentle creak of the swing. "This whole divorce thing sucks but leaving all my friends, that's been the hardest part. I hope you never have to go through that."

She stared out into the distance, the weight of her emotions palpable between us. I looked at her, feeling the burden of my own past. "I do know what it's like. My parents split for a while, and my mom dragged me off to Hollywood. She got this fancy job doing hair on a soap opera and had a boyfriend—some jerk from high school who always wore snakeskin boots. What a poser. It was a mess. Then my cousin was kidnapped, and somehow, that brought my parents back together."

"That's so scary. I remember hearing about that. Grandma Talie started this prayer chain, we were so relieved when she was found alive."

"Lacey is okay now. Well, she's not quite her old self yet, but she's still with us, and my parents got back together. They realized how much they needed each other, and they've been trying to make it up to me ever since." I paused.

"I'm sorry you went through that. I guess nobody really gets their happily ever after. Let's promise not to end up like them, creating problems for ourselves. We've got each other now, and we've got a dream, too. One day, we'll be traveling the world together."

"One day," I replied.

For a moment, it felt like the world held its breath. Erin kicked her legs, making the swing sway.

"We'll get to make our own choices," she continued, her voice teeming with determination. "No one's going to tell us what to do or where to go."

"Yeah," I echoed, feeling that spark rise inside me again. "And when that day comes, we'll go wherever we want. No rules. Just us."

Erin smiled a little wider, her eyes meeting mine. "Promise?"

I wrapped my pinky around hers. "We'll take on the whole world."

In that moment, I believed every word.

CHAPTER 2

Girls Just Want to Have Fun

MONTCLAIR, CALIFORNIA

FALL, 1990

Starla Silverson
Fourteen Years Old

L acey's laughter echoed through the living room like a breath of fresh air. Her platinum-blonde ponytail whipped around as she jingled her car keys. "You girls ready to roll?"

"Absolutely," Erin and I echoed her excitement. Erin had been my shadow since she moved next door, becoming like a sister I never had. Even though she was a grade ahead of me at Montclair High, we were an inseparable constant in a world that seemed to shift with every passing day.

I grabbed my jean jacket and turned to Lacey, disbelief washing over me. "I can't believe Mom's letting you drive us to the rink. She's been so overprotective lately." My mind drifted back to the incident that changed all of our lives.

The memory of that spring break still haunted me— Lacey pale and shaken in that hospital bed. Now, as she fought to rebuild her life, I couldn't help but think of the nightmare she faced and how it impacted us all.

But now, sitting in my living room, Lacey looked like a different person. Her eyes still held a hint of that haunted look, yet a flicker of her former confidence crept back like dawn after a long night. She was determined to reclaim her life, refusing to let the past define her.

I was so proud when she managed to graduate from high school and began regaining control of her life, slowly but surely. "Hey, don't worry about me. I've got this. It's been a lot, but I'm finally feeling like myself again," she'd said tightly, gripping the wheel. This was the first time we were going somewhere without adults.

"That's great, Lace. Maybe you'll be able to go to college soon?" I encouraged. It was hard to believe it had only been six months since the incident.

"We'll see. My parents couldn't leave Hollywood fast enough after the incident, so I didn't get a chance to register. Something about escaping the big, bad city. I haven't checked out colleges around here yet. Maybe you could help me figure it out?"

"I'd love to. You know, I'm glad you guys moved closer. It's nice having more family around. Are you still thinking about majoring in psychology?"

"Yeah, my therapist is amazing. I want to be more like that. Pay it forward, you know? Help people like they helped me."

Lacey had a heart of gold. Everyone seemed to hold their breath, waiting for her next move. Before the abduction, being with her felt like glimpsing the person I wanted to be—beautiful, confident, and peppy. It warmed my heart to see her finding her way back to that girl she once was.

As we climbed into the back seat of Lacey's cherry red VW, the lively beat of Cyndi Lauper filled the air. The crisp fall breeze whipped through the open windows, carrying with it the promise of a joyful night ahead. Skating, root beer floats, and maybe even flirting with some boys at the local rink. Erin shot me a grin, and I could see the excitement reflected in her eyes too.

"You think Brandon will be there?" Erin asked, her words laced with amusement.

"Brandon who?" Lacey glanced at us through the rearview mirror.

"Only the cutest boy in ninth grade," Erin replied with a giggle.

"All the girls are totally obsessed with him." I twirled a lock of my hair, attempting to play it cool. Deep down, I knew I'd be scribbling his name surrounded by hearts and doodles later. It was my thing—writing down all my thoughts and dreams in my trusty journal.

Lacey smiled at me. "So, what about you? Are you into him, too?"

"I mean, maybe? But he doesn't even know I exist."

"Oh, come on. That can't be true! You know he's noticed you, too. Don't sell yourself short," Erin advised.

As we pulled up to the roller rink, neon lights flashed red, blue, and green, casting colorful reflections over the crowd lining up outside. My stomach tightened with a familiar mix of nerves and anticipation. The night stretched ahead, full of possibilities, and I couldn't wait to lace up my skates.

Inside, the rink buzzed with music and laughter, the steady hum of skates rolling against the polished wood floor providing a rhythmic backdrop to the evening's excitement. The scent of buttery popcorn wafted through the air, mingling with the faint aroma of leather from my rental skates.

The less confident skaters clung to the outer rim, hands grazing the wall like it was the only thing keeping them upright. The cool kids dominated the center, spinning under the disco ball as if they'd been born with wheels on their feet. I watched them, feeling a little thrill of hope rising in me, wondering if I could ever belong there too.

Would I ever belong in that circle?

"You ready?" Erin asked as she elbowed me. She was always so sure of herself. I nodded, even though I wasn't, but I didn't want her to know.

As we rolled onto the rink, I stuck close to Erin, letting her confidence guide me. Lacey was something else altogether, gliding across the rink like she owned it. Graceful and effortless, she was mesmerizing.

"We need to be more like that." I motioned toward Lacey as she spun effortlessly under the lights.

"You're right. Let's get her to teach us how to skate backward. Come on!"

Erin pulled me forward, and soon, I found my balance. As the cool air whirled past, an exhilarating rush of freedom engulfed me. For a moment, I forgot about trying to fit in or worrying about what anyone else thought, and I started to believe that maybe I could look as natural as my cousin.

As I attempted my first spin, a boy in ripped acid-washed jeans crashed into me, sending me sprawling across the slick floor. I quickly tried to regain my footing and shot him an annoyed glare, but he seemed unfazed and offered his hand. "Want to skate with me?"

"Sure," I replied, my anger softening into something closer to flattery. Wow, I thought, skate couples with him? Erin would be impressed—I'd actually caught the interest of an older boy.

He executed a perfect spin in front of me, showing off his moves. "I'm Jarrod."

"Star," I replied.

"Who are you here with tonight?" he asked, running a hand through his spiked blond hair.

"My cousin and my neighbor."

"That's fun. Do you live around here?" He shifted on his skates nervously.

I looked for Lacey as unease began to grow in my stomach. Why was he asking so many questions? Something felt off about my new friend.

"Yes, why do you ask?" I replied.

"How old do you think I am?" he ignored my question, and a troublesome smile spread across his ruddy skin.

I laughed nervously. "I don't know, fifteen?"

He threw his head back and cackled. "Nope, I'm eighteen. People always think I'm younger."

The word 'eighteen' clanged in my head like an alarm. Eighteen. That's an adult. I shifted on my skates, trying to steady myself, feeling small and out of place.

As Jarrod leaned in closer, I caught a whiff of his cologne—sharp, like cheap pine mixed with something metallic. My stomach twisted. His grip tightened around my hand, just enough to make my skin prickle, and I had to fight the urge to pull away. Every instinct told me to step back, but my feet felt frozen in my skates.

"Come on, we can still skate together. What's the harm?"

"I—I don't know," I stammered, my gaze dropping to my skates. I felt clumsy and trapped. "I just turned fourteen. I don't think I should be skating with you."

His hand was still hovering between us, waiting. He finally said with a syrupy tone, "Don't be shy. You're a cute kid. Just one skate, and then you can run back to your little friends."

I felt my heart thumping in my chest as I looked for

Lacey. She would know how to handle Jarrod. Something about the way he said 'little friends' made me flinch. My breath caught, and I didn't know how to say no or how to make him stop without causing a scene.

When I caught sight of Lacey out of the corner of my eye, she was gliding through the crowd, her skates smooth and fast, her eyes locked onto us with a fierce, unwavering intensity. She wasn't smiling. Her gaze was sharp, cutting right through him, and I felt my breath begin to steady, the tight band around my chest slowly loosening.

Still, Jarrod kept pushing. "Let's go. Unless you're afraid?"

My heart pounded harder, and my palms grew damp as I turned my gaze back to Lacey, who was getting closer. Erin wasn't far behind. I swallowed and tried to steady my voice. "I'm not scared."

The boy's smile grew, but it didn't reach his eyes. His grip was tight enough to make my wrist ache. "Stop being such a baby."

That word stung, sinking into me like a thorn. I opened my mouth to say something, anything, but before I could, Lacey skated up to us, sliding between him and me, like a protective barrier. "Is there a problem here?"

The boy's smirk faltered, and he finally let go of my wrist. "Chill out. We were just going to skate."

Lacey didn't move as she stared him down. Her voice didn't waver, not once. "Find someone else. She's too young for you."

The boy rolled his eyes and skated off, muttering under his breath. I didn't care. My legs were still shaky, a knot tightening in my stomach, but Lacey was with me. Somehow, that made everything okay.

I glanced back just in time to catch the look on Jarrod's face—defeated, his shoulders slumping in his too-baggy Guess jeans.

"I didn't think he was *that* much older than me."

"I can't believe he's that old. He looks our age," Erin chimed in.

"What a weird guy, and he's still watching us. We need to call Aunt Twyla," Lacey explained gently but firmly.

"Ugh, please don't. Mom overreacts with stuff like this ever since…well, you know. Do we have to call her?"

Erin draped a comforting arm around me. "Lacey's right. That kid creeped me out too. Better to be safe. There's a pay phone by the entrance."

Lacey hesitated, her eyes flicking between us. "Starla, you don't have to handle everything on your own, you know? It's okay to ask for help."

After she ended the call, Lacey turned to us. "Your dad's on his way. Aunt Twyla said to get a Coke and wait at the snack bar until he gets here."

Even though I'd objected to calling my parents, I did feel better knowing Dad was on his way.

He must have dropped everything and raced straight over to the skating rink because moments later, I saw his unmistakable silhouette filling the doorway. His tall, broad frame stood rigid, shoulders squared like he was bracing for something. The neon lights from the rink flickered over him, catching the strands of his shoulder-length hair, which recently began to thin on top. But it wasn't his posture or his hair that held my focus—it was his hands. Those massive hands, the ones that used to hoist me onto his shoulders with ease, were clenched into tight fists at his sides.

"Hey, girls. Everything okay?" Concern reflecting in his eyes.

"You didn't have to come, Dad. We took care of it," I said, wrapping my arms around him in a hug. Dad was only twenty when I was born, and he looked so much younger and stronger than the other dads. To me, he was the most powerful man in the world—a former motocross legend with countless wins under his belt.

"Of course, I had to come, kiddo. That's what dads are for. Enjoy the rest of the night, I'll be close by, okay? First, I want you to point out this guy to me, so I can keep an eye on him."

My stomach twisted as I spotted Jarrod at the Pac-Man machine. The last thing I wanted was a scene, but seeing Dad's steady presence gave me a strange mix of relief and something else—something a little like impatience. I knew he would always be there, but didn't he realize it was time for me to learn to be there for myself?

I skated back to the rink, my heart racing as I caught sight of Dad out of the corner of my eye, walking toward the arcade. A part of me wanted to run over and pull him back, keep him from confronting Jarrod, keep him from being so protective. And yet, I had to admit, I felt safer with him there.

Suddenly, there was a commotion near the arcade. I heard Dad raising his voice and saw his chest puffing out, fists clenched.

"What's your deal, asking a fourteen-year-old to skate with you? You freaked her and her friends out."

"I'm sorry, sir. I didn't mean anything by it. I was showing off for the older girl she's with," Jarrod stammered, sounding terrified.

Dad didn't back down. "It's not okay to approach young girls like that. Make better choices next time, young man."

Jarrod tilted his head, sheepishly. "Yes, sir. It won't happen again."

Dad caught my eye and gave me a thumbs up, his face softened, and he flexed his right fist one last time before letting it relax.

Just then, the DJ's voice crackled over the loudspeaker, announcing it was time for the final song. As the neon lights dimmed, the haunting beat of "In the Air Tonight" echoed through the rink. The energy shifted as couples skated close together, caught in the moody rhythm. Erin, Lacey, and I stayed side by side, gliding along as the song pulsed in the background. The night was winding down, but under the fading disco lights, with music filling the air, it felt like a moment we'd never forget.

As we stepped out of the roller rink, a blast of cold night

air hit my face, and I heard the distant sounds of young people chatting and laughing from across the parking lot. Everyone who was anyone usually went to In-N-Out after skating. The smell of fries and burgers wafted over, making my stomach rumble.

"Dad, can we get a burger before we leave? Everyone else is going." I glanced hopefully at the line of kids already piling inside for a late-night treat.

"Sure thing, kiddo. I'll walk you to Lacey's car. You're welcome to go through the drive-through, but head right home with your food. I'll make sure no one's following you out of the parking lot. There's something else here I need to take care of."

"Don't hurt him, Dad, you already scared the daylights out of him."

"I want to let him know I have my eye on him."

The car smelled like salt and grease, the red and white bags carrying our burgers radiating warmth onto my lap as we drove home, everyone talking nonstop in an unspoken attempt to lift my spirits. Lacey, true to form, kept it upbeat. "You guys killed it out there tonight. And Star, don't even worry about your dad yelling at Jarrod. He had it coming—you were just being nice, but always, always trust your gut."

Her words made me feel a little better, but my brain was still swirling with everything that happened.

"I just don't want everyone at school gossiping about my family." I leaned back in my leather bucket seat. It was bad enough that there were rumors going around about Lacey's kidnapping; now we'd be the center of attention yet again.

"Look, there's Brandon." Erin practically launched herself out of the window of Lacey's VW. "Hey, Brandon! What're you up to tonight?"

Brandon turned, grinning when he saw us. "Hey, ladies. I was at the high school football game with my brother. Sorry I missed you, but I'll catch you at school?"

Lacey giggled, her eyes sparkling as she glanced over at him. "Maybe we'll see you on Monday."

Moments later, we pulled into the driveway of our little bungalow. I let out a huge sigh of relief. It felt good to be home. I glanced at Erin and Lacey, my heart feeling lighter. Sure, tonight got a little intense, but I wasn't going to let it mess everything up. If anything, things like this just made us closer, like we were this tight little girl gang.

The screen door creaked as we pushed it open, the sound breaking the quiet night. The familiar scent of home, Mom's lavender candles and freshly polished wood floors, wrapped around me like a warm hug.

Mom sat at the kitchen table, her face softened by the dim light, offering us a tired smile. Dressed in her favorite animal print pajamas, the fuzzy fabric draped comfortably over her toned frame. Her platinum-blonde hair framed her face in relaxed waves. The crow's feet around her green eyes deepened as she smiled. Mom taught songwriting classes at the local college part-time and seemed to be correcting some of her students' work. "How was the skating?"

"It was great! We grabbed burgers on the way back," I replied, forcing my voice to stay steady. The nerves still churned beneath the surface. If Mom caught on that I was scared, she might not let me go back without her.

"You did the right thing by calling home. Trust your instincts, okay? If something feels off, call me or come right home," she said, ruffling my hair like I was still a kid.

"Yes, Mom. I will." I rolled my eyes at her little speech. I loved my mom, but she could be a bit overactive at times.

"I'm heading to bed. Don't stay up too late. I'm proud of you, lovebug." She pulled me in for a gentle hug before heading to her bedroom.

"Okay, so, are we ready to see Brandon at school on Monday? He was totally flirting in the drive-through line." Erin remarked.

I giggled, shaking my head. "I can't believe you practically flung yourself out the window."

Erin threw a fry at me. "Whatever. He loved it, and you know it."

We all burst out laughing, the earlier tension fading away. Everything was back to normal.

"Let's put on a movie," Lacey suggested, grabbing a VHS tape from the shelf. "How about *The Breakfast Club*?"

"Perfect," Erin and I chimed in together.

We slipped the tape into the VCR and heard the soft hum of the machine as we nestled into a cozy pile of blankets and pillows on the living room floor. The familiar scenes of our favorite movie surrounded us. We giggled at the funny parts, gasped at the tense moments, and shared a timeless bond.

When the moment came up where Claire puts on her lipstick using her bra, Erin and Lacey exchanged grins.

Lacey reached for her purse and fumbled around inside, "I bet I could."

"Me too, I wanna try."

We all giggled as we took turns trying to push the lipstick tube up with our bras. We laughed so hard, and by the time the movie ended, it felt like none of that business with Jarrod mattered.

I was drifting off, nestled in our cozy pile of blankets, that perfect mix of warmth and sleep pulling me under. BRRRIIING! The phone blared through the silence, yanking me awake. My heart pounded as Mom stepped into the doorway, her face tightening as she listened, then catching my eye with a tense whisper, "Go wake your dad."

"Mom? What's going on?" I asked, as a chill settled in my stomach.

Mom turned to me, her face pale, her eyes wide with a mix of shock and concern. "It's Aunt Susan. There's been another kidnapping."

CHAPTER 3

Policy of Truth

MONTCLAIR, CALIFORNIA
FALL, 1990

Starla Silverson
Fourteen Years Old

T he temperature seemed to drop around us. Erin and Lacey exchanged worried glances.

"Another kidnapping?" Lacey whispered, her voice barely audible, the color drained from her face. "Is the girl alive?"

"A fourteen-year-old girl named Yvette Wilson and her sister. The sister didn't make it." Mom gripped the phone tighter. "But this time, they caught him. He's in custody in San Diego. He kidnapped them from Pacific Beach."

A chill raced down my spine. The man who hurt Lacey had killed someone else and had finally been caught.

Silence enveloped the room, the weight of the news

crashing down like a thousand bricks. Erin reached for my hand, squeezing it as if clinging to a lifeline. Lacey looked utterly overwhelmed. The girl who passed away—that could have been her.

"I'm coming over," Aunt Susan's voice crackled through the phone, each word sharp and urgent.

"We'll see you soon," Mom replied before gently hanging up the receiver.

We'd been longing for the day this man would be caught and locked away, but not like this. Now that it was here, fear twisted in my gut.

What if Lacey had to confront him in court?

"I'll be fine," Lacey seemed to read my mind, her voice steady but distant. "I need to see him locked up. Then I can really move on from this. I just feel so bad for that other girl."

"Lace, are you sure you're up for this?" I asked, almost afraid of her answer. I didn't want her to go. I didn't want her to relive that nightmare. I didn't want to think of that other girl.

"I'm sure," Lacey replied, meeting my eyes. "I'm not letting him get away with this again. He needs to be locked up forever."

A short time later, there was a loud knock on the door. Aunt Susan had arrived, her face tight with worry as she stepped inside. "Lacey, the police will be waiting for us in the morning, we don't have to go now. We'll go when we wake up, your father will drive us. Everything is going to be okay." She wrapped my cousin in huge hug.

Lacey dipped her head, pulling away from Aunt Susan, her face resolute. "I'm ready."

"I'm coming too, we are in this together." Mom ran a hand through her thick hair.

"Do you want me to drive you?" Dad jumped in, his tone steady, but I could sense the tension beneath.

"No, you stay here with Star. Susan and I can handle this," Mom replied, her voice firm but strained.

The house was suddenly alive with tension, everyone moving with purpose but saying very little. I could feel the weight of what was coming, the inevitable confrontation Lacey would face.

As I glanced at my beautiful cousin, my chest tightened. Once vibrant and full of ambition, Lacey now seemed adrift, her spark dimmed by fear once again. *What if seeing him again broke her all over again?*

"I love you, Lace," I said.

"Don't worry, Star," she replied. "I'll be okay."

"Let's go home. We'll come back in the morning to get you, sis. We can ride down to the police station together." Susan gave Mom a hug goodbye.

As the door closed behind Aunt Susan and Lacey, a cold dread settled in my stomach. I stood frozen in the kitchen, an unsettling feeling gnawing at me, whispering that something bigger lurked just out of sight.

My heart raced. I tried to focus on the mundane sounds.

The ticking clock, the hum of the refrigerator, but the tightness in my chest grew, squeezing like a vise.

"Dad?" I called, my voice shaking as I stumbled onto the sofa.

"Hey, Star, you okay?" Mom rushed over, sensing my unease.

"No, I don't feel good," I cried, the room spinning around me. The walls felt like they were closing in, and panic ignited in my veins. "I think I need to go to the ER."

Dad stood up, his expression shifting. "Star, listen to me. You're having a panic attack. I've read about this." He approached slowly, hands outstretched as if to catch the air between us. "It's okay. Breathe with me."

I struggled to focus on his words, my breath quickening, each inhale jagged. "I can't breathe! It feels like I'm suffocating."

"Just breathe into this paper bag," he urged gently. "You're safe here, I promise."

I mirrored his breaths, trying to find some rhythm amid the chaos. With each exhale, the tightness eased ever so slightly, but the panic still loomed large in my chest. "I've never felt like this before. It's too much."

"I know it feels overwhelming," Mom said, her gaze steady as a lighthouse in a storm. "We're going to get through it together. I think you should talk to that counselor Lacey has been seeing."

"I want to talk to someone," I blurted, tears brimming in my eyes. "I get so scared sometimes."

"We were all impacted by what happened to Lacey. It's best to face our fears head-on," Dad replied, his hand resting solidly on my shoulder. "I'll make an appointment. You're not alone in this, I promise. We'll tackle it together, one step at a time."

His words hung in the air, grounding me, even as a knot of worry lingered in my chest. Dad was right—I had to face this. With a shaky breath, I latched onto that glimmer of hope, letting it push back the shadows, if only for a moment.

As my breathing steadied, a fragile sense of calm began to settle in. I was still shaky, but knowing I wasn't alone made the weight a little easier to bear. I crawled into my cozy bed, letting the warmth of the blankets cocoon me, their softness the only armor I had for the night. My eyes grew heavy, and I could feel myself drifting. But just before sleep took over, a single thought broke through: I'd need to toughen up—to be strong, not just for me, but for everything Lacey was about to face.

THE NEXT MORNING, AFTER A RESTLESS NIGHT, I SAT ON THE porch swing, staring at the empty street. The early stillness was comforting, even as my heart felt heavy. My journal lay beside me, its pages blank—I had tried to write, but the words wouldn't come. I traced the grooves of the wooden armrest, grounding myself.

Mom was on her way to San Diego with Lacey's parents to confront the man who had kidnapped her. They left in the quiet of early morning, Dad having called in a favor to get a mug shot and rap sheet. Now we had a name for the person who had turned our lives upside down: Johnny Roche.

The name alone sent a chill down my spine. He was a small-town crook from Chula Vista, just twenty-two. At first glance, he looked almost ordinary—maybe even attractive —but his eyes gave him away. They were cold, like a predator's, devoid of any trace of humanity.

Lacey should have been getting ready for college, falling in love. Instead, she was facing her worst nightmare all over again. The thought of her walking into that identification room to confront him made my stomach churn. She was finally beginning to heal, and now she had to relive the trauma once more.

"Star!" Erin's voice cut through my gloom. I glanced up to see her bouncing up the porch steps like she'd consumed five cups of coffee. She always seemed to be a morning person, brimming with boundless energy, whereas I took a little while to wake up.

"Hey, Erin," I mumbled, trying to sound more enthusiastic.

"Did everyone leave for the police station?" Erin plopped down next to me.

"Everyone, apart from Dad and me."

"Are you okay? You don't look so good."

"Last night, after you left, I had, well, I guess it was a panic attack."

Erin settled beside me, worry etched on her face. "Oh, Star, I'm so sorry. How are you holding up now?"

"I'm feeling better, but my parents want me to talk to someone about it."

"That makes sense. It's tough being close to someone who went through something so traumatic."

"I guess so."

"Hey, it's going to be a while before we hear anything. What do you say we head to the skate park and watch the boys skate? A change of scenery might be good."

"I dunno," I said, shrugging. "I'm not in the mood for a bunch of kids showing off their tricks."

Erin gave me her best puppy-dog eyes, which usually worked. "Come on, Star. It's just a short walk through the dog park. Sitting here and worrying isn't going to help. Lacey would want you to be out having fun, living your life."

"How do you always know what I need?"

"Let's say I've been through enough to recognize when my friend could use a boost."

It was true.

We took the ten-minute walk to the park, bringing my husky, Princess, along for some exercise.

"It feels like every time my life settles down, something else happens," I sighed, kicking a loose pebble on the side-walk. "First my parent's separation, then the move to

Hollywood, and now this. It's like the universe is against me."

"You're tougher than you think, Star. We both are. And honestly, it's not the universe out to get you. It's just life doing its thing. It throws twists and turns at us, some harder to handle than others. You're managing it. Grandma Talie always says to take things bit by bit, and I promise, it will get better."

I wanted to believe her. Really, I did. With everything happening, it was hard to feel like I was handling anything at all. I pressed my lips together, unsure of what to say next, when Princess darted forward, yanking me out of my thoughts as she tugged on the leash, eager to chase after a squirrel.

"See?" Erin laughed. "Even Princess knows how to keep moving forward."

I couldn't help but crack a smile. "She's not worried about much beyond squirrels and treats."

"And you shouldn't be worried about anything beyond today," Erin replied.

I hesitated, the weight of everything heavy on my chest, but the spark of hope in Erin's eyes made it clear she wouldn't let me wallow in my thoughts all day.

"Okay, but I want to be home by lunchtime to wait for news from Mom. She said she'd call with an update."

As we approached the skate park, I felt my shoulders relax a little. My worries hadn't vanished, but maybe Erin was onto something. Perhaps I could focus on the present and set aside the showdown at the police station, if only for a little while.

MOM EVENTUALLY RETURNED FROM THE IDENTIFICATION process, drained and emotionally spent. She shared that the moment they saw Johnny Roche in the lineup, Lacey had gotten sick and shaken uncontrollably.

The weeks that followed were tough on all of us, especially Lacey. It was as if a light inside her had dimmed. She slipped back into old habits, isolating herself at home and pulling away from everything. The idea of pursuing a psychology degree was set aside as she insisted, she wasn't ready to face people yet.

At last, the day had come for my first appointment with the therapist.

The waiting room was bright, filled with plants and soft, calming colors. A part of me wanted to bolt back to the safety of home, but I reminded myself why I was here. I needed to do this for me, for Lacey.

When Robin called my name, I stood up, my heart racing. She smiled warmly, instantly putting me at ease.

"Hi, Starla. It's nice to meet you," she said, leading me into a cozy office adorned with inspiring quotes and art.

"Hi," I replied, trying to sound more confident than I felt.

"Let's talk about what's been going on," Robin said as

she settled into her chair, her notepad on her lap. "This has been a difficult time for you and your family, especially with what happened to your cousin."

I nodded, the tightness in my chest returning. "It's been hard. I don't know how to handle it."

"That's completely normal," Robin said gently. "When someone close goes through something as traumatic as Lacey did, it impacts you, too. Have you talked to her?"

"Not recently. She's been staying home a lot. I had a panic attack when I found out they caught the kidnapper. Another girl got hurt, like Lacey. One girl died."

Robin's expression softened with a knowing look, her eyes full of understanding. "That is a lot for a young person to process. Panic attacks can happen after hearing upsetting news. It's your body's way of coping. But remember, it's temporary. Your body is trying to protect you, even if it feels out of control."

"Can I do anything about it?" I asked, feeling small.

"Absolutely. I'll teach you some grounding techniques. Have you heard of butterfly tapping?"

I shook my head.

Robin demonstrated, crossing her arms over her chest and tapping her collarbone. "You tap lightly while focusing on your breath. Let's try it."

We spent a few minutes tapping and breathing. It felt oddly soothing, like a gentle wave washing over me.

Robin smiled. "That's perfect. Take it one step at a time,

and lean on the people around you for support. You're not alone in this."

"Thank you," I said. "But will Lacey ever be the same again? She's given up on her dreams."

Robin nodded, her expression empathetic. "It's natural to worry about Lacey. Trauma can change us, and it might feel like she's lost her way. Remember, healing isn't a straight path; it's full of ups and downs."

"But what does that mean for her future?" I replied.

"Lacey may not return to exactly who she was before, but it doesn't mean she won't find a new sense of purpose. It's normal to feel uncertain about the future. Encourage her to take small steps towards what once inspired her, even if they seem insignificant. As she works through her feelings, she might discover new dreams, which are more in line with the person she is now."

As our session ended, I felt lighter, as if I had a small toolkit of strategies to help me navigate the storm that had become my life. I wasn't just carrying the weight of my fears. I had tools to fight back, and I was going to fight.

THE FOLLOWING EVENING, I SPRAWLED OUT ON MY BED, flipping through a travel magazine filled with glossy images of far-off places like Paris, Tokyo, and London—each one a tempting promise of adventure. Erin was curled up on the floor beside me, her sketchbook open, pencil dancing across the page.

Depeche Mode pulsed softly from the radio, its electronic rhythm a comforting backdrop to our thoughts.

Lately, Erin was always around, like a big sister who never left. We spent our days laughing and sharing secrets, never once fighting.

"I don't want to end up like that," I remarked, breaking the silence.

"Like what?" Erin looked up from her doodling, her curiosity piqued.

"Like Lacey. Stuck. Afraid of everything. It's like she's living on a rollercoaster, but too afraid to get off. I want to see the world, for both of us."

Erin set down her pen, her brow furrowing. "I get it. But Lacey's been through hell. I don't blame her. It's just a setback. Once the court case is finished, she'll bounce back."

"You're probably right." My gaze shifted to a picture of the Eiffel Tower in the magazine. "That won't be us, though. We're going to explore the world."

Erin nodded, determination in her eyes. "We just have to keep focusing on our dreams."

I sighed. "My mom's been so protective since the kidnapping. I feel like I'm trapped in a bubble."

Erin shifted, sitting cross-legged. "It feels like we're stuck here, but our time will come."

Dave Gahan's haunting voice played softly in the background, blending with our conversation. For a moment, our dreams felt within reach, and a boldness rose in me—I felt we could do it. Erin's expression hardened with determination.

"We just have to keep focusing on our dreams."

"I can't keep living like this. Sometimes, I just want to pack up and run away."

Erin turned to me, eyes lit with determination. "Okay, let's make a pact. Nothing will get in the way of our dreams. No boys, no parents, nothing. We have to promise each other."

A wave of excitement washed over me. "Absolutely! Let's make it happen. I'm more ready than ever to see the world. I'll send Lacey a postcard from every place I visit. Maybe she can join us someday."

Erin propped herself on her elbows, a spark of delight in her eyes. "I have an idea. I heard airlines hire people who speak another language. What if we took French lessons? Get ahead of the game?"

I blinked, surprised at how quickly she jumped into action. French? It sounded so daring, so exciting—like a secret promise of something bigger than Montclair, California. "French? That's a great idea," I said, the words tumbling out. "I can see it now—us sipping coffee, strolling through the streets. And hey, being flight attendants means free travel, right?"

I pictured the two of us in crisp uniforms, wheeling suitcases through international terminals. This wasn't just a plan; it was a ticket out—away from locked doors, worried looks, and everything that happened to Lacey. This could be freedom.

"Exactly." Erin grinned. "We could start now, get fluent. By the time we're old enough to apply, we'll be miles ahead."

The idea settled in my mind, feeling concrete. A way to escape—not just from Montclair, but from everything painful and suffocating.

"Okay," I said, smiling. "Let's do it. I'll talk to my mom about it tomorrow. She's still trying to make things up to me."

"Enjoy it while it lasts."

"Hey, did I tell you my friends from Hollywood are coming during Christmas break? You're going to love Shawn and Shannon. They're edgy but fun."

"Your mom's letting them come stay? Maybe she's not as overprotective as we thought."

"I guess she's not all that bad." I replied.

"I've been dying to meet them. What are they like?"

"Shawn's cute. He's in eleventh grade. Shannon's in ninth grade, like me. You'll love them. Shawn's sleeping in Dad's office."

"I can't wait, we'll have to take them skating." Erin flicked her hair over her shoulder.

"Great idea."

"Now, back to our plans. I'll grab the English-to-French dictionary my uncle gave me last Christmas," Erin said, eager to dive in. Once she decided on something, there was no turning back.

A few moments later, she clambered through my window—quicker than the front door. Flipping through the pages, I asked, "Okay, where do we start?"

"Let's start with something useful—like asking for directions," Erin suggested, her eyes sparkling.

"Perfect. How do you say, 'Where is the Eiffel Tower?' in French?"

"Let me see... Où est la Tour Eiffel?" Erin said, watching me intently.

"Okay, let me try." I cleared my throat, adding some flair. "Où est la Tour Eiffel?"

"That sounded great, Star. You're a natural."

A smile crept onto my face, and I felt a new sense of purpose. "Who knows, maybe one day we'll be sitting beneath the real Eiffel Tower, chatting in perfect French and living our best lives."

"You bet we will," Erin replied, her laughter ringing like music. We both fell into giggles, filling the air with a lightness I hadn't felt in ages.

Wiping tears of laughter from my eyes, I leaned back, hope swelling in my chest. "Imagine it—croissants for breakfast, wandering cobblestone streets, and not a care in the world."

"Sounds perfect," Erin said, eyes sparkling with dreams.

For the first time in forever, I allowed myself to believe

the world was full of possibilities, waiting for us to seize them.

THE FOLLOWING WEEKS DRAGGED ON, EACH MINUTE stretching endlessly, as I anticipated Shannon and Shawn's arrival. Finally, the day arrived. The winter air nipped at our cheeks as the cousins from Hollywood stepped off the bus, their presence like a burst of energy, crashing into my life and mingling my old world with my former life. Although I was glad to be back in good old Montclair, sometimes I did miss the buzz of living in a big city.

Erin and I exchanged an excited glance, knowing this was going to be one of those weeks we'd never forget. The house vibrated with anticipation of our visitors.

"Hey, babes! Look at you, all grown up. You must have grown three inches since I last saw you!" Shannon exclaimed as she jumped off the bus and ran over to give me a huge hug.

"So, what's the plan for this week?" Shawn asked, slinking behind her. "You girls got anything exciting lined up?"

I shot a quick glance at Erin, my grin widening. "Oh, you know, we're gonna give you the grand tour of small-town life. Roller rink, late-night burgers, maybe even a little bonfire in Dad's fire pit."

Erin gave me a playful nudge. "But don't worry, we've got a few surprises up our sleeves."

Shawn raised an eyebrow, curiosity piqued. "Surprise plans?"

I exchanged a glance with Erin, the thrill of our little secret buzzing between us. "You'll have to wait and see."

Once we got Shawn and Shannon settled, and the initial excitement of our reunion faded, Erin and I slipped into the living room.

"Okay, you didn't mention how cute he is! This game of spin the bottle is about to get way more interesting. And Brandon should be here soon. What time do your parents head out for their date?"

"Date? More like a counseling session. They've been hitting up all these marriage support groups since they got back together. They call it date night, but let's be real—it's couples therapy."

"That's a good thing, right?"

"I guess, but the best part is they'll be gone for a few hours, which means more time for spin the bottle," I giggled, feeling the excitement build.

That evening, Erin, Brandon, and the rest of us were sprawled across the old, hard wood floor. We spun the bottle as fast as it would go. It wobbled a little before it slowed and stopped, pointing right at me. My heart was pounding with a weird mix of anticipation and nerves I hadn't really felt before. Giggles and whispers infused the air. In the background, *Yo! MTV Raps* was playing, the music thumping along with the vibe of the room, making everything feel more intense.

Shannon leaned in, her wild red hair a fiery halo around her face. She was dressed in a baggy, oversized sweatshirt hanging off one shoulder, paired with her signature Doc Martens, scuffed and worn, and undeniably cool. Her eyes sparkled as she nudged me with her elbow. "Looks like it's your turn, Starla."

Shawn shot me a playful wink, his blue mohawk standing tall and defiant. He'd tossed his leather jacket over a chair, his ripped jeans adding to his bad-boy vibe. He was like a punk rock James Dean, all attitude and swagger, but with a softness in his eyes making my stomach flutter. "Come on, don't be shy. It's just a kiss."

I swallowed hard, my eyes flicking from the floor to everyone around me. This was it—the moment every girl talks about but secretly freaks out over. The rules were simple, but it felt like a huge deal. Everyone was watching me, waiting to see if I'd go through with it.

Shawn's face was now just inches from mine. The faint scent of spearmint gum and Drakkar Noir surrounded me, catching me off guard in a way I hadn't anticipated.

It was true, I'd always had a crush on Shawn, since the first moment I met him on the rooftop of our old apartment building in Hollywood, but he seemed so much older then. I still felt like a little girl, until recently.

Since moving back to Montclair, I had grown a few inches and was now taller than Mom. My curves had filled out, and my style had matured. The remnants of my neon pink crop top peeked out from beneath my denim jacket, and a ring of bracelets jingled on each arm as I leaned forward, my honey blonde waves cascading over my shoulders. I caught my reflection in the window, noticing the confident glint in my eyes that hadn't been there before. It was strange, almost like I was seeing myself for the first time—a version of me ready to take on whatever came next.

I closed my eyes, my heart hammering in my chest, feeling Shawn's breath warm against my skin. It was a slow kiss, enveloping me in a moment that felt both fragile and profound. The rest of the room faded away as the tip of Shawn's tongue caressed my bottom lip, sending shivers up and down my spine.

When I pulled back, heat rushed to my cheeks, and I cast my gaze downward, my heart fluttering in my chest. Shawn flashed a confident grin at me—a smile that made my heart race.

Shannon clapped her hands together, her laughter breaking the awkward silence. "Somebody call the fire department," she declared playfully. "Starla's burning up."

Before I could fully absorb the moment, the sound of the front door creaking open cut through the laughter. My heart sank as I recognized the familiar sound of my parents' footsteps. The sudden intrusion of reality into our little world.

My parents stepped into the living room, their eyes

immediately sweeping over the scene. Mom's expression shifted from surprise to anger mixed with disappointment.

The laughter faded, leaving us in an awkward silence, everyone too afraid to make a move.

"Starla," she said, her words full of frustration. "What's going on here?"

I scrambled to my feet. "We were just playing around. It's nothing."

Her gaze flicked to the bottle lying on the floor, and I saw understanding dawn in her eyes. "Time for everyone to leave. Shawn and Shannon, you two go to the office while I speak with my daughter," she commanded, her expression stern.

The room filled with the sounds of chairs scraping against the floor, shoes scuffing as my friends hurried to gather their things. Shawn gave me a sympathetic wink as he passed, his earlier confidence now tinged with awkwardness. Shannon paused beside me, giving my hand a quick squeeze.

"Don't worry, Star," she murmured. "We'll wait in the office until you're done."

My mouth clamped shut, my cheeks burning as I struggled not to cry. The door closed behind them, leaving me alone in the living room with my red-faced parents. The silence that followed was thick, almost suffocating. I could tell Mom was trying to keep her cool.

"I'll handle this," she said, her voice steady as Dad also left the room, his face flushed with anger—or maybe embarrassment. It was hard to tell. All I knew was the awkwardness was thick, a tangible weight that lingered.

Mom sat on the edge of the sofa, her shoulders slumped. She looked at me, and for a moment, the frustration melted away, replaced by something softer, more vulnerable.

"Starla, we need to talk," she said, her voice quieter now and tinged with weariness. "I know things have been tough these last few years, and I'm trying my best to understand. You're growing so fast, and I'm just trying to keep up."

Dark circles shadowed her eyes, nearly concealed by makeup, remnants of fatigue she couldn't completely mask. Her emerald-green eyes flickered with a hint of understanding.

She seemed almost fragile, still navigating her own journey. It struck me how young she really was—barely in her thirties yet expected to have everything figured out.

"I'm sorry, Mom," I said, running a hand through my hair, as if it might untangle the mess of emotions swirling inside me.

The air between us felt heavy with unspoken words, each one lingering, waiting for the right moment to escape.

"I know I've made mistakes, but that doesn't mean you can run wild. I want to trust you," Mom continued.

"It's not a big deal. It was just spin the bottle. Don't you remember being a teenager? I want to do things before I settle down. See the world, kiss boys. It's not a big deal."

"Of course, I remember being a teenager, wasn't that

long ago, you know? Sometimes it's like we're all growing up together." She ran her finger down the tip of my nose.

"I've known that for a while now."

"You're too smart for your own good. But I need you to make better choices. Okay?"

A lump formed in my throat. "Okay, Mom. I know it's been hard for you. It's been hard for me, too."

Mom reached out, her hand warm and reassuring as it enveloped mine. "We'll get through this. We're all making changes. I've changed careers, and you're turning into a woman, much too fast."

I nodded, a small spark of hope flickering in my chest. "Don't worry, Mom. Nothing bad is going to happen."

Mom sighed, concern etching itself across her face. "You need to focus, Star. No more slacking off. Your grades are slipping, and the school called to say you're struggling in every subject except writing."

I looked away, the shame rising inside me. "I know, Mom. Writing feels like the only thing that really belongs to me, the one thing I can control when everything else feels so out of hand."

"You were always a straight-A student. I'm worried you're going down the wrong path."

"I'll try harder. It was difficult leaving everything behind while you chased your Hollywood dream. Then, everything happened with Lacey. I just don't feel like the same perfect little girl I used to be."

Mom's face softened, though her eyes were still troubled.

"I'm trying to understand, Star. Your dad and I have talked, and we want to start family counseling together. Can you meet us halfway?"

I swallowed hard. The tightness in my chest was back, but this time, there was something I had to say. I took a deep breath and looked at Mom, my heart pounding in my ears. "There is one thing really important to me that I've been wanting to ask you."

Mom's demeanor softened, waiting for me to continue. "I want to take French lessons. If you'll pay for them, I promise I'll work harder on all my grades." Learning French felt like my ticket out of this place, out of feeling stuck, I added silently.

Mom blinked, clearly surprised. "French lessons? Why French?"

"There's a new boy at our school, his family speaks French, it sounds so exotic," I said. I didn't really know why I lied. Maybe I was afraid if I told her the real reason—I wanted to leave this place and see the world—she'd say no. Mom always talked about the importance of family and keeping everyone close together.

She studied me. "Improve your grades, and I'll look into those lessons. Deal?"

"Deal!" I jumped up and gave her a big hug, feeling a spark of hope ignite. Maybe this could be the first step to something bigger—something beyond this town.

CHAPTER 4

All I Wanna Do

MONTCLAIR, CALIFORNIA
OCTOBER 31, 1993

Starla Silverson
Sixteen Years Old

A s the bell rang, cutting through the buzz of Montclair High's hallway, I settled into my desk. The familiar creak welcomed me like an old friend, even if today felt different. Posters lined the walls, advertising upcoming events, motivational quotes, and the Homecoming dance. Up front, Ms. Thompson bounced on her toes, her curly hair bobbing as she clasped her hands together like a child eager to share a secret.

Ms. Thompson beamed, her eyes lighting up as if she were introducing them to her new pet. "Alright, class. Today, we're exploring something set to change the future. Email!"

She paused for effect, scanning the room to let the weight of her words sink in. "Trust me, it's going to revolutionize how we communicate. Your assignment? Set up your very own email address on AOL.com and send your first email message."

A few curious murmurs rippled through the class, but Ms. Thompson pressed on. "Don't worry, I won't be checking it. You can send it to anyone you know—or to yourself, if you don't know anyone else with email. Think of it as a digital letter."

She offered a reassuring smile. "This is just for practice. No pressure."

A wave of murmurs rippled through the room as students exchanged glances of curiosity and confusion. I couldn't help but grin; the idea of sending an email felt revolutionary. Like I was unlocking a portal to a world beyond the confines of Montclair. I powered on the Apple computer in front of me, listening to the hissing sound as it connected to the internet. Taking a deep breath, I focused on the words I wanted to share with Lacey, feeling that comforting flow I always felt when I focused on my writing.

Subject: My First Email

Dear Lacey,

I hope I got your email address right. You're one of the

only people I know who has one, so here it goes—my first email ever!

I'm not sure if I'll need an email when I'm a flight attendant, but I guess it could be a good way to keep in touch while I'm off traveling the world.

Can you believe it's been three years since I begged Mom for French lessons? I'm practically fluent now! Who would've thought? The world feels a little more within reach, and I'm officially on track to become a flight attendant—my ticket out of here.

You know how much Erin and I want this. I haven't even told Mom yet, but there's still time for that. I've got a few more years before I turn twenty-one, and the airlines won't even look at me until then. So, I'm stuck here for now, finishing high school and applying to local colleges. Mom wants me to stay close to home, and I hope she doesn't take it too hard when I announce my big plans.

Honestly, I get it. She's still so worried something might happen to me, and I don't think she'll ever stop. But enough about me—how are you? I'm so proud of you for earning your degree in psychology! I still don't know how you managed to do it in just three years. I guess if you want something badly enough, you can make it happen. You inspire me to keep moving forward.

And guess what? I passed my driver's test! One more step toward freedom. Still no boyfriend, though—I'm

not getting tied down. Seeing how that played out for
Mom, I know I want more for myself.
It's not just about boys or this town; it's about wanting
to feel free and experience everything.
Anyway, the bell just rang for the next class—another
day closer to figuring it all out. Who knows? Maybe one
day I'll be sending you postcards from all the amazing
places I dream about. Email me back if you get this.
Love you,
—Star

The bell rang, signaling the end of class and the beginning of lunch break. I hit send on the email, crossing my fingers that I'd remembered Lacey's address correctly before gathering my things.

Soon, the high school corridors buzzed with the familiar energy of teenage laughter, and gossip floated around us like a warm breeze, wrapping us in the chaotic warmth of friendship and freedom.

I spotted Erin across the hall, her confidence radiating as she strode toward me. We moved through the corridors like seasoned pros now. As a junior, I could feel the weight of time pressing down on me, each moment slipping away like sand through my fingers, taking a piece of my childhood with it.

Together, Erin and I navigated crushes, family drama, and late-night study sessions, emerging stronger together. As we stood on the brink of something new, the bond of our shared history connected us, making every moment feel significant.

In fact, the best thing about moving back to my hometown was Erin. The bond we'd forged in the drama of adolescence had only grown stronger over the years. No matter what was happening around us, we never stopped dreaming about our future—about escaping this place and taking to the skies. We were both only children, but once Erin moved into the neighborhood, it felt like I had a soul sister.

Coming back to Montclair and Erin moving in next door was Like slipping into an old, well-worn jacket. Comfortable and familiar. My time in Hollywood now seemed like a faraway dream, filled with months of yearning to get back home. Yet now that I was here, all I wanted was to leave again. Reminding me to be careful what you wish for.

Would I ever feel truly content with where I was?

"You think we'll do it?" I asked, glancing over at Erin. "Get out of here, see the world? Or is it one of those things people say but never follow-through with?"

Erin turned serious for a moment, her eyes locking onto mine. "We will, Star. You know why? Because we're not like everyone else. We don't let life get in the way of our dreams."

A warm rush spread through me at her words. Erin had

this way of pushing me forward, reminding me our dreams were more than just fantasies. They were real, and we were inching closer every day.

"And hey," she said, her playful grin illuminating her face, "if nothing else, we'll always have French, right? We can gossip about other people right in front of them, and they'll be none the wiser."

I laughed, her confidence contagious. She was right. We were different. We were going to get out of here, and nothing was going to stop us. "I love your costume, by the way."

We'd spent the entire month of October scouring thrift shops for the perfect vintage pieces for our Halloween costumes. Channeling the glamorous TWA stewardesses from the nineteen seventies, I was thrilled to see how closely our outfits resembled the retro ad we'd unearthed in one of Grandma's old *Ladies Home Journal* magazines.

"Those go-go boots you scored from Aunt Rory? Totally rad," she said, admiring my look. "I wish people still dressed with that much style."

Just then, a lanky guy with shaggy hair, ripped jeans, and a flannel shirt came barreling into Erin, sending books flying everywhere. Our conversation screeched to a halt. He muttered, looking sheepish as he helped gather the scattered textbooks. "Um, sorry about that."

"You should be. Now sit down and put your tray table up, this plane is about to take off," Erin giggled.

"Yeah, right," Elijah said, rubbing the back of his neck. "Erin, uh, I wanted to ask you something."

Erin raised an eyebrow. "What is it, Elijah? By the way, I love your Kurt Cobain costume."

Elijah looked down at his clothes, clearly puzzled. "What costume?"

Erin and I burst into laughter, as the absurdity of it hit us. Elijah's flannel shirt and disheveled hair were so unintentional. It was hilarious.

"Never mind," Erin said, still chuckling. "So, what was it you wanted to ask?"

Elijah shifted, avoiding eye contact. "I wanted to know if you'd go with me to Homecoming?"

Erin's eyes widened. "Both of us? Star needs a date, too."

"Well, I was thinking my cousin Scott and Star could go together."

"Perfect. Pick us up at eight." Erin's face glowed.

"Will do," Elijah said, his relief clear as he walked away. Erin and I exchanged triumphant glances.

"Looks like we've got dates," Erin said, flicking her hair back with a grin.

"You know I've had a crush on Scott since last year," I admitted, my heart racing at the thought. Scott Cruz was a junior who played in a local garage band called *Mother Tongue*. Those blue eyes and that smile. Every time he looked my way, my heart did somersaults.

"Okay, so what are we going to wear?" Erin asked, her eyes sparkling with excitement.

"Looks like we need to hit up the mall again soon," I laughed as we made our way to our next class.

"Alright, how are you feeling about this French test? I expect you to ace it." Erin gave me a playful nudge as we headed to our next class. Her confidence radiated, leaving me feeling a little less sure of myself.

"Easy for you to say. Your uncle's French Canadian, and you've got someone to practice with who speaks the language. Meanwhile, I'm just trying not to confuse my étudiant with my étudiante," I grumbled, rummaging through my bag for my crumpled notes.

"There's Scott, he's looking this way. Okay, act natural," Erin whispered conspiratorially, her eyes darting mischievously between Scott and me.

"How do you act natural? Is there a manual for this?" I hissed back, trying not to choke on my apple juice as Scott headed in our direction.

"Just smile and say hi. Wait, not like that. You look like you're constipated." She giggled, elbowing me gently.

"Hi, ladies. I hear we're going to Homecoming together?" Scott's voice, smooth and confident, broke through my panicked thoughts. He had a classic grunge vibe—tousled dark hair and a relaxed style that gave him a laid-back charm. I could get lost in his crisp blue eyes, and his easy, lopsided smile made him effortlessly likable.

"Hi, Scott, great performance last Friday," I managed to say.

"Thanks. You were at See's Cafe?" He had a hopeful lilt to his words as he looked at me.

"I wouldn't miss it," I said a little too eagerly.

The conversation was short, but it sent me soaring for the rest of the day. Erin raised an eyebrow at my dreamy expression. "Star and Scottie, the perfect pair."

"Shut up, Erin," I laughed, tossing a crumpled piece of paper her way.

THE NIGHT OF THE HOMECOMING DANCE QUICKLY ARRIVED. Erin and I were both buzzing as we finished getting ready. The boys were due to arrive at my house any moment, and the atmosphere was electric.

"Star, I'm telling you, tonight's gonna be epic. You ready?" Erin twirled in her slinky dress, her voice a mix of eagerness and anticipation.

"Yeah," I replied, adjusting the hem of my dress with a half-smile. "As ready as I'll ever be."

"Let's go make some memories."

We were about to leave when Mom appeared in the doorway, her Polaroid camera in hand. "Wait! Let me grab some photos of you two before you go. Won't your dates come in for a few pictures?"

"Mom, seriously? That's so embarrassing. They take

professional photos at the dance. You'll see them in a few weeks." I rolled my eyes, trying not to sound as exasperated as I felt.

Mom meant well, but she always went overboard with high school milestones—probably because she'd missed out on them herself. While her friends were off at dances, she was dealing with being pregnant with me.

"Okay, but can you at least take this disposable camera? I want to see some pictures from tonight." She offered it to me with hopeful eyes.

"Fine, fine. We've got to run." I stuffed the camera into my purse just as the boys pulled up, honking obnoxiously.

"In my day, the boys came to the door with a corsage." Dad appeared in the front room in time to see us off.

"Times have changed, Dad."

He shot me a half-smile. "Not always for the better. I want you girls to be smart tonight, no shenanigans."

"Don't worry. We'll be smart," I responded as I gave him a quick hug goodbye.

"Come on, let's go." Erin grabbed her cardigan as we made our way out the door.

"Be safe and have fun, but not too much fun," Mom called after us.

"We will!" Erin shouted over her shoulder as we rushed down the steps. The cool night air hit me, sharp and exhilarating, and suddenly I felt like anything could happen. My stomach did a little flip, the kind you get when you're right on the edge of something big, something that might just change you a little.

The boys were already out of the car, leaning against it like they'd stepped out of a teen movie. Scott's blue eyes landed directly on me. "You ladies ready for the night of your lives?"

Erin giggled. "We'll see about that."

As we piled into the classic Nova and drove off, I stole a glance back at my childhood home, watching it recede into the distance like a fading memory.

When we arrived at the high school and stepped into the gym, it felt like entering a different universe. One where all that mattered was the moment we were in. The air vibrated with excitement, music pulsing through the crowd like a heartbeat.

"Want to dance?" Scott asked, his eyes sparkling as he held out his hand. It wasn't really a question. It was an invitation, and before I could overthink it, I took his hand in mine. Behind Scott's back, Erin gave a thumbs up, her grin illuminated the entire room.

"Go get 'em, Star," she mouthed, her enthusiasm infectious.

As we swayed to the music, the noise of the gym faded into a soft background hum. Scott didn't say much, but still managed to make me feel like I was the only person in the room. "Did you have fun at the café the other night?"

"Yeah," I replied, aiming for a casual tone. "You guys are really good."

He smiled and it was like the entire world tilted for a second. "We want to record a demo, you know?"

"That's so cool." The music slowed, and my palms dampened as Scott moved a little closer. We swayed in a quiet, comfortable silence, our bodies softly touching, but somehow it felt like more.

The band launched into an upbeat number, and the dance floor flooded with people again, bursting the intimate bubble we'd been wrapped in. Scott stepped back slightly, his eyes locked on mine, a knowing smile tugging at the corners of his lips. A stab of disappointment settled over me —I wasn't ready for this closeness to end.

"You want to go outside for some fresh air?" Scott asked.

Before I could answer, Erin was by my side, a hint of trouble in her eyes. "The cool kids are heading to the football field. One of the seniors has a bottle of Strawberry Hill. You coming?"

I glanced at Scott, my heart racing. He looked at me in a way that made my stomach flip. "I'm in, if you are."

"Sure."

We slipped out of the gym, Erin and Elijah leading the way, their laughter echoing through the dark hallways. On the field, the grass was damp, and the stars were bright. It felt like the night could go on forever.

A few kids were already there, passing around the Boones Farm bottle like it was some kind of secret treasure. Erin grabbed it first, took a big swig, and handed it to me. "Your turn."

I wrapped my fingers around the cool glass of the bottle and took a sip. The wine was sweet, maybe a bit too sweet, there was a satisfying burn as I swallowed. "Not bad," I said, passing it to Scott. He took a swig, then stretched out on the grass, gazing up at the stars.

"Pretty cool night, huh?"

I lay down next to him, feeling the slightly damp grass beneath me. "Yeah. Really cool."

Scott's hand found mine, feeling utterly natural. When his lips brushed against me, soft and a little uncertain, I eagerly kissed him back. For a moment, everything else faded away. The stars, us, and the lingering taste of cheap wine.

Erin was a short distance away, flirting with Elijah.

In between kisses, we'd gaze at the stars and Scott would quote song lyrics. The world felt bigger and smaller at the same time, like anything could happen.

Then, in the distance, I heard it. The unmistakable sound of a car door slamming, followed by the crunch of footsteps on gravel.

Erin pulled away from Elijah and sat up suddenly, her eyes wide. "Did you hear that?"

Scott and I froze, and I could feel the tension ripple through the group. We all turned toward the parking lot, where two flashlight beams swept across the field, cutting through the darkness.

The school police.

"Shit," Elijah uttered, already scrambling to his feet. "We've got to go."

Erin was on her feet in a flash, grabbing my arm and yanking me forward. "Come on, Star, move!"

Panic surged through me as we all bolted, our hearts pounding in time with our footsteps. The laughter and whispers were gone, replaced by the rush of adrenaline as we sprinted toward the shadows, hoping to disappear before the lights found us.

Scott grabbed my hand, pulling me along as we ducked behind the bleachers. "Stay low."

The lights swept over the field again, and we all held our breath, pressed against the cold metal of the bleachers.

The footsteps got closer, and I could hear the school police talking to each other, their words low but stern. "They couldn't have gotten far. Check the bleachers."

My heart felt like it might explode as I squeezed Scott's hand, my mind racing with thoughts of what would happen if we got caught. Then, as the flashlight beam swept toward us, Scott tugged me deeper into the shadows.

"This way," he motioned toward a narrow gap beneath the bleachers.

We crawled through, the metal scraping against our clothes, but we didn't stop. The voices of the school police were too close, too real, and all I could think about was getting away.

"Hold on," one of the officers called out. "I think I saw something."

We froze, the beam of light flickering inches away from where we huddled. My hand gripped Scott's so tightly I was losing the feeling in my fingertips.

"Come on," the other officer said. "Let's check the other side."

The beam of light moved away, and I exhaled, trembling. We held our breath, hearts pounding in our ears, every muscle tense, until the footsteps faded, leaving only the echo of our fear behind.

Erin was the first to speak. "Are they gone?"

Scott nodded, his breath warm against my ear. "Yes. But we can't stay here. Let's go."

We crept out from under the bleachers, still moving in the shadows, our nerves raw but our spirits still intact. As we reached the edge of the field, the adrenaline still pumping through our veins, I couldn't help but glance back. How close had we come to getting caught?

We didn't stop. We kept running. The thrill of the chase mingling with fear, leaving us with the knowledge that this night—this wild, unforgettable night—was just the beginning.

THE REST OF THE SCHOOL YEAR FLEW BY IN A BLUR OF LATE-night study sessions and spontaneous adventures. Erin was dating Elijah, and I was with Scott. Every moment together felt electric, charged with laughter and stolen glances, which hinted he was wanting more from our relationship.

"Don't forget our pact," Erin said one Friday evening as we got ready to head to their band practice. "We're just having fun with these guys. They're small-town boys, and we're not getting locked into anything serious."

"Nothing's going to stand in our way," I said, though I couldn't shake the uneasiness in my stomach. "But lately, Scott's been dropping the 'L' word. It's kind of sweet, honestly. I mean, he could really be the one I lose my virginity to. He's so charming and, well, incredibly hot. He's a great kisser."

"Just be careful, sex always complicates things, and for goodness sake be safe. My mom keeps some condoms in her top drawer. Let's put some in your purse, just in case. We don't want you following in your mom's footsteps."

"Oh, hell no. You don't think she'll notice a few are gone?"

"She might notice, but she won't say anything, she's terrified I might get pregnant and she's not ready to be a grandma."

An hour later, we found ourselves at band practice, Scott's garage had been transformed into a makeshift stage, filled with instruments and amps. As the guys jammed, I settled onto a worn-out couch, enjoying the music filling the air. After a few songs, Scott shifted away from the mic, wiping the sweat from his brow, his eyes lighting up when he spotted me.

"Hey, you made it," he called, jogging over to give me a warm kiss.

"I wouldn't miss it," I replied, feeling a thrill at his attention.

"My parents are out of town this weekend. How would you feel about staying late. Maybe even spending the night?"

"That sounds tempting. I could tell my mom I'm staying at Erin's house. She'd never suspect a thing. Let me check with Erin." I tried to sound confident, but I wasn't so sure Mom wouldn't notice.

As practice continued, I watched him lose himself in the music, the way he moved with the beat, completely in his element. When the last song ended, the room erupted with applause, and Scott took a bow, his smile wider than ever.

"Want to head outside for some fresh air?" he suggested, his voice softening as he looked at me.

"Sure," I said, excitement bubbling inside me.

We slipped out of the garage into the balmy night, the stars twinkling overhead. I leaned against the railing of his porch, inhaling the crispness of the evening, feeling the energy between us.

"Pretty clear night, huh?" Scott said, gazing at the stars.

"It really is," I replied, glancing at him. There was something in his eyes that made my heart race.

As we stood there, a comfortable silence surrounded us. His hand found mine, fitting perfectly, and when his lips brushed against mine—soft and tentative—I kissed him back, losing myself in the moment. Just us, the stars, and the thrill of the night. We pulled away slightly, breathless and smiling.

"You're really good," I said, my cheeks flushing. "You know that, right?"

"Thanks," he said, his gaze warm. We exchanged a few more kisses, the world around us fading away.

"I don't think staying the night is a good idea," I said, feeling a twinge of regret. He looked down, with a hint of disappointment in his expression.

"Hey, don't look so crushed. My curfew isn't until midnight. We still have plenty of time to have some fun." I met his gaze, a playful spark in my eyes.

"In that case, let's go to my room," he said, gesturing toward the house. "I'll make sure everyone clears out. Erin and Elijah can stick around, but the rest of these bone-heads? They're getting the boot."

I entered Scott's room and flicked on his lava lamp, watching the warm glow fill the space. A mix of excitement and uncertainty swirled inside me. We'd gone pretty far before; our make-out sessions had been practically electric. Was I ready to take it all the way? The thought lingered, tempting yet intimidating, as I leaned back against the wall, trying to calm the nerves within.

"I'm back," Scott said, stepping in with a grin that lit up the room even more than the lava lamp. He closed the door behind him, and my heart jumped.

"Nice ambiance," I teased, motioning to the glowing lamp.

"I thought you might like it." His expression shifted to something more serious. "So, what are you thinking?"

I took another sip, gathering my thoughts. "Honestly? I'm feeling a little nervous."

Scott caressed my arm, his eyes locking onto mine. "I get it. I'm still a virgin too, you know?"

His words eased some of the tension, but the thrill of the unknown still lingered in the air. "I'm glad I'm not the only one."

"Let's enjoy ourselves and see what happens." He reached for my hand, pulling me toward him.

With slow exhalation, I let go of my worries, the warmth of his presence making everything seem insignificant. Our kisses intensified, filling the room with the kind of electricity that promised something more.

We sank into the moment, the glow of the lava lamp cast soft shadows on the walls. Time slipped away, our laughter mingled with whispered words. Hours felt like minutes, and the tension between us ignited in a way that was both exhilarating and comforting.

As the night deepened, we found ourselves wrapped in each other's arms, the heat of his chest against mine making my body tingle with anticipation. When we finally drew back, breathless and smiling, it was clear we'd crossed a line, but in the best way possible.

As the lamp's glow flickered, I knew whatever happened next would be just ours. A shared secret in the soft shadows of the room.

Bang, bang, bang.

"Star, it's past midnight. We better get home, or our moms are going to kill us," Erin shouted through the bedroom door.

"I must have dosed off," I mumbled, throwing the tangled sheets off.

"I think we should get home." Erin replied.

"I've got to go, Scott." I said as I pulled on my jeans.

"Next time, it'll be longer. I promise." He ran a hand through his hair, looking sheepish. "I love you. You know that, right?"

"Yeah, love you too. I'll call you tomorrow." The words felt foreign on my tongue.

I gave him a quick kiss before opening the bedroom door. "Let's get home. Hopefully, Mom went to bed and wasn't waiting up for us. What time is it, anyway?"

"It's 12:15. So, what were you two doing?" Erin asked, raising an eyebrow.

"Why, do I look any different?"

"I want details. You better spill it all."

As we headed to the car, a whirlwind of nerves and excitement tangled in my chest. Every step felt heavy yet exhilarating, like I was teetering on the edge of something I desperately wanted but couldn't quite grasp. "There's not much to tell. It all happened so fast. It didn't really hurt, but it didn't feel all that great either."

Erin's eyes widened. "Don't worry, it gets better. My first time with Elijah wasn't great either."

I shrugged, biting my lip as we climbed into the car. "Yeah, I was expecting more. Like fireworks or something."

Erin tilted her head slightly, her expression softening. "Just don't go falling in love. Sex complicates things."

"Don't worry, Scott's sweet and all, but I know he's not the one I want to spend forever with. He just felt safe, you know."

"I get it, I really do."

I glanced back at Scott's house, a wave of uncertainty crashing over me. It hadn't been the fairy tale I'd envisioned, but standing there, I sensed we were on the brink of something new and uncharted, and it sent a thrill coursing through me.

IN THE WEEKS THAT FOLLOWED AT SCHOOL, THINGS FELT A bit awkward with Scott. Now that we'd crossed that line, it seemed he expected sex every time we found ourselves alone together.

"Hey, babe, what are you doing after school?" he asked one day during passing period, his eyes sparkling with that familiar hopefulness.

"I have my French lessons on Tuesday. Remember?" I replied, trying to keep things light.

"I thought you could blow it off just this once." He

looked at me with those puppy dog eyes, and my heart did a little flip. "Don't you want to come to band practice? We could spend some time alone together afterward."

I hesitated, torn between the thrill of being with him and my commitment to those lessons. "Maybe I'll swing by afterwards?"

"Wow, don't sound too excited," he shot back, sarcasm lacing his words. I could see the hurt flicker in his eyes, and it stung a bit.

"Don't be like that. These lessons matter to me, like your band matters to you."

"Right. I'll catch you later," he muttered, storming off.

He could be so immature sometimes. I didn't want to hurt him, but I also couldn't shake the feeling I was losing a part of myself in this relationship.

By mid-afternoon, I'd finished my French lesson and headed over to Scott's house. The familiar thrum of the band practicing spilled out into the neighborhood, and with each step closer to the garage, my heart picked up speed, a fluttery mix of nerves and excitement.

I hoped Scott was done being mad at me, but the second I stepped inside, the warmth in my chest iced over. In the corner, Scott was tangled up with some wannabe groupie— dyed black hair and a skirt a little too short for its own good. She was the exact opposite of my easygoing, natural vibe. A total cliché, yet it still hurt like hell.

I froze, the anticipation turning to dread, like a punch in the gut. Just last week, it had been us, caught up in our own world, with him saying he loved me.

"What's going on here?" I shouted, my voice shaking.

Scott pulled away, guilt in his eyes, mixed with something disturbingly close to enjoyment. "Relax, it's not what it looks like," he muttered, but his words fell flat.

"Well, it looks like you've got your tongue down another girl's throat," I shot back, the anger sharp in my voice. "I'm done. You can have him," I said over my shoulder, willing myself not to look back.

As I stormed away, my heart raced with anger and hurt, our moments together already feeling like a distant memory. Whatever we'd had was slipping away, like a feather blowing in the wind.

"He's such a jerk. I can't believe I caught him kissing another girl," I said, pacing as I vented to Erin over the phone.

"You're way too good for him," Erin sighed. "I'm so sorry, Star. Elijah mentioned some girls hanging around practice, but I thought it was harmless flirting. Scott always acted like he was obsessed with you."

"It doesn't matter. I just need to stay focused on my goals and not get sidetracked by people like that." I tried to sound indifferent, but the tremor in my voice betrayed the hurt I was hiding.

Erin paused for a moment, then said, "Look, I know this

feels awful—like beyond awful. But don't let him make you feel like you're not enough. You're better than some guy who's too blind to see what he has. You have dreams, Star, and you're going to make them happen. One day, someone will see you exactly for who you are, no doubts, no hesitation. He'll be all in. I promise."

I contemplated her words, as I stared at the fading light outside my window. No matter how hard I tried to let them sink in, the doubt was there, twisting its way through me.

What if I'm never enough? What if true love doesn't exist, and we're all just pretending?

Erin's pep talk was playing on repeat in my head, but it felt like she was describing someone else. Someone who had their life together, someone who wasn't sitting in a room, replaying the most embarrassing moment of their life. I wanted to believe her. I wanted to be the girl about whom she was talking. But right now? I felt broken.

I tried to block out the memory of seeing Scott's lips on someone else's. It wasn't even the fact that he'd kissed her that hurt the most. The real pain came from this gnawing feeling in my chest. I wasn't good enough to hold on to him. Not Scott specifically. I didn't even know if I really loved him, but the idea that if I couldn't keep him, then who could I keep? It was like the universe had slapped a label on me that said *replaceable.*

If I wasn't enough for someone who seemed obsessed with me, how could I be enough for anyone? Or was this just how it worked. Everyone pretended for a while, until something better came along?

"I can't stand him," I whispered, but it didn't make me feel any better.

Erin's voice pulled me out of my spiraling thoughts. "Star? You still there?"

"Yeah," I said, swallowing the lump in my throat. "I'm here."

"Okay, good. I'm coming over. We're going to binge on ice cream and watch *16 Candles*, we don't need Scott when we have Jake Ryan."

"I'd like that," I replied

"I've got cookie dough ice cream," Erin announced. "Tonight, we're bingeing cheesy teen romance, eating our weight in ice cream, and fully embracing the wallow. But tomorrow? Tomorrow, you're going to wake up over him—even if it's a total 'fake it till you make it' situation."

"I love you, you know that?"

"Of course I know, I'm the best," she joked. "I'll be right over, you fire up the VCR. Okay?"

"Yes, ma'am," I teased back.

After hanging up, I forced myself off the bed. The ache in my chest was still there, heavy and relentless. However, knowing Erin was coming made it a little easier to breathe. It was like I didn't have to carry all of it by myself anymore.

I grabbed some blankets from the closet and tossed them on the couch, tying my hair into a messy bun. By the time I heard the knock at the door, I wasn't all better, but I wasn't as upset as I had been.

Erin didn't even bother with a greeting when I opened the door. She hugged me tight, handed over the ice cream, and collapsed onto the couch. "Okay," she said, grabbing the remote. "Let's forget about Scott and pretend Jake is our guy."

As the opening credits rolled, I took my first bite of ice cream, and something slowly shifted inside me. The ache was still there, but the throbbing pain in my heart had subsided. Maybe I wasn't over this betrayal yet, but I wasn't going to let this guy ruin me. Not tonight, not ever.

CHAPTER 5

Don't Want to Miss a Thing

MONTCLAIR, CALIFORNIA

SEPTEMBER, 1998

Starla Silverson
Twenty-One Years Old

Subject: Birthday Plans

Hey Star,

So great to hear from you! Your high school English teacher was onto something—email really is the way to go! Do you think physical letters will ever go extinct? Maybe we should get Grandma set up with an email account; can you imagine her face? LOL (That's "laugh out loud," just in case you didn't know!)

I can't believe you're turning twenty-one already! Seriously, where did the time go? Any news from the airlines? Now that you can finally apply, I bet you've thrown your application at every airline from here to Europe. It feels like just yesterday I was cheering you on through high school, and now you're on the edge of adulthood!

I'm so proud of you for chasing those dreams. Turning twenty-one is a big deal, and I can't wait to see what's next for you. As for me, I've finally been able to put my darkness behind me, and I'm living the life I was meant to live. I love my job working as a counselor at Montclair High—right in our own backyard! It's honestly amazing to help students find their way. Going back to school for my Psych degree? Best decision ever! It's empowering to learn how to turn my struggles into strength while giving back to the community that means so much to me.

But enough about me! I know someone's birthday is coming up, and we have to celebrate! Dinner at Don Jose's sounds perfect—just the two of us! How does Saturday at 7 PM sound? I'd love to celebrate your big day. Let me know if that works for you!

Gotta dash—my next student is about to walk in!

Love you tons,

Lacey XOXO

T folded the printed email, tucking it beside the Luxe Air offer letter, letting the excitement and nerves mingle in my pocket. Meeting Lacey over tacos and margaritas sounded perfect, just the way to share my big news. As I climbed out of my little Ford Escort, the warm evening air wrapped around me, and the light drizzle fell like a gentle kiss from the sky.

September was my favorite time of year—still warm in California, yet that perfect moment when fall began to fold into summer. It felt like a season of change.

The golden glow of streetlights danced on the damp pavement, creating a shimmering canvas that mirrored the joy bubbling inside me.

I made my way into the restaurant, ready to share my news with Lacey when, out of nowhere, a chorus of "Surprise!" erupted around me. I blinked, caught between laughter and disbelief as Don Jose's sprang to life in a riot of colors. Streamers hung from the ceiling like festive ribbons, while balloons in every shade danced gently above a long table filled with family and friends, their faces glowing with excitement. Laughter and the clinking of glasses echoed in the air, enveloping me in a warm embrace that turned my anticipation into pure joy.

Mom stood in the middle of it all, grinning like she'd pulled off the heist of the century, her eyes crinkling with pride. "Did you really think I'd let your twenty-first slip by without a celebration?"

I hugged her, trying to hold back a squeal. "I didn't see this coming at all! You really went all out."

"Only the best for my girl. Lacey and Erin helped me plan the whole thing. Were you surprised?" Mom asked, guiding me to the head of the table where a giant plate of chicken taquitos awaited, topped with melting cheese and warm guacamole.

"Surprised is an understatement." I thought of the folded offer letter from the airline that was now burning a hole in my pocket.

"We've got all your favorites. And don't worry, I ordered your favorite Tres Leches Cake."

As I scanned the room, I couldn't help but feel over-whelmed by the love and support surrounding me. Grandma Dawn sat with Aunt Rory and Susan. Colorful gifts were piled high in the corner, and Mom had even hired a karaoke host who was setting up nearby.

Uncle Randall and his family were seated in another corner, their faces glowing with pride. Lacey smiled at me from across the table, her eyes twinkling with laughter. "Hey, little cousin, looks like we surprised you after all." Lacey took a sip of her margarita. She looked fantastic, not a hint of the darkness that had lingered for so many months after her abduction.

"This is fabulous," I said, smiling at everyone. "Thank you all for being here."

"We wouldn't miss it for the world," Lacey replied, squeezing my hand warmly. "You only turn twenty-one once, right? Let's get you a drink!" With that, she jumped to her feet and bounded off toward the bar, her platinum-blonde ponytail swinging with every step.

I smiled as my thoughts drifted back to my first taste of rebellion. It's astounding that five years have slipped by since that wild junior homecoming, when I first felt the burn of alcohol sliding down my throat.

The rest of high school unfolded in a perfect storm of fleeting crushes and cherished moments—a rollercoaster ride unique to those teenage years. Erin and I navigated the bittersweet transition of teetering on the edge of adulthood while still feeling like kids at heart. Throughout it all, Lacey stood by us, guiding us through as she battled her own demons.

When graduation finally arrived, the choice to live at home and attend the University of La Verne eight miles away felt instinctive. Despite my best efforts to convince Mom community college was a better fit, she swayed me toward a university. Now, it was time to let her know I was leaving.

The familiar aroma of sizzling fajitas and fresh tortillas tickled my nose as I took a seat next to Erin. The sounds of laughter and clinking glasses surrounded me, but my mind kept drifting back to the letter from Luxe Air.

I turned to Erin. "How did you manage to get off work? I thought your route was Paris to London?"

Erin leaned in with a playful smile, giving me a quick once-over. "You know, I'd never miss your birthday. I traded shifts with another flight attendant and got the New York to LA route this week. Elaine jumped at the chance to go to Paris."

"Thank you, bestie. It means the world to me. You look fantastic, by the way."

"Me? Look at you! You've got that classy biker babe vibe down. I love those boots. They're so edgy."

My style had matured. My long, honey-blonde hair now flowed sleekly in a side ponytail—a far cry from the teased chaos of my teen years. My green, cat-like eyes still held the fierce determination that had seen me through countless challenges, though I'd traded heavy makeup for a more polished look. I was finally coming into my own. The delicate white babydoll dress hinted at softness, while my red biker boots symbolized the rebellious spirit I couldn't quite shake.

"Thank you, now tell me all about Paris. I want to know everything."

"It's all that we imagined, and more." She added with a grin, her voice held an enthusiasm that made it impossible not to smile along with her.

"It's really happening for you." I squeezed her hand.

"Have you heard back from the airline yet? I put in a good word for you with my boss. I can't wait to have you flying with us."

Before I could respond, a familiar laugh echoed from across the room. I turned to see Shawn DeLeon, now sporting a short spiky hairstyle but still flashing those smoldering dark eyes, standing next to the DJ booth. His magnetic presence made my heart skip a beat. Beside him was Shannon Simone, her red hair as untamed as I remembered, and her smile as infectious.

Mom had outdone herself with this surprise.

"Shawn? Shannon?" I gasped, my eyes wide. "Wow, this is a total surprise."

Shawn gave an impish grin. "I was wondering how long it would take you to spot us."

"I didn't recognize you without the blue mohawk," I retorted.

"Your mom pulled some strings. Said you needed 'a little Hollywood magic' for your birthday," he said with a wink.

"And I couldn't miss it. The three musketeers reunited," Shannon exclaimed, wrapping me in a tight hug.

The room was suddenly alive with memories. For a moment, I let myself be swept away by the laughter, the music, and the feeling of being surrounded by people who had seen me through it all.

Maybe it was better to wait until the end of the night to share my news. Everyone looked so happy, their laughter filling the air, and I didn't want to spoil the moment by revealing that in just a few short weeks, I'd be leaving for Chicago for flight attendant training.

As we reveled in an unforgettable night of dancing and karaoke, I tried to build up the nerve to make my announcement while also having the time of my life.

Soon, the last bite of Tres Leches cake had vanished,

and Mom stood to raise her glass. "To Starla, my little sea star," she said, her voice rich with pride and love. "Our beautiful, talented daughter—I'm so proud of the woman you've become. You're going to do exceptional things in your life."

The sentiment behind her words wrapped around me, and for a moment, I basked in the night's happiness, the laughter, the dancing, the off-key karaoke filling the air. Deep down, I knew it was time to stop procrastinating.

The time had come to share my news.

I felt the weight of the envelope in my pocket, a reminder of the decision I had made long before this celebration. I glanced around at the smiling faces of my family and inhaled deeply, knowing the joy of this night would soon be intertwined with the uncertainty of my next chapter.

My throat tightened as I reached into my pocket, pulling out the white envelope. "Mom, there's something I've been meaning to tell you."

The room quieted around us, the hum of conversation fading into the background as I carefully unfolded the letter and handed it to her.

"Dear Ms. Silverson," she read aloud. "Congratulations. We are pleased to offer you the position of flight attendant with Luxe Air. We were very impressed by your interview, and your enthusiasm for aviation and commitment to customer service will be a valuable asset to our team. You are invited to attend our six-week training course in Chicago."

She trailed off, shock and disbelief etched across her face. "Starla, this is incredible. But what about school? You've worked so hard. I thought we'd decided you'd apply after graduation—you only have one year left," Mom added.

I could feel the tension in the air as exhilaration and fear battled within me. "I've thought about this a lot. I love studying journalism and I'm proud of what I've accomplished, but being a flight attendant is my true calling. I want to leave school."

The worry in her eyes deepened with her smile faltering. "But you're such a talented writer. You're so close. Couldn't you finish your degree and then reapply? You don't want to leave something so important unfinished."

"I don't want to wait. You didn't chase your dreams until your late twenties, and I've seen how much time you lost because of it. I don't want to make the same mistake. I want to start my dream chasing now."

The mention of her past struck a deep chord, and for a moment, I saw a flicker of hurt in her eyes. "What if something happens to you while you're gallivanting halfway around the world?" Her voice trembled as she absently twisted the worn band of her wedding ring.

"I know you're trying to protect me," I replied, my voice growing more determined. "But I can't live in fear my whole life. I've worked hard for this dream, and I'm leaving school to chase it. If it doesn't work out after a year, I'll go right back. I'll be careful. I promise."

Her gaze softened slightly, and I could tell she was wrestling with the worry etched in her heart while also knowing it was time to let me go.

The room seemed to hold its breath, the air thick with unspoken fears and dreams. We stared at each other, the weight of my words lingering between us. Slowly, mom nodded, a small, bittersweet smile tugging at her lips.

"If this is what you really want, then we'll support you," Dad interrupted, his crystal blue eyes piercing and unwavering. He gently rested his giant hand on Mom's petite back, a quiet reminder that despite their rocky past, they remained partners in life, no matter what.

"Promise me," she said softly, her voice tinged with hope, "that you'll finish your degree someday."

"I promise." Relief washed over me like a warm wave, easing the tension knotted in my stomach. "But, I have to do this. I hope you understand."

We embraced, the tension dissolving as we held each other close. The music of the restaurant fading into the background, leaving only the steady rhythm of my heart, certain and sure.

This was my time to spread my wings. The world was out there, waiting for me, and I was finally ready to fly.

PART TWO
Starla Silverson

"I want to see the world. I want to see everything, even though it may mean goodbye to home, goodbye to love, goodbye to everything that was once familiar."

— *Zelda Fitzgerald*

CHAPTER 6
Here I Go Again

NEW YORK, NY

NOVEMBER, 1998

Starla Silverson

Twenty-One Years Old

Had I made a mistake?

T his was it, New York City—everything I'd dreamed of, but somehow, standing here now, the reality felt heavier. The city's roar enveloped me as I exited the plane at JFK, the faint smell of jet fuel lingering in the air. My heart raced with a cocktail of excitement and nerves.

This would be my new home and the launchpad for the life I'd always envisioned.

Was I really ready for such a big move?

As I maneuvered my suitcase through the crowded

terminal, I tried to swallow down the wave of uncertainty consuming me. The city loomed large outside the window—larger, more intimidating than I had ever imagined.

I scanned the crowd of unfamiliar faces until I spotted Erin, exuding her usual confidence and grace as she waved me over with a warm smile. After flying the Paris route, she had blossomed into the woman I'd always known she'd become, fully embracing the glamorous flight attendant lifestyle. Her striking red uniform hugged her figure, with a fitted blazer and a sleek pencil skirt falling just below her knees, complemented by a crisp white blouse that added an elegant touch.

Her dark hair was styled in a chic, half-up look that highlighted her sharp features and aquiline nose, while the rest of her hair cascaded in soft waves over her petite shoulders. A vibrant red scarf tied neatly around her neck added a striking pop of color, and her expression radiated authenticity and professionalism. She looked every bit the part—effortlessly polished and ready to conquer the skies.

"Starla," Erin's voice cut through the noise.

I smiled, but underneath, a flicker of doubt lingered. "I can't believe it! We're actually here."

"You look amazing, as always. Ready to take on the world?" she asked, giving me a quick hug.

"As ready as I'll ever be," I said, but I wasn't sure I believed it. Erin had always been a step ahead, pushing me to take risks. I wasn't sure I could keep up.

Erin quickly hailed a cab, and we slid into the backseat,

her grin widening as she leaned forward to give the driver directions. "We're headed to Brooklyn—take the Williamsburg Bridge," she said, then turned to me with a mischievous smile. "So, how was Chicago? Did they put you through the wringer?"

"Oh, definitely. The most stressful six weeks of my life. They're trying to replicate the golden age of flying—napkin folding and all. They even brought in a makeup artist so we could master the Luxe Air look."

Erin chuckled. "Yeah, they did that during my training too. Don't stress it. Sure, they're strict on the dress code, but it becomes second nature soon enough. Besides, you've got a secret weapon."

"What's that?"

"Me!" She flicked her hair over her shoulder, flashing a playful grin as she batted her eyelashes, dripping with mock innocence.

I smiled, trying to mirror her confidence. "I still can't believe you snagged the Paris route already. I just hope my French is up to snuff. So, how's it going? Still loving it?"

Erin laughed, leaning back into the leather seat of the cab. "Absolutely. That's the beauty of joining a newer airline. You build seniority fast."

I nodded. "Good to hear."

"Don't worry, you'll get there too. Just picture it. Champagne, Paris, everyone dressed to impress. It doesn't get better than that. Don't overthink it."

Her words painted a future I craved deeply, and for a moment, I let her boldness wash over me like a warm tide.

As the taxi sped toward Brooklyn, Erin filled me in on our apartment. "It's close to the airport, and we're sharing it with two pilots."

"Wait, what?" My practical side kicked in, alarm bells ringing. "Dad will freak out if he finds out I'm living with pilots. I thought we'd have female flight attendants as roommates."

Erin smirked, a playful spark in her eye. "Relax. That's the only way we can afford such a cool place. Seriously, you have nothing to worry about. One's married, and the other's gay. They're like big brothers. They're hardly ever home, but tonight we got lucky. The stars have aligned and they're both waiting to meet you."

"I guess it makes sense to meet my new roommates *before* I move in," I laughed, half-amused, half-nervous. Erin had a knack for making things fall into place—she could breeze past details that would leave most people sweating. But as I thought about meeting my new roommates, a tiny knot of anxiety twisted in my chest. I silently crossed my fingers, hoping for good vibes. This whole whirlwind of change was thrilling, yes, but the uncertainty buzzed at the edges, refusing to let me relax completely.

Taking a deep breath, I exhaled slowly, imagining my doubts and fears drifting out the open window and into the sprawling New York sky.

"Are you ready? You look nervous." Erin observed.

"It's a lot," I admitted.

"Are you still having those panic attacks?" She took my hand in hers.

"No, remember the therapist Mom took me to when I was younger? She taught me some techniques that helped tremendously. I haven't had one in years."

"That's great, Star, you've been through a lot and I'm proud of you for facing it all. But this is a new beginning. We're here to chase our dreams."

I gazed out at the city lights twinkling like stars, reminding me of the infinite possibilities ahead. "I know. Sometimes I feel like I'm not ready for all this. What if I can't handle it?"

Erin squeezed my hand tighter. "You're stronger than you think. Remember, you've already conquered so much. This is just another adventure. And I'll be right here with you."

I took a deep breath, letting her words sink in. "Okay, you're probably right. Just some last-minute nerves."

"Exactly. Let's go out and celebrate. New city, new job, new life."

We arrived at our apartment, a loft with exposed brick and mismatched furniture. It was rough around the edges but full of charm and the location was ideal. Erin dropped her bag on the couch and grinned. "Welcome home. What do you think?"

"I love it," I said, my sincerity shining through. It felt like something straight out of a movie. Having watched countless TV shows and films set in New York, I couldn't shake the feeling that something exciting lingered around every corner.

As I took in my new home, the front door swung open, revealing two tall figures. One of them said, "Hey, you must be Starla."

"Yeah, that's me," I replied.

"I'm Mark," he said, extending a hand. "And this is Josh."

"Nice to meet you!" I shook their hands, trying to hide my nerves.

"Erin's told us a lot about you," Josh said with a welcoming grin. "Welcome to the family." He was tall with sandy blond hair, exuding that effortlessly cool charm, while beside him, Mark stood slightly shorter, his dark caramel skin and warm brown eyes making him equally striking. *Did the airline only hire models as pilots?* I couldn't help but wonder which one was married.

I exchanged a glance with Erin, who winked at me, her enthusiasm contagious. "Can you believe we're here? We need to celebrate!"

"Definitely. What's the plan?" I asked, a thrill creeping into my chest.

"Let's hit that new rooftop bar I read about. The views of the skyline at night are supposed to be the best," she said, already digging through her bag for her phone.

"A rooftop bar? We should dress up," I suggested, anticipation bubbling inside.

Erin's eyes sparkled. "It's our first night in the city; let's make it a night you'll never forget. Josh, Mark, are you coming?"

"Sorry, I've got an early flight in the morning," Mark replied, but he looked genuinely disappointed.

"I have a later show time tomorrow, so I'd love to join you for a quick drink," Josh said, his smile brightening the room. The faintest hint of a dimple appeared in his left cheek, and my heart skipped a beat, as if time momentarily paused.

"And I'll finally break out those new heels," I said, glancing at my suitcase.

Erin squealed. "This is it. The Fly Girls are taking over New York."

"Make that the Fly Girls and Fly Guy," Josh chimed in, and I couldn't help but smile at their enthusiasm.

In that moment, all my earlier doubts melted away, giving way to a night filled with unforgettable adventures and laughter. The city felt electric, alive with possibilities, and I was ready to embrace every moment.

LATER THAT NIGHT, WE HIT THE CITY. ERIN HAD BEEN raving about this club for days, so we dressed to impress— Erin in a sleek black dress that looked custom-made for her, and me in a shimmery silver number that I hoped distracted from my nerves. Josh was a lively addition, cracking jokes and keeping the energy high, but midway through his second drink, he grinned and raised his glass. "Alright, ladies, I know when I'm outmatched. I'll leave you two to work your magic. Just don't do anything I wouldn't do." With a wink, he made a graceful exit, leaving Erin and me to dive into the nightlife on our own. The city pulsed with energy, every beat of music echoing my excitement. For the first time, I felt like I might actually belong here.

"Welcome to the rest of your life," Erin said, handing me a drink at the bar. "This is where the magic happens."

"Goodbye, California. Hello, New York! Hello to my new life," I responded, a smile spreading across my face as the lights in the nightclub flickered like stars.

We danced to the pulsating techno beats until our feet throbbed, completely immersed in the music. The outside world dissolved, and the only thing that mattered was the rhythm coursing through us.

The next morning, Erin whisked me around the neighborhood, excited to share her favorite haunts. She led me to her go-to bodega for the perfect cup of coffee, then to a quaint bakery renowned for its irresistible everything bagels. We stopped by a charming boutique she swore by, where the owner greeted her like an old friend. Everywhere we went, locals waved and smiled, enchanted by Erin's warm and welcoming spirit.

Erin became my guide in this new world. She helped me navigate the sometimes exhausting but incredibly rewarding life of a flight attendant. I put in my bid for the monthly schedule and ended up on reserve. It wasn't ideal, but it gave me time to explore the city. Time to find my footing.

On my days off, New York transformed into my playground. I strolled through Central Park, losing myself in the vibrant colors of the changing leaves, and hopped on the subway to explore new neighborhoods I read about. I savored hot dogs from street vendors, their simplicity feeling almost magical. I even saw my first Broadway play, the energy of the audience swirling around me like a warm embrace.

The city was everything I dreamed it would be—and then some. While I loved the moments exploring with Erin, our busy schedules often left me to navigate the city solo. I was getting more comfortable exploring on my own. It was an adjustment, but I learned to embrace my new independence.

By my second month at Luxe Air, I got my first real route: New York to Dublin. The quick turnarounds were tiring but exhilarating. It wasn't Paris, but I was finding my rhythm, and Dublin was the perfect city to cut my flight attendant teeth on. The people were welcoming, the city vibrant, and each trip felt like a new adventure waiting to unfold.

"It'll come," Erin said when I shared my route with her. "Paris is just around the corner. You're moving up quickly with Luxe and I heard they're hiring tons of new employees. You'll get the route you want soon."

Eventually, Erin and I were paired together, and it started to feel like I was getting the hang of things.

"How do you manage to keep so energetic?" I asked one night over a spaghetti dinner in Little Italy.

"Lots of Coffee and Green Tea," she replied.

"Is that all?" I laughed.

"And water. Make sure to drink eight glasses per day. Don't forget to start a good daily vitamin too."

"Help me, Obi-Wan Kenobi," I teased.

"Roll your clothes, don't fold. Keep a spare uniform. And always carry lip balm, a little black dress that you don't have to iron, and a good book. You never know when a plane you're on will get grounded."

I grinned. "I'd be lost without you."

"You'd be fine," she teased. "It just wouldn't be as much fun."

Erin had an incredible knack for turning our layovers into unforgettable adventures. She knew the coziest hidden cafés in Paris, where we'd linger for hours, people-watching and savoring the aroma of fresh croissants. Then, there were the trendiest jazz spots in New York, where the music swirled through the air like a comforting embrace in the dim light. With her as my guide, those in-between moments transformed from mere pauses in our hectic schedule into vibrant snapshots of joy that lingered long after we boarded our next flight.

Whether we were sipping rich espresso in a charming

Parisian café, laughter spilling into the street, or gazing at the twinkling city lights from our hotel room, those experiences became the bright spots that anchored me amid the long hours and constant travel. Each adventure served as a reminder that no matter how chaotic our lives became, there was beauty to be found in every moment.

I quickly settled into my new life, finding my rhythm with each flight. My confidence bloomed as a flight attendant, and I began to feel at home in my own skin. Yet, in the cozy solitude of my hotel room, I couldn't quite shake those old, nagging doubts that clung to me like smoke.

I gazed out the window at the gentle rain pattering against the glass; everything looked so perfect, for Paris was even more beautiful in the rain. Yet despite the beauty, an unsettling feeling twisted in my chest. I pressed my forehead against the cool glass, hoping to quiet the unease swirling within me.

I reminded myself how much I loved this life—the thrill of takeoff, the endless stream of unique passengers, the intoxicating feeling of having the world at my fingertips. But as quickly as that warmth filled me, the old shadows crept back in, whispering that happiness was a mirage, something too fleeting, too fragile to hold on to for long.

Would I wake up one day to find it all slipping away?

I could almost hear the echo of my past, a reminder that I had built a life full of light, yet I still found myself waiting for the other shoe to drop. It was a delicate dance, this new joy intertwined with the weight of my former trauma, and I could only hope I was strong enough to keep the darkness at bay.

CHAPTER 7

My Kind of Scene

NEW YORK, NY

SPRING, 1999

Starla Silverson
Twenty-One Years Old

Subject: Thinking of You

Hey Star,

Just a quick note to let you know I'm thinking of you and miss you. I hope you're soaking in all that Paris magic. I can just picture you and Erin wandering the charming streets, indulging in croissants, and having the time of your lives.

Please keep sending the pictures and postcards; I've

117

never left the country again since Mexico, and I feel like
I'm living vicariously through you. I love that! Please be
safe, and don't forget to put a chair against your hotel
door at night.

Make sure to carve out some time for exercise whenever
you can. A quick workout or a long hike in nature can
work wonders for your mental well-being and get those
endorphins flowing. Eric and I have been hiking at Mt.
Baldy, and it's been incredible to immerse myself in
nature again. I only wish I'd gotten back into it years ago
—but I guess I just needed the right hiking buddy.

Speaking of buddies, things are going pretty well here. I
started dating Eric a few months ago, and he's incred-
ibly kind—in that cute, slightly nerdy way. It's still early
days, but part of me wonders if he could be the one,
which is exciting! But I don't want to jinx it, so let's keep
that between us for now, okay?

I'm still enjoying my work—it's so fulfilling to help kids
find their way.

Take care of yourself, and remember to stay safe out
there. I'm cheering you on from this side of the pond!
Let me know the next time you'll be in town—are you
coming home for Thanksgiving? If things are still going
well with Eric, I'd love to invite him to the family dinner.
It would be amazing if you were there too.

Love you tons,

Lacey XOXO

P.S. Honestly, I've been daydreaming about visiting you

*and Erin in Paris. I just need to work up the nerve to
book that ticket!*

A s I settled into the back of the taxi, New York's
sights whizzed by—charming cafés nestled
between towering skyscrapers, the crisp spring
air mingling with the scent of leather from the car's seats. I
carefully folded Lacey's printed email, eager to share it with
Erin—a sweet reminder of home. It warmed my heart to
know that Lacey was building a future with someone special,
sparking a flicker of hope within me. Maybe, just maybe, I
could do the same.

Optimism surged within me, and the shadows that once
threatened to creep back in began to dissipate like mist in
the morning sun. The vibrant city mirrored the dreams I
had buried deep inside. As we passed historic brick buildings
bathed in sunlight, I felt a thrill of possibility.

I loved being a flight attendant. It wasn't just about the
destinations; it was about the people I met and the stories
we shared. Each flight from New York to Paris brought fresh
faces and new stories, and I welcomed them with wide-eyed
wonder, feeling more connected to the world with every
journey. It had been an adjustment, but I was actually
thriving.

Everything was falling into place.

This had always been our dream, and now that Erin and
I were finally on the same route, there was a rare sense of
alignment, as if the universe had been quietly working

behind the scenes to bring us together in this vibrant new life.

As I took in the New York skyline, its electric energy wrapped around me, igniting a spark of confidence. Everything pulsed with life, and by the time I arrived at JFK, I could feel myself growing bolder and more self-assured with each passing day.

By the time I arrived in the crew lounge, I was absolutely buzzing.

"Hey there, early bird! I thought we were coming in together this morning," I greeted Erin with a smile.

"Did you get my note?" she asked. "I woke up early and decided to run some errands."

"I saw it—thanks for letting me sleep in. I really needed that extra hour. By the way, I got an email from Lacey," I said, grinning at her.

"How's she doing?" Erin asked, her eyes lighting up with curiosity.

"Still working at the school, and guess what? I think she's falling in love. She sounds so happy and even mentioned booking a flight."

"That's incredible. We can get her a buddy pass, you know, after your one-year anniversary, you'll start getting those."

"I'll let her know. I hope she gets the nerve to see the world. She still tends to stick close to home."

"That's understandable. She's not like us. The Fly Girls."

"I get it. Stepping out of her comfort zone isn't easy, especially after everything she's been through. I'm just glad she's finally hitting her stride."

Erin nodded, her expression turning thoughtful. "I agree. Everyone is not meant to walk the same path. I'm happy to hear Lacey is thriving. Just like us! Now, let's get this plane put together. We have a quick turnaround today."

Once we had prepped the plane and were in the air, the familiar scent of jet fuel and coffee enveloped me, sparking a thrill of anticipation. Every moment hummed with the promise of adventure. As we ascended, I stole a glance out the window at the patchwork of clouds below, and a wave of nostalgia washed over me, reminding me of all the dreams we'd shared. Dreams that were, at last, taking flight.

Seven hours later, we landed, and the cabin buzzed with electric energy. Flying into Paris felt like stepping into a world where anything was possible. My heart raced as the plane taxied to the gate. For years, we had imagined ourselves wandering the streets of Paris, sipping espresso in charming cafés, and losing ourselves in art-filled museums.

"Ready for Paris?" Erin asked as we exited the plane, her voice barely containing her glee.

"Absolutely, let's do this!"

As we navigated the bustling airport and stepped into the crisp Parisian air, exhilaration surged through me. A French announcement crackled over the intercom, grounding me in the realization that I was finally here. We hopped onto the airport shuttle, anticipation thrumming between us as we made our way to the hotel.

And then it happened. The Eiffel Tower came into view, looming in the distance like a beacon of our dreams. My words caught in my throat, and awe washed over me. It was even more magnificent than I had imagined, a symbol of everything I had hoped for. Gratitude swelled within me, filling every corner of my being as I soaked in the sight, knowing this moment would stay with me forever.

"Can you believe it?" Erin exclaimed, her eyes sparkling with excitement as we arrived at the hotel to check in. "I'll set the alarm for thirty minutes, and after a quick nap, we'll hit the town together. I've dreamed of this moment for so long!"

Hours later, well-rested and refreshed, we wandered through the charming cobble stoned streets, the soft glow of the streetlights guiding our way. As we approached a quaint pâtisserie with "Angelina" emblazoned on the awning, Erin paused, her eyes sparkling with excitement as she turned to me. "We *must* stop here. This is your first croissant in Paris. Only the best for you, my dear."

"It's like a dream," I murmured as we entered Angelina. The heavenly scent of freshly baked pastries and rich chocolate wrapped around me. The charming interior, adorned with elegant marble tables and ornate chandeliers, felt like a step back in time—a cozy haven amidst the crowded streets of Paris. The soft sounds of voices and the clinking of cups created a warm ambiance, inviting us to linger.

"Oh my gosh, this is the best thing I've ever tasted," I exclaimed after my first bite, savoring the rich, velvety chocolate that seemed to melt away all my worries. "How are French people so thin when they have food like this?"

"Tell me about it. Hey, I'm so glad we're finally here together. It means a lot to me," she said, a hint of affection in her voice.

Later, as we strolled through the quiet corners of Paris, Erin turned to me, her voice softening. "Let's pick up the pace. There's so much to see, and we're flying out tomorrow afternoon."

I chuckled, shaking my head. "Don't worry. We don't have to do everything tonight."

With a sense of reassurance, we settled into our routine, and I realized just how worthwhile every sacrifice had been. Leaving university, memorizing endless airport codes, and practicing my French had all led to this moment. And this was only the beginning—I could feel the endless possibilities and unforgettable memories waiting for me in my new life ahead.

ONE NIGHT, AFTER A PARTICULARLY CHALLENGING FLIGHT, the last passengers disembarked. Erin and I slumped against the galley counter, exhaustion settling in as we took a moment to catch our breath. Around us, the half-empty coffee pots and crumpled snack wrappers told the story of a grueling transatlantic haul—a reminder of the relentless pace we kept. Yet in that rare, quiet pause, with the cabin finally still, a moment of calm washed over us.

Erin wiped her brow. "Well, that was a doozy, huh? It's not always glamorous, I guess there is a downside to all the traveling we get to do."

I returned her smile, even through the exhaustion. "It's tougher than I thought, but I'm loving it. Every flight feels like a new adventure, and Paris is like a dream. I can't wait to explore more of it with you."

"Right? Nothing beats traveling with a buddy. Makes those layovers so much more enjoyable."

I snickered as I leaned back against the bathroom door. "I still can't believe how you talked your way into the VIP room of that club on Avenue Montaigne. What was it called again? We need to go back."

Erin laughed, shaking her head. "It was called Le Queen. It's amazing what a little charm and *je ne sais quoi* can do. Hey, did I tell you about Elaine's wedding? She's getting married in Cheltenham, and you could be my plus one. I'm sure she wouldn't mind. She met this rugby player on one of her flights, and they're tying the knot."

"A British wedding? Sounds like a dream," I said, grinning. "But don't you want to take a date? What about that pilot you went out with?"

"Ryan? No way! I'd rather keep my options open. There are going to be hot, English rugby players there. Why would I ruin that by bringing a guy with me?"

"Sounds like things aren't going so well with Ryan, huh?"

"Don't get me wrong, he's nice and all, but dating a pilot is tough. Our schedules are too different. It's been impossible."

Just then, Elaine strode into the crew lounge, her face glowing. "Hey, you two. Guess what? This is my last flight!"

I turned to her, surprise washing over me. "Wait, what? You're leaving?"

"Yup. I'm switching to the ticketing department. Less travel, more time with my honey," she said, her eyes sparkling with enthusiasm.

"Wow, that's huge," Erin exclaimed. "I didn't know you were going to change careers."

Elaine was practically bouncing on her feet. "I've been a flight attendant for a few years, and it's been hard keeping a social life and relationships going when I'm gone all the time. So, when Jake asked me to marry him. I quickly put in a transfer. I'm going to be a British subject soon. Can you believe it?"

"No way. I'm so happy for you," I responded, my heart racing at the thought of Elaine finding her happiness.

"I already invited Erin to the wedding, but Star, I'd love for you to come, too," Elaine said, her words brimming with enthusiasm. "It's going to be in a beautiful venue, and Jake's Rugby team will be there, too. I promised him I'd invite some of the girls." She winked.

A rush of joy washed over me. Elaine's happiness was

downright infectious. "I wouldn't miss it for the world! I'm so happy for you, Elaine."

Erin clapped her hands together, her excitement bubbling over. "This is going to be perfect!"

Elaine beamed, practically glowing. "It's going to be really traditional, but don't worry—I'm keeping all our American traditions too. Planning it has been such a blast! And there'll be plenty of dancing and celebrating."

As the three of us chatted about the upcoming nuptials, the anticipation continued to spread throughout my chest. Elaine's journey gave me hope that some people could fall in love and live happily ever after.

"I can't wait to experience a real British wedding," I said.

"Trust me, you're going to love it." Elaine's eyes sparkled with giddiness.

"Let's make a whole weekend out of it. We have a few days break in our schedule. How do you fancy exploring London?" Erin flicked her hair over her shoulder.

"I literally can't wait," I replied.

"Okay, ladies, enough chit-chat. Let's get this plane ready for the next flight," Renee, the head attendant, interrupted our little gathering and ordered us back to work.

Surrounded by my closest friends and colleagues, I experienced an undeniable sense of belonging. On the edge of exploring a city that had been on my bucket list for years. Moments like these were precisely why I had chosen this career path. I was beginning to believe that leaving school had been the best decision I'd ever made.

THE DAYS LEADING UP TO THE WEDDING FELT LIKE A whirlwind of passengers and unfamiliar faces—not all of them kind. Some men made unwanted advances, their touches lingering a moment too long. One man leaned in with a smirk as he slipped a business card into my hand. "Just in case you're free tonight," he murmured, his wedding ring glinting under the cabin lights.

I kept my expression neutral, slipping the card back to him with a polite smile. "Thank you, sir, but I'm spoken for," I lied, maintaining my professionalism. He shrugged with a chuckle, unfazed, and turned back to his seat, leaving an uncomfortable edge to the rest of the flight. *Maybe I should start wearing a fake wedding ring,* I thought.

But there were wonderful moments, too. Amid the hustle and bustle, I especially loved engaging with the young kids on our flights. Their eyes sparkled with wonder as we lifted into the sky, reminding me of the magic woven into every journey.

Finally, the time for our London trip had arrived. Erin and I flew standby from Charles de Gaulle to Heathrow, excitedly discussing our plans for our short jaunt to Old Blighty. We arrived a day early to explore the city, wandering lively streets, browsing charming shops, and enjoying pints of lager, as if we were seasoned locals before heading to the Cotswolds.

As we settled into the train for our brief journey, gliding through the rolling English countryside toward Cheltenham, Erin's excitement was contagious. "Star, I can't believe we're finally on our way. I know we're going to love this place. Have you seen any pictures of the venue?"

I shook my head, grinning. "Nope. This is all a surprise."

Her eyes full of curiosity. "Elaine showed me a postcard, and it looked like a dream. I can't wait to hear all the British accents. I mean, a guy could casually say he's going to the bathroom, but with a British accent? I'm daydreaming he's inviting me on a romantic getaway."

"Right? I could listen to them all day," I replied, envisioning the charming locals we might encounter. "Don't be surprised if we end up speaking like that."

"Let's not embarrass ourselves, okay?" Erin laughed, her enthusiasm bubbling over. "I have a feeling this is going to be an unforgettable night."

"It's all happening. The Fly Girls have officially landed," I said, slipping into my best English accent.

"From a small town in California to the cobblestone streets of England. Look out, boys," Erin chimed in, playing along with her best rendition of a Cockney lilt.

"That sounded more Irish than British," I chuckled. "But honestly, it wouldn't have been the same without you. I'm glad we're doing this adventure together."

As we chatted, the anticipation swelled around us like a warm breeze. The quaint streets of Cheltenham unfolded like a scene from a Jane Austen novel, with cobblestones glistening under the dappled sunlight. Church bells chimed melodically in the distance, their rich tones echoing through the air, guiding us closer to the magnificent St. Giles Church. Its weathered stone façade rose majestically, adorned with climbing ivy and delicate stained glass that shimmered like jewels. The fragrant scent of lavender and freshly cut grass filled my lungs, mingling with the gentle rustle of leaves overhead.

"Oh wow, check out all these hats," Erin whispered, her eyes wide with wonder as we arrived at the venue. "I feel a bit underdressed."

"Wait until they see your fly dance moves," I teased, adjusting the simple hat I'd snagged at a second-hand shop in London. "The boys will be lining up in no time."

We settled into our seats, and as the ceremony unfolded, I was swept up in the perfect blend of British elegance and American traditions. The romance of it all pulled me in, and for a moment, I found myself wondering if, just maybe, some people really did find their fairytale endings.

When the newlyweds strolled down the aisle, radiant with joy, Erin leaned in with a playful grin. "Ready to dance the night away?"

"Naturally, I packed my favorite dancing shoes, didn't I?" I shot back, using my best British accent. We both stifled giggles, as if we were back in high school. We joined the other guests in the courtyard for the reception. I sipped a glass of Taittinger sparkling wine, letting the bubbles tickle my nose.

As the sun began to set, everything was bathed in a warm golden glow, and we were all grateful that the weather had held for the beautiful bride. I caught sight of Erin across the way and was about to make my way over when—bam!—I collided with a solid wall of muscle.

My glass slipped from my hand, and in an instant, wine splattered across the front of my dark green dress. I gasped, stepping back to assess the damage to find a pair of dark amber eyes looking at me.

"Well done," the man said, his British accent laced with a teasing tone as he reached for some napkins on the table. He looked me up and down, a smirk playing at the corner of his mouth. "Were you in need of a cool down? It is getting a bit warm in here."

I frowned, stunned not only by the wine now dripping from my dress but also by what I assumed was his failed attempt at humor. "Excuse me?"

"Oh, don't get your knickers in a twist. Accidents happen," he said, waving a hand dismissively. "It will dry." His voice was smooth, but there was an edge to it that I couldn't place.

"If you weren't so massive and paid attention to where you were walking," I shot back, trying to keep my cool while I wiped at the wetness spreading across my dress. "A simple apology wouldn't hurt either."

He tilted his head, a smirk playing at the corner of his lips. "Apologize? For what? Walking? If that's a crime, I'm guilty as charged." I noticed a slight slur in his words.

I narrowed my eyes, trying to ignore the way his dark hair caught the fading sunlight just right. "Or maybe think about having a coffee instead of another beer.

"You're a feisty one." He chuckled, a low, easy sound only fueling my irritation. I couldn't tell if he was serious or trying to get a rise out of me, but either way, I wasn't having it.

"You're impossible," I muttered, turning away in frustration, wishing I could ignore the way his laughter lingered in the air.

"Glad we agree on something," he called after me, but I didn't turn back. As I made my way to Erin, my heart was still racing. His gaze seemed to follow me. Erin and I found a spot near the dance floor, where I recounted my disastrous run-in with Mr. Too-Handsome-For-His-Own-Good.

"You should have seen him, Erin. He was so smug, and the way he talked to me. Like it was all a joke," I huffed, still fuming as I relayed the incident.

Erin snickered, clearly amused by my frustration. "Sounds like he was just flirting with you. The Brits have their own brand of banter, you'll get used to it."

"It came across as arrogant and rude," I muttered, taking a sip of my drink.

"Methinks the lady doth protest too much," Erin teased, nudging me with a grin. "I haven't seen you this flustered since we were dodging the school police. Now, was he good-looking in that polished British way like Rick Astley, or more like David Beckham, all muscles and that roguish charm?"

"Okay, fine. He was definitely more of a David, only darker hair," I admitted, a reluctant smile creeping onto my face.

Erin snickered again, her eyes twinkling with mischief. "I'd say that makes it all the more interesting."

Soon, it was time for the bouquet toss, and I found myself swept into a crowd of eager women. All vying for a chance to catch the flowers. The bride, perched on a small platform, threw the bouquet with a flourish.

In an instant, the delicate arrangement of roses and lilies was soaring through the air. Right toward me.

Without thinking, I raised my hands, and the bouquet landed perfectly in my grasp, the soft petals of the red roses brushing against my fingertips as cheers and applause erupted around me. I couldn't help but laugh, the earlier tension melting away as I held the bouquet high, feeling as if I'd won a mini lottery.

"It's not too late to drop it. I know you're not planning to tie the knot soon." Erin nudged me playfully, and I swayed a little in response.

"Not if I can help it," I shot back with a grin, but the moment was short-lived. As I turned to leave the dance floor, I found myself face-to-face with the tall man from earlier. This time, there was no wine to spill. He stood tall and strong, his tousled auburn hair framing a face that radiated spirited charm. His deep-set amber eyes sparkled with confidence, effortlessly drawing me in. He wore a tailored indigo suit that hugged his muscular body perfectly.

He raised an eyebrow, a smirk dancing on his lips as he nodded toward the bouquet in my hands. "Looks like fate's got a cheeky sense of humor, doesn't it?"

I stared at him, momentarily at a loss for words. "I guess so."

He chuckled, his tone softer this time but still laced with that sarcastic edge. "I think we are destined for a dance together. Let's call a truce?" He held up his hands in surrender. "I'm Seb."

"Pardon?" I asked, caught off guard by the casual introduction.

"Sebastian, but my friends call me Seb," he corrected, a playful twinkle in his eye. "Is that alright with you?"

I hesitated, unsure if he was teasing or just being charming, before finally shaking his hand. His grip was firm, his touch warm. As I looked into his eyes, I couldn't shake the feeling that our paths had crossed for a reason—whether I liked it or not.

"I'm Star," I said, feeling a bit shy under his gaze.

"Sorry about the spillage in the village earlier," he replied with a playful grin. "I swear, I'm usually more graceful on the pitch."

"So, you're a rugby player then?" I asked, my eyes widening in surprise.

"Guilty as charged." He raised his hands in mock surrender.

"What position do you play?"

"I'm a Full-Back."

"Is that like a quarterback? Sorry, I don't know much about rugby."

He chuckled. "Not quite. I think they call it a safety in American football, kind of like the last line of defense."

"Got it. So, you're basically the hero of the field?"

He laughed, a genuine sound that made my heart skip. "Something like that. I promise I'm not as clumsy as I seem. How about I make it up to you with dinner tomorrow night? You can even bring your friend," he added, the playfulness in his tone giving way to something more sincere, a hint of vulnerability breaking through.

"You're on probation, but okay," I replied, unable to suppress a smile despite my better judgment.

"Fair enough," he said, his smile growing as he let go of my hand.

"Let me text you my number," I said, tapping out my digits while trying to ignore the flutter in my stomach.

"Now, how about that dance?" He asked, a playful spark in his eyes.

"Is that really part of the tradition?" I hesitated, glancing at the garter belt he was holding. "I haven't been to many weddings. I try to steer clear of them."

He chuckled, effortlessly charming. "I think it's an

American thing. The bride is from New York, and the groom's my cousin."

"I work with the bride. I tagged along because I've always wanted to visit the Cotswolds."

"So, you're a flight attendant, then," he said with a wink. Before I could protest further, he gently took my hand and led me to the dance floor.

The band played a soft, melodic tune, and Seb wrapped his arm around my waist, pulling me in close. All the earlier tension between us melted away, replaced by an unexpected electric heat. As we moved in perfect harmony, the rest of the world slipped into the background, fading away until there was nothing but the feeling of his warm body against mine.

"I must say," he murmured, his lips brushing against my ear, "you may be a clumsy walker, but you dance beautifully."

"You're not so bad yourself," I teased back. We swayed together, perfectly in sync, our movements smooth and effortless—as if we'd been dancing forever.

The reception blossomed around us in a spacious yet intimate garden, enclosed by neatly trimmed hedges and vibrant flower beds. Fairy lights danced between the silver birch trees, casting a soft glow over round tables draped in crisp white linens. Each table showcased vintage China, gleaming silverware, and centerpieces of wildflowers in delicate, mismatched vases arranged around the dance floor.

The air was infused with the soothing scent of English

lavender, mingling with the warm glow overhead. An enchanting atmosphere, and the chemistry between us was magnetic, drawing me deeper into the moment.

"Who knew crashing a wedding could turn out like this?" I teased, feeling more at ease with him than expected.

"Perhaps, it was meant to be," He replied, his tone light but with a hint of something deeper.

As we continued to dance, the distance between us seemed to close with each step until there was no room left for anything but us. The music played on, but I scarcely noticed, too absorbed in the feel of Seb's rock-hard body against mine and the way his hand caressed my back.

"Maybe weddings aren't so bad after all," I admitted, almost to myself, as the song faded.

Seb leaned in, his breath warm against my cheek. "Especially when they end like this."

Before I could respond, he pressed his lips against mine, a rush of electricity coursed through me. Like the crackle of a live wire. The kiss began softly, a gentle brush that sent shivers down my spine, but it ignited into a wildfire of sensations. The world around us was a haze of unknown faces. All that mattered was the heat of his mouth against mine, the way his hands cupped my face, drawing me deeper into the rush of fire swirling between us.

When we finally pulled back, the air seemed to hum with that lingering electricity. The moment was too perfect.

"So, about that dinner tomorrow?" Seb grinned, still

holding me close, his eyes reflecting the thrill of the unexpected.

"Text me the address and I'll be there, but I have to be back in Paris on Monday, for work," I said, looking up at him.

"You work in Paris?" His eyes locked on mine, playful but with a hint of something deeper. "I thought you lived in America."

"I do, but I'm a flight attendant, remember? I'm in Europe a lot."

"That's convenient."

"For what?"

"Well, I might want to see you again. After tomorrow." He ran a hand through his hair, revealing a hint of vulnerability in his face.

"My schedule's all over the place," I said, trying to keep things casual. Dinner was one thing, but he was starting to come on a bit strong.

"Okay, I get it," he said, a slight smile tugging at his lips. "No pressure."

The song wrapped up too quickly, leaving me craving more. As the night wound down, an unexpected heaviness settled over me. Saying goodbye to Seb felt harder than it should. He was such a puzzle; I couldn't help but wonder— was he the cocky guy who'd spilled my wine or the charming romantic who'd utterly thrown me off balance?

The feeling that he was an enigma lingered, and part of

me wanted to peel back his layers, eager to see what lay beneath his cocky exterior.

As guests began trickling out, the fresh air invigorated my senses. The evening hadn't been perfect, but it was alive with laughter and romance. Unexpected yet surprisingly welcome.

Erin and I found each other by the entrance, lingering as if trying to absorb the last moments of the celebration.

"Ready to head out?" Erin asked, glancing at her watch. "We've got enough time to grab a nightcap in the hotel lobby."

"Let me grab my things," I said, reaching for my bag. Then it hit me. "Wait. Where's the bouquet?"

My heart sank as I glanced around. I could've sworn I'd set it down right here while I was chatting with Seb. Erin frowned, scanning the area around us. "It was right here a moment ago, wasn't it?"

"Yeah," I replied, my eyes darting around the now-empty room. "It's gone."

We retraced our steps, looking under tables, behind chairs, and even asking the remaining staff if they'd seen it. But the bouquet was nowhere to be found.

"Maybe someone picked it up by mistake," Erin suggested, though her tone was uncertain.

"Maybe," I echoed, but a nagging feeling tugged at the back of my mind. It wasn't just a bouquet. It felt like something more. A symbol, perhaps, of the evening, of the possibilities laying ahead. It was missing. I couldn't shake the disappointed feeling that settled in my chest.

The streetlights flickered as we made our way down the sidewalk, and I couldn't help but glance over my shoulder, half-expecting to see someone watching us from the shadows.

"Let's call tomorrow and leave a message at the venue for them to look for the bouquet. I'm sure it'll turn up," Erin said, trying to lighten the mood.

"I guess it's not important," I replied, forcing a casual tone, but the knot in my chest only tightened.

"Not important? You caught the bouquet—that's a dream come true for every single girl at a wedding." Erin raised an eyebrow, a teasing smile playing on her lips.

"Yeah, but it feels like a bad omen," I confessed, looking away. "Like love can just disappear. Just like with my parents and with Scott."

"Hey, that's the alcohol talking. Don't spiral on me now," she nudged me playfully. "You're amazing, and you'll find someone who appreciates you. Look at Seb. He's into you."

I couldn't help but roll my eyes, a reluctant smile forming. "Yeah, but he's so hot and cold. I'm not sure we're compatible."

"You looked pretty compatible smooching on the dance floor; don't think I didn't see that," she grinned, nudging me again. "But don't let a lost bouquet ruin your night. Let's focus on how fabulous this evening has been. Don't read too much into it."

I inhaled deeply, letting her energy pull me back. "Alright, you're right."

"How about we head back to the hotel for a midnight pig-out session? I think I spotted a kebab shop across the street."

"Sounds like a plan," I replied, eager to push the negative thoughts aside. As we turned to leave, I caught a glimpse of Seb in the crowd, laughter ringing out like music. He was walking with another girl, their closeness unmistakable, sending a chill of doubt through me.

"Hey, you coming?" Erin called, already a few steps ahead.

I hesitated, the familiar tightness creeping back in. What if I was setting myself up for heartbreak? Seb felt like a tornado, sweeping me off my feet one moment and leaving me in the dark the next. The thrill was intoxicating, but was I ready to gamble my heart on someone who felt so volatile?

"Yeah, just a sec," I managed, torn between Erin's enthusiasm and the uncertainty swirling in my mind. Watching Seb, I couldn't shake the feeling that I was on the edge of something both exhilarating and intimidating.

CHAPTER 8
How's It Going To Be

CHELTENHAM, ENGLAND
MAY, 1999

Starla Silverson
Twenty-One Years Old

"Do you really think I should go for it? He looked pretty cozy with that girl last night."

"Don't get mad, but I did a little detective work last night."

"Oh no, Erin, what did you do?'

"I texted Elaine to thank her for the wedding and casually dropped Seb's name. She said it was another cousin he was talking to."

"I can't believe you bothered her on her wedding night. Don't you think she had other things on her mind?"

"You worry too much. If she was busy, she wouldn't have responded. I was trying to protect you."

"What else did she say?"

"Only that he's available. And quite a catch. Stop worrying. He's perfect."

"Alright, let's call a taxi to take us to his place."

Twenty minutes later, Erin and I arrived at Seb's house, a charming stone cottage tucked away in the heart of the Cotswolds. It exuded rustic charm and elegant simplicity, with ivy climbing the walls and warm golden light spilling from the windows. Erin, ever the protective friend, insisted on coming with me, and I was grateful for her support.

As the moon peeked through drifting clouds, casting its light across the cobblestone path, it pierced the encroaching shadows of the night. The cool air carried the scent of damp earth and blooming flowers, filling our lungs, while a gentle breeze rustled the leaves, creating a soft symphony of nature that stood in stark contrast to the nerves twisting inside me.

As we walked along the cobblestone path, Erin squeezed my arm. "Remember, mention Jim Morrison, if you want me to leave."

I smiled, my heart racing as I knocked on the door. It swung open almost immediately, revealing Seb, who seemed even taller than I remembered. In the daylight, his hair was a richer shade of auburn than at the wedding, and he had a faint smattering of freckles dancing across his nose. He wore a tailored shirt that hugged his muscular frame, paired with jeans that showcased his build.

"You alright?" he asked, his grin broadening, revealing a

hint of playfulness that made my stomach dance. All my nerves seemed to dissipate, replaced by the thrill of possibility that pulsated in the air between us.

"Ladies, welcome," he said, stepping aside to let us in. He had to be at least six-foot-three, with a lean, muscular frame that hinted at serious athleticism. His deep-set amber eyes held a roguish charm. "I'm glad you both could make it."

As we entered, my eyes were drawn to the dining table, where the wedding bouquet from the night before sat in a crystal vase, the flowers still fresh and vibrant. My heart skipped a beat.

"Is that?" I began, pointing to the bouquet.

Seb's gaze followed mine, a small, almost sheepish smile tugging at his lips. "Ah, you noticed. I found it when I was leaving the venue. I thought it would be a shame for it to go to waste, so I figured I'd keep it safe until I could return it to its rightful owner."

"Well, that's thoughtful," Erin flicked her hair back, her tone light but with an underlying hint of approval. "Aren't you full of surprises?"

His sexy grin spread even wider. "I try my best."

"Why don't we grab a drink before we head out?" Seb motioned toward a cozy sitting area by the fireplace.

"Sounds perfect," Erin agreed, giving me a knowing glance.

We settled into the plush armchairs, and Seb poured

each of us a wine spritzer. "So, what's it really like to be a flight attendant?"

"She's been doing it longer; got any wild stories to share?" I added.

Erin's eyes sparkled with amusement. "Where do I even start? You wouldn't believe the stories I have. Like the time I caught an older couple trying to sneak into the restroom together. I knocked on the door, and they stumbled out like kids caught with their hands in the cookie jar. I quickly ushered them back to their seats—you should've seen how red they turned! People are always trying to join the mile-high club, but not on my watch."

Seb burst out laughing, "You could've charged them for the privilege."

"So, what's the plan for tonight?" Erin asked, taking a sip of her wine.

"I thought we'd nip out for a drink at Montpellier," Seb replied. "It's a local favorite—swanky but not too pretentious. Figured it'd be a good spot to relax and get to know each other."

Erin shot me a look, her eyes sparkling with amusement. "Sounds perfect. Before we go, Star, don't forget our flight leaves tomorrow around noon. It will be back to Paris for both of us."

"Oh, right!" I said, playing along after catching the meaning in her eyes. "This time, let's make sure to visit Jim Morrison's grave."

Erin smiled as she sat her glass down. "Actually, I'm

suddenly feeling a bit tired. I think I'm going to head back to the hotel. I've got the latest Anne Rice waiting for me. You two can drop me off at the hotel on the way to the pub, if it's not too far out of the way."

"Not at all. It'd be my pleasure. There's a taxi stand five minutes from here," Seb said.

"Thanks, Erin," I replied, grateful for the smooth exit plan we had contrived earlier. "We'll drop you off on the way."

Erin gave Seb a quick nod and a warm smile. "It was great meeting you, Seb. Take care of my girl tonight, okay?"

"Will do," Seb replied as we prepared to leave.

A short while later, the three of us caught a taxi to town, the drive filled with easy conversation and Seb's charming wit. Once Erin left the cab, the initial tension between Seb and me melted away, replaced by comfortable banter.

Seb turned to me, a playful smile tugging at his lips. "So, Paris, huh? I've always wanted to go back."

"It really is one of the most exquisite places I've ever been."

"How do you like Cheltenham? Wait until you see this pub—it's only two hundred years old, but it has so much character. The atmosphere is warm and inviting. It might not be as grand as Paris, but some people say it has a charm all its own."

"It sounds perfect. I absolutely love Cheltenham; everything feels so old compared to California. I've always wanted to visit England—I really love to travel."

"Sounds like you have the perfect job for it, angel. The pub's just around the corner. You ready?"

His use of the pet name caught me off guard, sending an unexpected flutter through my stomach.

"Absolutely," I managed to regain my composure long enough to choke out the single word.

With a warm smile, he took my arm and guided me through the lively streets of Cheltenham toward the pub. The air buzzed with laughter and conversation, and I felt a sense of excitement bubble within me, eager to experience this new adventure together.

Montpellier welcomed us with its rustic charm, the air rich with the scent of aged wood and polished brass. Dim lighting illuminated the original wooden beams overhead, while sleek, contemporary furnishings offered a striking contrast. As we settled into a cozy corner booth, the warm glow and the echo of laughter enveloped us, and I couldn't shake the feeling that this was the beginning of something more.

"Tell me more about yourself." Seb leaned back with a relaxed smile. "I feel like I've been doing all the talking."

"Not at all," I replied, taking a sip of my wine. "I've been enjoying your stories."

"Flattery will get you everywhere," he quipped, his eyes twinkling with amusement.

I snorted, feeling the electricity between us again. "Well, I'm a Virgo, which explains why I'm a bit of a perfectionist. I'm also a flight attendant, but you knew that. I love to travel, obviously, and I'm a bit of a bookworm."

"Sounds like the perfect mix of adventure and smarts," Seb said, his tone playful but with a hint of curiosity. He bit his lip, a gesture that made him look even sexier. My defenses faltered for a second, and I hated that he could disarm me so easily.

"But what about the things that don't fit neatly into your plans? How do you handle those?"

I paused, considering his question. "I'm still working on that part. I guess I'm learning to embrace the unexpected, even if it scares me a little."

Seb gave a slight, thoughtful smile. "I get it. I'm a planner too, in my own way. Sometimes life throws you a curveball, and you go with the flow."

"Like a wedding bouquet landing in your lap?" I teased, a smile tugging at my lips.

"Exactly," he agreed, chuckling. "Or like meeting an American girl who challenges you in ways you didn't expect."

His words hung in the air between us, the underlying tension evident. There was a vulnerability in his eyes that hadn't been there before, and it drew me in, making me wonder what else there was to discover beneath his rugged exterior.

We talked and laughed for hours, our conversation flowing effortlessly. There was an undeniable spark between us, something I'd never experienced so quickly before. By the time we exited into the crisp night air, it seemed as if I'd known Seb far longer than two days.

As we stood outside, the soft glow of the streetlights illuminated us, and Seb's expression shifted to something more serious. "Star, I've had a fantastic time tonight," he said, pausing to gather his thoughts. "But I should probably mention, there's a chance I might be moving to Australia next year. I've had scouts from there at my games, and it's an opportunity I can't ignore."

His words caught me off guard, stirring a strange mix of emotions, disappointment, curiosity, and something else I couldn't name. "Australia?" I repeated, trying to process what this meant. "That's fabulous, Seb. Really. But it's so far away."

"I haven't gotten the offer yet, but it's always been a dream of mine. It's a big decision, and it's something I've been working towards. Let's not stress about it now. I just wanted to be upfront with you about the possibility."

I nodded, appreciating his honesty even if it complicated things. "Thanks for telling me. If it's your dream, you shouldn't let anything get in your way."

Seb's smile transformed his face, but I caught a flicker of uncertainty in his eyes. "I don't want you hoping for something serious, when I might be moving halfway around the world."

"Well, since we're sharing secrets." I took a breath, feeling oddly brave. "I've never been in a serious relationship, not since High School. I usually avoid them like the plague. How's that for real?"

His eyebrows shot up in surprise, and a grin spread across his face. "You're quickly becoming the most interesting girl I've ever met. I haven't had much luck in the love department either. Most girls bolt when they realize rugby takes priority."

"Let's enjoy the moment and not worry about the future," I suggested, the words feeling both exhilarating and a little reckless. Seb wasn't looking for anything intense, which felt refreshing. Every guy I'd dated before had tried to pull me into a relationship, promising me the moon but never delivering. Maybe without those promises hanging over us, there were no expectations to shatter.

He leaned in, desire dancing in his eyes. "I like your style, Star. So, what's the plan? Back to my place, or should I drop you at the hotel?"

"Let's go back to my room." I daringly responded.

"Taxi!" He quickly hailed a black cab zipping around the corner. Without hesitation, he took my hand and pulled me inside the vehicle. As the driver sped off, he rattled off the hotel name, squeezed my hand reassuringly, and leaned in for another kiss.

The air between us was electric as his lips brushed mine, a kiss both tender and urgent. As if we knew this night could be all we ever had, and we wanted to make the most of it. We continued to nuzzle when the elevator doors closed and soon, I found myself fumbling for my hotel key as he gently caressed my lower back. We tumbled into the hotel room and made our way to bed with an urgency that surprised me.

His hands moved with deft ability as he unzipped my dress, pulling me even closer as his embrace deepened. My body tingled in anticipation. There was no turning back.

The atmosphere was charged with an unspoken understanding. There was no need for words. Everything we felt was communicated in the way we touched.

Seb's hands were gentle and tender, as if he was trying to savor every moment. As much as I appreciated his sweetness, there was a fire inside me that had been smoldering for far too long, and it was about to combust.

An overwhelming need for something more intense surged within me. The anticipation had been building all night, and finally alone, I was ready to let go. When we came together, Seb's movements were controlled, as if he feared I might shatter. His hands explored me with a tenderness that suggested I was something fragile, and it was sweet. But I wanted more.

"I'm not going to break, you know," I murmured, my voice laced with a teasing edge. I leaned in, playfully biting his ear before sucking on his lobe, letting him know I wanted more.

The careful restraint he'd been showing began to slip, replaced by something more primal, more in tune with the pent-up tension I was feeling. As we moved together, the intensity built. Tenderness shifted into a raw connection. We were caught in a moment defined by passion, not perfection.

Afterward, as we lay there, our bodies still entwined under the sheets, a deep sense of satisfaction washed over me. The tension had been released, but the connection between us lingered, leaving me with a mix of peace and contentment that I hadn't expected.

"That was," Seb began, his voice trailing off as he looked at me with a soft smile, his earlier intensity replaced by something gentler.

"Yeah," I replied, my own smile mirroring his. "It was."

We didn't need to say more. I nestled into his chest, feeling the steady rhythm of his heartbeat against my cheek, the warmth of his body grounding me in the moment. I didn't know what the future held, but with him, everything felt right.

"Will you stay?" I asked.

"Overnight?"

"Yes."

"Let me check in with Erin and let her know I made it back to my room safely." I grabbed my cell phone from the nightstand and quickly shot off a text.

> Hey, things are going really well.
> Better than expected. Sebs here at
> the hotel with me.

> Ooh la la! Looks like someone's
> having a very good night. Enjoy
> yourself, babe—details tomorrow!

"Done." I tossed my phone back onto the nightstand, a playful grin on my lips. "So, what should we do next?"

Seb's eyes sparkled with mischief as he leaned in closer, his voice low and teasing. "I've got a few ideas in mind."

Before I could respond, his lips found mine again, the kiss deepening with a promise that made my pulse quicken. As his hands began to explore again, I knew sleep was the last thing on either of our minds.

CHAPTER 9

Every Morning

CHELTENHAM, ENGLAND
JUNE, 1999

Starla Silverson
Twenty-One Years Old

W*hat did last night mean?* I wondered as I awoke, momentarily disoriented before the events of the previous night flooded back. Seb's arm draped over my waist, his breath slow and steady against the back of my neck. The comfort of his body beckoned to me, and for a moment, I savored the tranquility of it all. But then reality began to creep back in, bringing with it an inevitable surge of nerves.

Carefully, I slipped out of bed, trying not to wake him as I reached for my phone on the nightstand. A quick glance at the screen revealed it was early morning, and Erin had already sent a follow-up text.

> Good morning. How was the rest of your night?

I couldn't help but smile. I quickly typed back,

> Morning! I'll give you the details later, but let's say it was unexpectedly incredible. Talk soon.

I set the phone down, glancing back at Seb, who stirred, his hand reaching out as if searching for me. I felt a prickle of something. Was it guilt? Or was it the realization that things could get complicated?

Seb's long dark lashes fluttered open, a slow, lazy smile spread across his face. "Good morning sunshine."

"Morning," I replied, suddenly feeling a little shy under his gaze. The confidence of last night had melted away in the stark daylight, leaving me more vulnerable than I cared to admit.

He propped himself on one elbow, the sheet slipped down to reveal the toned muscles of his chest. "What's on your mind?"

I hesitated, not wanting to spoil the moment but knowing that we couldn't avoid the conversation forever. "Last night was...fantastic," I began searching for the right words. "But, I'm just wondering what happens next?"

Seb's smile faded, and he sat up fully, raking a hand through his messy auburn hair. "Good question."

The room fell into an awkward silence, heavy with unspoken words. My heart raced, the uncertainty gnawing at me.

"I don't want to complicate things," I said, finally breaking the silence. "We agreed to keep this light. I'm not looking to get tied down, especially with everything you've got going on, and I've got my career to focus on too. How would this ever work?"

Seb explained, his expression thoughtful. "I know. And I meant it when I said I'm not looking for anything serious." He trailed off. "But I also don't want to pretend last night wasn't special to me."

The sincerity in his words caught me off guard, and I felt my defenses slipping a little. "It did mean something. I've only been with one other person. Back in high school."

He reached out, taking my hand in his. "Star, why didn't you tell me?"

"I don't know. I guess I didn't want to scare you off. I mean, all that talk about moving to Australia, and I'm not planning on settling down either."

"I'm speechless for once."

"Forget I said anything."

"Star, you are one of the most interesting people I've ever met. I don't have all the answers, but I know I like being with you. Maybe we don't have to figure everything out right now. Maybe we'll just take it one day at a time."

I looked at him, trying to read the intention behind his eyes, searching for a flicker of hope. "One day at a time," I echoed, liking the sound of it. "Yeah, I think I can do that."

Subject: Update from Star

Hey Lacey,

I hope you're doing well! Things are wonderful here. Being a flight attendant is like a dream, but I won't lie— it can be grueling. Don't get me wrong, I love it, although it can be a bit like a slog. I sometimes feel like I've become a professional suitcase packer and starting a new relationship with Seb while I'm in transit feels like I'm running through quicksand.
We've been in this 'no strings attached' situation for six months now, and honestly, it's more complicated than I thought it would be. It sounds great on paper, but it comes with its own challenges. He's traveling with his rugby team, and our schedules hardly ever line up. Thankfully, the flight benefits have been great, and we've shared some unforgettable moments in London and Paris. Still, my emotions are all over the place. When I'm with him, things feel so right, but it seems like he doesn't realize what we have together. I'm starting to

feel like a close second to his real love—rugby. It gets frustrating.

I'd love for you to meet him. Seb is gorgeous, funny and charming (in his own way). If you're up for it, maybe you could come to London during your summer break? I'd be thrilled to pick you up at the airport and show you around. It would mean a lot to share my world with you.

How's everything going at school? Are you still seeing that handsome teacher? I'd love to hear all the latest gossip when you get a chance. I really miss our talks and just hanging out together.

Write back soon. I can't wait to catch up!

Love,

Star

I CLICKED SEND AND SETTLED INTO THE COMFORT OF MY couch, the familiar softness of the cushions enveloping me as I savored this rare night off in my New York loft. Now that I was back in the States, I had a few days to recharge before my next flight. Just as I got comfortable, the landline rang, and Mom's name flashed across the screen. I answered with a smile, eager to hear her voice.

"Hey, Mom!"

"Starla, honey, it's not too late for you, is it? I hope I'm not interrupting anything," she said, her warm voice stirring a tinge of homesickness within me.

"Not at all. Enjoying a rare night in," I replied, leaning against the cushions.

"Oh, that sounds lovely. How's your jet-setting lifestyle? Is it everything you imagined?" she asked, curiosity lacing her tone.

I sighed, feeling the weight of my thoughts. "Funny you should ask. I was just emailing Lacey about it. You should consider getting an email account. It would make keeping in touch so much easier."

"I have one at school. I'll text it to you when we get off the phone."

"Look at you, embracing technology," I teased.

"Okay, enough sidestepping. How are things with you and your new life?"

"I love it, but it's harder than I expected."

"How so?"

"I enjoy traveling, but after hours in the air, I'm utterly shattered. The time changes are brutal, and the customers can be demanding. I'm not sure I can maintain this long-term, and I'm trying to figure out how having a family would fit into this lifestyle."

"I'm sure living your dream is a lot different than fanta-sizing about it. You're always welcome to come home and finish school."

"Oh, I'm not ready for that yet. There's so much I want to see, and forfeiting my flight benefits would be hard."

"I understand. Remember, you have options."

"Thanks, Mom. The crazy flight schedules also make it tough to build relationships and have a social life outside of work. Thank goodness for Erin."

"I'm glad you have her. How's it going with the British guy?"

"He's great, but he also has a knack for driving me insane."

"Insane in a good way or a bad way?" she probed, clearly intrigued.

"Both," I admitted. "When we're together, it's like fireworks. Romantic and attentive."

Mom chuckled softly. "So, what's the catch?"

I hesitated. "The problem is, everything he does suggests he's falling for me, but then he reminds me he'll be off to Australia one day. His actions and words just don't align. And then there's his humor."

"Oh, sweetheart. What about his sense of humor?"

"Sometimes it feels like arrogance wrapped in a British accent," I explained, exasperated. "Just the other day, after a rough flight, he said, 'If you can't handle turbulence, maybe you should stick to a nice, safe desk job.' Then he told me to stop whingeing! Ugh, what even is that?"

Mom gasped. "Did you tell him where to stick his sarcasm?"

"Not exactly," I replied, biting my lip. "I let it slide because I know he didn't mean it that way. But it's infuriating! One minute he's aloof, and the next, he's writing love letters."

"Sounds like he's sending mixed signals," she said, concern evident in her voice. "Have you talked to him about how you're feeling?"

"I don't know how," I admitted, feeling the familiar knot in my stomach. "We agreed this would be casual. I don't want to be that girl who suddenly demands more."

"Starla," Mom said, "if it's not working for you, maybe you need to redefine your relationship. If he's got you feeling all over the place, it's not 'no strings,' is it?"

I nodded, even though she couldn't see me. "You're right. I just need to approach it without making things worse."

"You'll figure it out. And if he's worth it, he'll listen."

"Thanks, Mom. I know I need to talk to him. I just hope it doesn't blow up in my face."

"Remember, you're strong, Star. Whatever happens, you'll handle it. You need to figure out what you both really want."

As our conversation subsided, my cellphone buzzed. I glanced down, and there it was: a message from Seb, as if he knew we were talking about him.

"Speak of the devil," I said to Mom.

> Hey gorgeous, my parents are having a little get-together this weekend. It might be nice if you came along. No pressure; I thought it could be fun. What do you think?

I didn't know how to reply. Meeting the parents? That felt like relationship territory, and we weren't supposed to be anywhere near that. Yet now here I was, trying to convince myself it was a casual invite, even though, in my heart, I knew it wasn't.

"You still there?" Mom asked, noticing my silence.

"Seb wants me to meet his parents," I said, letting out a sigh of mixed excitement and a twinge of nerves.

"Wow. That sounds like a step in the right direction."

"Yeah," I muttered, more to myself than to her. "It is."

"And why don't you sound happy?" she asked.

"That's the thing," I said, my thoughts racing. "I don't know. I'm not sure if I'm ready for what this means or if I should walk away before it gets even more complicated."

"So, what are you going to do?"

I bit my lip, my mind a frenzy of uncertainty. "I don't know, Mom. Part of me wants to go, to see where this could lead. But the other part of me is terrified. Maybe it's time to end things before it's too late."

Mom's voice was gentle but firm. "Whatever you decide, make sure it's what you really want. Don't let fear make the choice for you."

"You're probably right." I had a decision to make, and whatever I chose, there would be no going back. I wasn't sure if I was ready to face the consequences. "Thanks for letting me vent."

"That's what moms are for."

"Do you think I should go?"

"I know you're going to. I can hear it in your voice."

"Thanks, Mom. You know me too well."

"I love you, dear. Stay safe and trust your instincts."

"I will, Mom. Love you."

As our call came to an end, one question loomed larger than ever: why would Seb invite me to meet his parents when he was always talking about moving away? That night, I tossed and turned, the uncertainty gnawing at me. Sleep came fitfully, my mind racing with unanswered questions.

When dawn broke, soft light filtered through my curtains, casting gentle shadows across the room. An undeniable weight settled on my chest, a tangible reminder that things were shifting into more serious territory. I grappled with the uncertainty: was I truly ready for this, or would I end up hurt again?

After a quick shower, I decided to clear my head with a stroll to the local bodega for an everything bagel. On my way, I swung by the mailbox, half-expecting nothing but junk. Instead, my heart skipped a beat as I discovered a letter postmarked from the UK. I recognized Seb's handwriting on the envelope, sending a rush of affection through me.

Dear Star,

I hope you've been enjoying these letters. I know I could just email you, but there's something about sending a personal letter that makes me feel closer to you. Just so you know, I've never been one to send love letters to a girlfriend—until now.

First off, cheers for coming to dinner last weekend. Since meeting you at the wedding, my world has been turned upside down, and I wouldn't trade that mishap for anything. I hope you can forgive my clumsiness and how I acted afterward. I probably should have told you all this sooner, but I have a knack for putting my foot in my mouth. I felt I could explain this better in a letter to you—this way, I won't accidentally put my foot in it again.

I'm not quite sure where this is heading, but you've made an impression on the lads from my rugby team. They get a kick out of the postcards you've sent. A few of them seem a bit jealous that I've snagged a hot air hostess! I'm definitely enjoying getting to know you.

Let's not let this distance or our crazy schedules keep us from creating more memories together. Let me know the best time to call you next; I love hearing your voice and learning more about you. We agreed to keep things light, but honestly, I think about you more than I'd like to admit. I find myself wondering what you're up to and if you're thinking of me too—sometimes it feels like you are. Does that sound bonkers? The harder I try to keep it casual, the more I realize I might not be able to. I suppose that's why I joke around so much—it's my way of shielding myself. We'll have to chat more about that when we see each other next. And about Australia, please don't let that weigh on your mind. When the time comes, we'll sort it out.

I'd hate for you to feel like it's something we can't overcome.

I'd love to see you again the next time you're this side of the pond. Let's not leave it too long.

All the best,
Seb xxx

P.S. Thanks for sending that photo of us dancing at the wedding. Tell Erin she's got a good eye. You looked stunning, and I could stare at that picture for ages. Your gorgeous green eyes have me all weak at the knees. I'm not sure what kind of spell you've cast on me, but I'm starting to enjoy it a bit too much.

As I sat on the park bench, finishing my bagel, I reread Seb's letter for what felt like the hundredth time. His unmistakable British accent echoed in my mind, each word making my heart quiver—exactly what I was afraid of. The easygoing plan we'd promised each other seemed to slip away with each read.

I couldn't shake the growing realization that I was falling for him, too—something we had agreed we wouldn't do. But with his potential move to Australia looming and my flight schedule pulling me further away, the situation felt increasingly complicated.

A squirrel darted across the grass, its little feet pattering against the earth as it scampered up a tree. I watched it for a moment, captivated by its carefree antics, wishing I could emulate that kind of ease. Until now, I'd always guarded my heart, but with Seb, everything felt different. The way he listened, smiled, and made me laugh was intoxicating.

As I glanced around the neighborhood park, I couldn't shake the thought of where this unexpected connection might lead us. I knew I was slipping, and that terrified me more than anything. *What if we couldn't keep things casual? What if I was already too far gone?*

CHAPTER 10

See You Again

ROSS-ON-WYE, ENGLAND

NOVEMBER, 1999

Starla Silverson
Twenty-Two Years Old

I should have known better than to let Seb talk me into this. Meeting his parents? That felt like a leap straight into relationship territory. Something I wasn't sure I was ready for. Here I stood outside a quaint brick house in Herefordshire, trying to convince myself that this was just a casual visit.

Nothing more, nothing serious.

But why was it that the more we attempted to keep things light, the harder it became to ignore the undeniable pull between us? Every smile and shared moment only deepened our connection, leaving me both maddened and exhilarated. Part of me wondered if I was already in too deep. With that thought swirling in my mind, I took a deep breath and knocked on the door.

"Hey sexy! I'm so glad you were able to get the weekend off," Seb answered, looking as handsome as ever, his grin easing some of my nerves.

"I got one of the girls to cover my flight home," I replied, the weight of my decision lifting as I stepped inside.

His family home was a charming mid-level house nestled among rolling green fields. The honey-colored brick walls, adorned with ivy, framed deep blue doors beneath an arched porch. A dormer window peeked from the slate-tiled roof, while flower boxes overflowed with petunias and lavender, infusing the scene with vibrant color and delightful fragrance.

As I entered, a stone path wound through a garden enclosed by a low wall, leading to the front door. The mix of well-tended flower beds and wild patches created a serene atmosphere.

Inside, exposed wooden beams and a central fireplace added coziness to the living room, where overstuffed armchairs and an immaculate cream sofa invited comfort. The kitchen, featuring wooden cabinetry and a farmhouse sink, overlooked a quintessentially British back garden.

It wasn't a grand home, but the family photos scattered about conveyed a warm and loving atmosphere.

"Are you ready for this?" I whispered, feeling a nervous twitch in my stomach.

"Look, I know this is really relationship-y, but I'm glad

you said yes," he admitted, a faint blush creeping across his cheeks.

"Relationship-y? Is that even a real word?" I teased, raising an eyebrow.

"Sure is," he quipped with a grin. "It felt like the right time you know?"

He paused, giving me that infuriatingly unreadable look. Dark amber eyes holding a thousand secrets. There was an intensity about him, as if he were always one step ahead in the game, both on and off the field.

"It's just dinner. No need to read into it," I said, unsure whether I was trying to convince him or myself.

"Dinners like this usually come with strings attached," he replied, crossing his arms as if that could shield him from what was to come.

"Strings? Like the ones you're tying yourself into knots with. You seem awfully nervous about all this," I teased him. Before he could respond, the door swung open, and in walked Seb's parents.

"Star, I'd like you to meet my mum and dad," he said, a hint of pride in his voice. His dad, Richard, stepped forward first. He was a quiet man, the sort who seemed more at home in his garage than in a social setting.

"Hello there," he said, giving me a polite nod as he shoved his hands deep into his pockets.

"Hi, Mr. Wylder," I replied, feeling a bit shy under his gaze.

"Don't mind him. He's a man of few words," Seb joked, shooting his dad a playful look.

Behind Richard stood Carol, Seb's mum, and I was struck by her beauty. She resembled an older sister more than a mother. Her dark hair was styled with effortless flair, framing her face perfectly, and she wore barely any makeup —a hint of lip gloss and mascara. She radiated a natural elegance.

"Starla, I've heard so much about you," Carol said, pulling me into a hug. Her embrace was welcoming, and I was enveloped in the scent of expensive perfume with a hint of hairspray. The kind of fragrance that immediately reminded me of my own mother. "Seb's told us all about how you've been turning his life upside down."

"Only the best bits, I promise," Seb chimed in, grinning as he leaned against the doorframe.

"Ah, I'm sure," Carol teased, looking between us with a knowing smile.

"Has he?" I replied, shooting Seb a look. "I hope he's kept it positive."

Carol laughed, a confident, rich sound that matched her perfectly. "Oh, don't worry. He's smitten, though he'll never admit it. I'm glad you're here, though. It's nice to have another woman around. Boys are fun, but I always wanted a daughter to ride horses with. These guys all prefer their sports cars to horses."

Richard, busy rearranging the logs by the fireplace,

glanced over with a grin. "Engines are just more reliable, that's all. Less chance of getting thrown off."

Carol rolled her eyes. "Please. You don't like that the horses don't come with a steering wheel."

"Well, that's part of it," Richard teased, shrugging with a playful grin. "Nice to meet you, Starla. I hope you're not a car snob like this one."

Carol smirked. "Oh, he's jealous he can't make the horses purr like his precious little sports car."

"Yes, dear, you're right," Richard replied, chuckling. "Starla, welcome to our home. Don't mind my wife. She loves to poke fun at my car obsession."

"Nice to meet you too, Mr. Wylder," I said, caught off guard by their banter.

"Please, call me Richard," he said with a warm smile before retreating to his corner of the room, happy to let Carol take the lead.

Seb looked at his mom with a mixture of amusement and mild exasperation. "Don't scare her off, Mum."

Carol waved him off, her eyes twinkling with mischief. "Oh, she's not scared. Are you, Starla?"

"Not in the slightest," I said, and I meant it. There was something about Carol that made me feel instantly at ease, like we'd known each other for years. She reminded me of Aunt Susan with her domineering yet well-meaning nature.

"Don't forget me." A tall, thin boy around fifteen stepped out from behind the Wylders.

"This is my little brother, Will," Seb said, giving him a light slap on the back.

"Nice to meet you." I replied.

"Hi, Starla. We've heard a lot about you," Will said with a smirk.

"Okay, enough about that, let's retire to the lounge and get better acquainted," Seb replied, looking slightly embarrassed.

As we moved into the living room, the evening unfolded smoothly, and I found myself drawn to Seb's mum. Conversation flowed effortlessly between us. Carol was a hairstylist like my mom had been, and she shared hilarious stories from her salon that had me in stitches. Her incredible ability to make everything sound fascinating made me realize she was the kind of person who could illuminate any room she entered.

"You're an only child, too, is that right? There's another thing we have in common," Carol commented as she poured me a glass of Cabernet.

"Yeah, it's just me. My mom's a professor back in California, she teaches writing at the local college, but she used to be a hair stylist when she was in her twenties, I practically grew up in her salon."

Carol's eyes sparkled with recognition. "It's a great way to grow up, don't you think? Surrounded by strong, independent women who know how to get things done."

I smiled, feeling a connection with her that was as unexpected as it was welcome. "Absolutely. My mom still enjoys giving the odd makeover."

Carol tilted her head with a knowing look. "Being a flight attendant isn't that different, you're still taking care of people. It's a handy skill, knowing how to care for others and making them feel special. Trust me, Starla, don't get too good at it. Otherwise, you'll turn out like me, with everyone thinking they can get away with anything."

"Mum, we're talking about hair, not world domination," Seb interjected, rolling his eyes.

Carol shot him a playful look. "And who says they're not the same thing? Anyway, Starla, remember. Don't let anyone tell you how to run the show, especially not this one here."

Did she know more about my situation with Seb than she was letting on? Carol possessed a sharpness that told me she didn't miss much.

"I'll keep that in mind."

Dinner was a flurry of conversation and laughter, Carol taking the lead as Richard sat back, content to listen. The table was set with all the fixings of a traditional Thanksgiving dinner. At least, in the way that a British family might imagine it. Instead of turkey, there was a roasted goose, its skin crisp and golden. Beside it sat a bowl of what Carol announced was pumpkin soup. Served cold, as per the recipe she found online.

I forced a smile, not having the heart to tell them that Americans go for turkey and warm pumpkin pie. The goose was delicious, and the soup was interesting. Still, the effort they put into making me feel welcome warmed me more than any meal could.

"I'm so touched that you went through the trouble of planning this Thanksgiving dinner for me. It's just like Grandma Dawn would cook." The white lie slipped out before I could stop it, but I didn't regret it. The last thing I wanted was to dampen their efforts with the truth.

Carol beamed at me, clearly pleased. "We wanted to give you a slice of home, Starla. Seb mentioned it was your first Thanksgiving away from your family, so we did our best to replicate a good old fashioned American Thanksgiving."

"It's perfect," I said, and surprisingly, I meant it. The food might not have been what I was used to, but the sentiment behind it warmed my heart.

"So, Starla," Will said with a clipped British accent, "how does it feel to be the one who finally tamed my big brother? He's been quite the commitment-phobe."

I raised an eyebrow, refusing to take the bait. "Is that what you think? I'm just here for the wine and the goose."

Carol laughed, her eyes sparkling with approval. "Oh, I like her, Seb. You may have met your match."

He shot me a playful look, a mix of teasing and warmth. "Keeps me on my toes, but I like it."

"I think so, too," Carol said with a knowing smile. "You two go ahead and relax in the lounge while your brother helps me with the dishes."

"But Mum," Will protested.

"No 'but Mum' anything. Star is our guest, and your

brother deserves a break after all that training," Carol said as she began to clear the dishes.

"Let me help with that," I said, grabbing a few plates. "I'll wash. You dry."

"Deal," he replied, joining in.

After dinner, Seb's parents had slipped away to the village pub, leaving us some alone time. As we settled by the fire, the weight of his earlier mention of moving to Australia hung between us, impossible to ignore. I turned to him, my voice softening. "So, about Australia. You're really serious about this, aren't you?"

Seb looked at me, his expression earnest. "Yeah, I am. It's something I've wanted for a long time. My gramps is a winemaker in Australia, and he always spoke about the country with such love. Nothing would make Grandpa Authur happier than having me over there learning his craft, but he'll settle for me playing the old footie. It's a nice consolation prize."

The admission caught me off guard, and I found myself staring at him, seeing him in a new light. "I didn't know that."

"Gramps moved there after grams died, to take over his father's winery," he said, his tone gentle but firm.

There was a long silence, the kind that felt like it held more meaning than anything we could say. I felt something shift between us, something I couldn't put into words.

"That really sounds ideal," I said, my tone half-teasing but entirely serious.

"Yes it is," Seb admitted, a small smile tugging at his lips. "I won't miss all this rain, I've got my sights set on living somewhere sunny and warm. Do you ever miss California?"

"I suppose I do," I responded. "Don't get me wrong—I love exploring this part of the world, and New York is exciting. But I guess I'm a California girl at heart."

"So, what?" Seb asked, his voice low, as if he was afraid to end the moment.

I tucked a strand of hair behind my ear, attempting to play it cool despite my racing pulse. "You tell me."

His smile widened, and he reached out to take my hand. "How about this."

He leaned in for a soft, slow kiss. As we sat by the fire, hands entwined, a sense of calm washed over me. The moment was almost perfect, a rare instance where everything seemed to align, and I allowed myself to believe, just for a second, that maybe this could work. Whatever 'this' was.

Will appeared in the doorway, a mischievous grin plastered on his face, his presence disrupting our intimacy.

"You haven't told her your news yet, have you?" he said, a smirk dancing on his lips and a glimmer of amusement in his eyes. Seb's hand tightened around my fingers, his jaw clenching as he shot his brother a glare.

"Will," Seb warned, but Will only smirked, as if he enjoyed the tension.

I looked between them, confusion and unease creeping into my chest. "Told me what?"

Seb turned to me, his eyes reflected a mixture of regret and fear, something I'd never seen in them before. My heart skipped a beat as the weight of whatever secret he was holding began to settle over us, threatening to shatter the fragile connection we'd built.

"Seb, what is it?" I pressed, even though every instinct screamed that I might not like the answer.

Before Seb could respond, Will's smirk broadened as he tilted his head, as if the whole situation were just one big joke. "Guess you'll find out soon enough."

Seb's eyes zeroed in on me, and I could see his struggle, the battle between telling me the truth and keeping whatever it was hidden. The fire crackled in the background, its heat had faded, replaced by a chill that crept into the room and settled deep in my bones.

"What is he talking about, Seb?" I asked again, my voice barely a whisper, but full of urgency.

Seb sighed, his shoulders slumping as if the weight of the world had dropped onto them. "There's something I need to tell you."

And just like that, the calm, the peace, the fleeting hope I'd felt only moments ago. All of it vanished, replaced by a gnawing sense of dread.

"I'm listening," I said, my voice steady despite the growing storm inside me.

He looked away, staring into the fire as if searching for the right words. "Star, I never wanted to hurt you. That's the last thing I ever wanted. I was honest with you from the start."

"What news?" My words came out sharper than I intended, I couldn't help it. The anxiety twisting in my gut was making it hard to breathe.

Seb finally turned back to me, his expression pained. "I've accepted an offer to play in Australia. I'll begin preseason training."

"What?" I uttered, barely able to comprehend what he was saying. "You've already accepted? So you invite me to meet your family, and then you're going to run off to Australia? Why bother inviting me here?"

"I invited you before I had the offer," he admitted, and his tone was thick with regret. "I'm sorry, I should have told you before you arrived, it wasn't something I wanted to say over the phone. I guess I hoped to have one more special weekend with you before I broke the news."

"You have every right to make a decision like that without talking to me first. But I kinda wish you'd told me— I'd have been happy for you."

"I know we haven't known each other that long," he said quickly, reaching for my hand. I pulled away, the hurt still too raw to let him touch me. "I thought. Maybe after this weekend, I could convince you to come with me. Picture it. You, me, the Australian sun."

"And what about my career," I snapped, anger bubbling up to replace the shock. "What if I have my own dreams that I'm not ready to give up?"

Seb's expression shifted, regret etched into every line of his face. "I would never ask you to forfeit your dreams, Star. I thought we could build something new together. Aren't there airlines in Australia you could apply to?"

"It's not that simple. I don't have a work visa for Australia." I rose, needing space to collect my thoughts before I completely unraveled. "Look, I knew you'd be leaving before we started this. I thought we'd have more time together."

"We can. Think of it as a gap year. Maybe Gramps could offer you an apprenticeship at the winery? He does that sometimes."

"I'm not going to follow you halfway around the world to learn how to make wine. That's not my dream."

"Star, please don't get mad. I'm trying to figure out how we can make this work," he pleaded, standing up too. "Despite everything, I've started falling for you. Can't we make this work?"

I shook my head, feeling the sting of betrayal. "I need time to think. I'm leaving. I don't want to have this conversation at your parents' house."

Seb stepped closer, his eyes full of desperation. "I made a mistake, Star. I never meant for you to find out like this. I should have told you sooner, but that doesn't change how I feel. I want you with me in Australia, living the life I've dreamed about."

Tears threatened to spill over, but I held them back.

"And what about what I want? Did you ever consider that? Or was this about what's best for you?"

He was silent, and in that silence, I had my answer.

"Seb, I don't think I can just drop everything for you," I said, my voice breaking. "I'm calling a cab. I need some space."

"No, I don't want you to leave this way," he insisted, stepping closer until he was in front of me, his hand reaching out to cup my cheek. "We are in this together. We can figure this out."

The sensation of his hand on my cheek sent a shiver down my spine, a familiar touch that felt both comforting and electrifying. I wanted to believe him, to let myself fall into the fantasy that we could make this work. Yet the reality loomed.

"I don't know if we can," I whispered, my body trembled with the effort of holding back my tears. "You've made your choice, Seb. And it wasn't me."

He opened his mouth to protest, I stepped back, shaking my head. "I can't do this. I need time to think. To figure out if I can even do this at all."

"Starla, please," Seb pleaded. "Don't go. Not like this."

I was already turning away, my heart pounding as I grabbed my phone and walked toward the door. I needed to escape, to get out of this house that felt too small, too suffocating. I couldn't breathe, couldn't think with him standing there, watching me with that same look of regret that twisted the knife deeper. As I reached the door, I paused, my hand hovering over the handle.

"Seb," I said, my voice barely above a whisper, "I need to figure out what's best for me. I don't know if that includes you."

I didn't wait for his response. I couldn't. I pushed the door open and stepped out, my heart breaking with every step I took away from him.

The sound of the door closing behind me echoed in the quiet night, and with it came the realization that this might be the end. I couldn't shake the feeling that something irrevocable had happened, something that would change everything. Even as I walked away, a part of me couldn't help but wonder if I was making a mistake. If leaving now meant losing him forever.

And that was the thought that haunted me as I dialed the cab and waited in the cold darkness.

"Are you mad?" Erin's voice crackled through the phone as I sat in the back of the cab, my pulse still racing. "A gorgeous Englishman is inviting you to spend the summer in Australia, and you're hesitating? It's clear you're head over heels for him. Take a leave of absence from work. Renee will give you the time off. If it doesn't work out, at least you'll have an incredible adventure."

I stared at the darkened streets, Erin's words echoing in my mind. Everything felt so overwhelming, so uncertain. There was something about the way she said it, like she could see the path forward even when I couldn't.

"I don't know, Erin," I replied. "It's not just about the job. It's about leaving everything behind to follow someone halfway around the world. What if it all falls apart?"

"Don't let fear hold you back from finding love. Star, life is all about risks," Erin said, her tone softening to something almost motherly. "This isn't just about him; it's about you. What's stopping you? Are those reasons enough to hold you back? You deserve to live fully and take chances. Take that leap of faith. Do something that scares you. Live. If you keep playing it safe with love, you'll miss out on something amazing. You're not your parents. You're stronger than you realize."

I slowly inhaled, trying to calm the storm within. "What if I'm not? What if I turn out like them. Their marriage has been an uphill battle. I mean, I'm glad they're together, but how could everything fall apart like it did when I was little? I never saw it coming."

"Listen to me," Erin said, her voice steady. "Don't overthink this. You're living a different life, making choices that are uniquely yours. This could be your chance to prove to yourself that you can take a risk and come out stronger. If it doesn't work out, you can always come back to work. With a year of experience at one of the top airlines in the world, you'll find another flight attendant job. If you don't take this chance, you'll always wonder what might have been with him. He's clearly head over heels for you."

I was silent, letting her words sink in. Could I really do

this? Could I take the leap and chase something unknown, something that could change everything?

"Alright," I finally said, my voice steadying. "I'll talk to Renee about taking a leave of absence. Erin, if this goes sideways, I'm holding you responsible."

Erin's laugh was bright, full of confidence. "Deal. But trust me, this is going to be the best decision you've ever made, and I'll come to visit. I can see us now, sipping wine on those Australian beaches."

"You're really too much, you know that?"

"I know, what would you do without me?"

"I'd still be stuck in Montclair, following my mom's dream for me," I laughed.

"True that," she responded. "Go back to that hot rugby player before he changes his mind."

As I ended the call, a surge of determination washed over me. Erin was right, I couldn't let fear control me anymore. I glanced at the cab driver.

"Turn around," I said firmly. "Take me back to where you picked me up. Please." I calmly added. The driver grunted and quickly made a u-turn.

My hands clenched as we retraced our route back to Seb's parents' house.

When we arrived at the familiar brick house, Seb was sitting on the porch, his head in his hands. The sight of him hit me like a punch to the gut. He looked up as I stepped out of the cab, quickly wiping his eyes, it was clear he'd been crying.

"Starla?" His voice was rough, a mix of surprise and vulnerability. "You came back."

I walked to him, my emotions bubbling just beneath the surface. "I'm not leaving things like this. I needed to come back. I guess I may have overreacted."

Seb stood, trying to compose himself, the rawness in his eyes was unmistakable. "I thought you were gone for good."

I shook my head, closing the distance between us. "Seb, we need to talk. We need to figure this out."

He nodded, relief visibly washing over him as he reached for my hand, gripping it tightly. "I never meant to hurt you. I just didn't know how to tell you."

I looked into his eyes, seeing the sincerity there, and felt the walls I'd built starting to crumble. "Let's go inside."

"I'm glad you came back. We'll figure out a way to make this work."

"Will you ask your Grandpa Authur about that winery position?" I quietly asked.

"Does this mean you're going to Australia with me?"

"It might. I just need to sort out a leave of absence. Erin thinks it won't be a problem to get at least six weeks, then we'll take it from there. I've been at the job for over a year now. Hopefully, that means something to them."

"Brilliant," Seb said, a hopeful flash in his eyes. "Because there's something else I want to ask you."

CHAPTER 11

Ocean Eyes

KO PHI PHI, THAILAND
DECEMBER, 1999

Starla Silverson
Twenty-Two Years Old

"I'm glad we're doing this." I smiled over at Seb as we disembarked from the Boeing 747.

He returned the smile, his eyes brimming with enthusiasm and a hint of nerves. "Me, too. It feels like the beginning of something special. Our great escapade."

The decision to backpack around Thailand before Seb's rugby training began was as spontaneous as it was thrilling. With ten days of freedom stretching before us, we set our sights on the stunning beaches, eager to soak in as much of Thailand's beauty and culture as possible.

Taking a leave of absence from work wasn't as straightforward as Erin had imagined, however, I managed to arrange for a coworker to cover my schedule until the end of the year. Renee, the head flight attendant, agreed to grant me January and February off as well, provided I promised to decide about returning by February fifteenth. I tried to push that date out of my mind. I'd worry about it later.

Always being an extreme planner, there was something liberating about leaving the itinerary loose, letting the adventure unfold naturally.

"This is going to be brilliant," Seb said, barely containing his excitement as we exited our flight to Bangkok. His amber eyes sparkled with that familiar intensity, the kind of drive that made him unstoppable on the rugby field. "Beaches, the sun, and us. It's perfect."

"And maybe a monkey or two," I added with a giggle, imagining the cheeky creatures running about.

Our arrival in Thailand greeted us with the signature warmth of Thai hospitality—and a blanket of heat that was both oppressive and oddly comforting. I could feel the beads of sweat forming at my temples, instead of discomfort, I felt alive. It was as if this new environment was arousing something dormant inside me.

"It's incredible here," I marveled as our tuk-tuk driver zipped through the chaotic streets of Bangkok with a speed that made my heart race. The small, three-wheeled vehicle darted between cars and buses, its open sides allowing the city's sounds and scents to wash over us. The hum of its engine, a constant buzz that matched the energy of the city around us.

Bangkok was alive and vibrant an amalgamation of new and old. Towering skyscrapers stood alongside golden temples, their intricate designs gleaming in the humid air. Street vendors lined the roads, selling everything from fake Rolexes to grilled meats and exotic fruits, their scents mingling with the exhaust from the busy traffic.

"Tomorrow, we'll catch a coach to the beaches of Krabi," Seb said, a flicker of excitement in his voice. The thought of trading the city's electric ambiance for Krabi's quiet shores stirred something in me. Seb and I had never spent more than two nights together, with work always pulling us in opposite directions. The idea of so much uninterrupted time together thrilled me, and made me a little nervous.

"Penny for your thoughts?" Seb asked.

"We've jumped from the frying pan to the fire, for a couple 'keeping things light,' don't you think?"

"Let's just forget we ever said that. We're together, and that's all that matters."

"Until February fifteenth."

"Ugh, don't remind me. Let's just live in the moment and tackle that, when the time comes. Deal?"

"Deal," I agreed.

We spent our first few nights at the Phra Nang Inn, nestled right on Railay Beach, where the vibrant energy of the shoreline was steps away from our bungalow. The scent of saltwater mingled with the sweet aroma of tropical flowers from the inn's lush gardens, while the gentle sound of waves provided a constant, soothing backdrop. We spent our days snorkeling in the warm, clear waters of the Indian Ocean, exploring the vibrant marine life beneath the surface.

As the sun dipped below the horizon, turning the sky a brilliant orange, we would retreat to our bungalow. Where we'd shower and change for some of the most spectacular evenings I ever had. Evenings were a culinary adventure, starting with selecting the freshest red snapper from a nearby vendor. The fish, glistening on a bed of ice, had been caught by local fishermen. For dessert, we'd indulge in warm banana fritters, their sweetness balancing the savory spices of our meal. These dinners were more than just food. They were an experience, a celebration of the vibrant flavors of Thailand that lingered long after the plates were cleared.

"Look at that sunset. This has to be the best one yet." Seb would exclaim as we walked the beach back to our hut where our nights were spent intertwined on a small bed, making love into the early hours of the morning.

"I could get used to this," Seb joked as we sipped coconut water straight from the fruit. Every evening on our walk back, he'd stop to buy one from a small, Thai boy who sold them for just a dollar. Seb always seemed so at ease, so in tune with his surroundings. I found myself admiring how he adapted to new situations. That was the thing about Seb.

He thrived on challenges, on pushing himself. I was beginning to see that his drive extended far beyond what I'd ever imagined.

THE MORNING SUN FILTERED THROUGH THE SHEER CURTAINS of our beach bungalow, casting a warm glow on the mosquito nets. I stretched, feeling the promise of adventure in the air, and turned to see Seb, his back to me as he fiddled with something on the dresser.

The scent of the sea mingled with the sweet aroma of coconuts and the mouthwatering smell of fresh seafood. It felt like a place where time seemed to slow, where every sound and scent would stay with me forever.

"Good morning, sleepyhead," he said, glancing over his shoulder with that familiar grin that made my heart flutter. "Ready for our last weekend in Thailand?"

"I'll be sad to leave. It's one of the most beautiful places I've ever been. I had no idea I'd love it so much." I caught myself reminiscing about all we had experienced here.

"There's that scary L-word," he teased, biting his lip, a playful glimmer in his eyes. "Seems you have no problem using it for inanimate objects."

"Well, inanimate objects don't hog the bed or leave their socks on the floor. What's not to love?" I quipped, nudging him playfully, feeling bold in my response.

"Is that so?" He feigned innocence, then lunged to tickle me as I grabbed my bathing suit from the peg on the wall.

"Come on, let's go for a swim. It's already warm."

"You're going to wear me out before basic training even starts," he laughed, but then his expression shifted. "Actually, I was thinking of doing something different today. I have a surprise for you."

"I love surprises! What do you have planned?" Curiosity bubbled inside me.

With a playful smirk, he held up a brochure that read "Ao Nang Elephant Sanctuary" in bright, bold letters. "I made reservations at an elephant sanctuary. We're going to feed and bathe the elephants by the river."

My eyes widened in delight. "Are you serious? That sounds epic!"

"Just wait until you see the place. It's supposed to be a hidden gem," he replied, his enthusiasm infectious. "Trust me, it'll be a memory to cherish."

Later that morning, we waded into the cool river water, the gentle current refreshing against my skin. I turned to Seb, who was kneeling beside an elephant, his hands reaching for a handful of bananas.

As the elephant's trunk came down for more fruit, we fell into a comfortable silence, enjoying the sounds of the sanctuary—the rustling leaves, the splashes of water, and the gentle trumpeting of our new friends. The sun's warmth and the moments we shared filled me with elation.

"Thank you for arranging this. It's one of the best days

of my life," I said, grinning at Seb as he handed another banana to the eager elephant.

He chuckled, his eyes sparkling with affection. "I'm glad you're enjoying it. I figured we could use one last adventure before we leave Thailand."

"I think we hit the jackpot," I replied, watching the elephant wrap its trunk around the banana, munching happily, its large eyes twinkling with intelligence.

As we continued to feed the elephants, the world around us faded into the background, leaving just the two of us and our gentle giants. The sunlight danced off the water, creating a shimmering backdrop for our adventure.

"Do you think we'll ever have days like this again?" Seb asked, looking thoughtful as beads of water dripped from his hair.

"Definitely. We should make it a tradition," I replied, the idea of future adventures with him filling me with excitement.

"Maybe we could come back here every year," I said, leaning against him as the elephant took a long drink of water from the river. "I think I could get used to this."

Seb laughed, the sound rich and warm. "You know, if we keep having days like this, I might just have to keep you around for good."

My heart raced at his words, and I felt a mix of excitement and uncertainty. "Are you sure you're ready for that kind of commitment?"

He turned to me, his expression serious for a moment

before a playful grin broke through. "I'm just saying, if you're willing to be my partner in crime for the next adventure, that's a pretty good start."

I smiled, feeling the sun's warmth on my skin and the comfort of his presence beside me. "Well, as long as I get to feed elephants, I think I can manage."

With that, we shared a laugh, our spirits high as we continued to create memories that would last a lifetime, the elephants playfully splashing in the water around us.

As our days in Thailand slipped away, we found ourselves on Railay Beach, watching the sun dip below the horizon and painting the sky in hues of orange and pink. One final watercolor masterpiece before nightfall.

"I'm really going to miss this," I sighed, leaning against Seb.

"Me, too. But we've still got Australia to look forward to. Who knows? I'm sure it'll be just as beautiful," he replied, kissing the top of my head.

"I'm looking forward to meeting your grandpa," I said, running a hand through my hair.

Seb tensed beside me, his smile faltering for just a moment before he recovered. "About that," he began, glancing away as the sun's fading light cast shadows across his face. Unease crept into his tone, and the warm glow of the setting sun suddenly felt cold.

"What is it, Seb?" I pressed, sensing he was holding something back.

He sighed, looking at me with an unreadable expression. "There's something I need to tell you before we get there."

My stomach tightened. What could be so important that he suddenly turned so serious?

Seb looked away, took a deep breath, and then turned back to me, hesitation flickering in his eyes. "You need to know about Gramps' new wife. She's a bit old-fashioned, very traditional, and she's made it clear that she won't allow us to stay in the bunkhouse together unless we're engaged."

I blinked, trying to process what he was saying. "Engaged?" I echoed, disbelief creeping into my voice.

Seb nodded, biting his bottom lip as if unsure how to continue. "My gramps knows about our situation. I thought, to avoid any awkwardness, we could pretend."

"Pretend?" I repeated, the word sounding strange. "You're too much."

Before I could react, Seb dropped to one knee and pulled a small box from his pocket. "I know this sounds crazy, but would you do me the honor of being my fake fiancée? It's just a harmless charade. What could go wrong?"

He opened the box, revealing a delicate ring with a small, sparkling stone that gleamed in the fading light. I recognized it from a market stall—simple yet elegant. "I bought this in Bangkok. It's a good fake, don't you think?"

I stared at the ring, then back at Seb, my heart racing as

the absurdity of the situation sank in. This was unexpected, yet I felt no urge to flee. The ring, though fake, felt like a step in the right direction. Maybe I was safe with Seb after all.

Gazing into his hopeful eyes, I swallowed and whispered, "Okay." A grin broke across his face, and with a soft chuckle, he gently slid the ring onto my finger.

"I guess this means you won't have to sleep alone," I teased, raising an eyebrow.

"Thanks for going along with it," he said, laughing. "I honestly had no idea how you'd react."

I smirked. "Does this mean we get to stage a dramatic fake breakup, too?"

Seb gazed at me, his eyes playful yet slightly serious. "We don't have to, you know."

"What do you mean?"

"Don't tell me you haven't thought about it—a future together."

I giggled. "Oh, Seb, I don't know. We're still so young."

He tilted his head, a twinkle in his eye. "We're the same age my parents were when they got married. Look, I'm not saying I'm ready now, but I do like where things are going."

"You mean this 'no strings attached' thing?"

"There are definitely some strings; otherwise, you wouldn't be coming to Australia with me."

"You're just going to have to settle for a fake fiancée," I retorted.

"Fake or not, this moment is ours," he murmured as the

sun melted into the horizon. A thrill sparked within me, whispering that this wild idea might be guiding us toward uncharted territory—somewhere unexpected yet undeniably meaningful.

"Erin's not going to believe this," I smiled to myself.

"You two are pretty close, aren't you?"

"Closer than sisters. It's a long story. Our grandmothers grew up on a Native American reservation, and since we're both only children, we've sort of adopted each other as sisters."

"That's sweet and kind of interesting. I'd love to meet your grandma someday. Think she'd approve of this?"

"She's going to find this hilarious. Knowing her, she'd say something like, 'Everything happens for a reason, and if you're pretending to be engaged, you might as well get married!'"

"She sounds like a sharp lady. Perhaps she'll be able to come visit while we're down under."

"I'd love that." I took his hand in mine as the sky transformed into a rich tapestry of magenta and violet. The horizon blazed with color, as if the sun were painting its final masterpiece before surrendering to the night. Wispy clouds caught the light, reflecting threads of gold, while a gentle breeze carried the salty ocean air and the aroma of fresh seafood from the nearby resort.

"We should get back and pack our things. Big day tomorrow," Seb said, brushing my hair away from my face.

"You're probably right," I replied, still captivated by the

stunning view. "It's just hard to tear myself away from something so stunning."

"I know the feeling," he said, yet he wasn't talking about the sunset.

"Careful, you might lose your bad boy rugby card," I teased, forcing a lightness I didn't quite feel. The heat in his eyes made my heart race again, sending a spark of nerves through me. His intensity was intoxicating, maybe even a bit overwhelming. What if this was all too much?

"Trust me, I'm still bad," he shot back with a grin. "I just happen to have a soft spot for beautiful sunsets. And American girls."

"You're terrible; I'm definitely questioning your bad boy credentials."

"A little charm doesn't ruin my reputation. Just don't tell anyone," he joked.

"Right, as long as you don't start serenading me. I might lose my cool," I teased back.

"Only if you promise to keep blushing like that. It's my new favorite pastime—making you blush." He gently nibbled on my earlobe.

"Ugh, you're impossible," I laughed, but I could feel the warmth spreading across my cheeks.

"Yeah, but you love it." He winked, and with that, my nerves slipped away. Under the vast evening sky, I realized that while the sunset had been stunning, it was this—this unspoken connection and promise of what might be—that felt like the night's true masterpiece.

WHEN SEB AND I TOUCHED DOWN IN CANBERRA, WE FELT A mix of exhaustion and eagerness, ready to embark on an exciting chapter of our lives. His new contract with the ACT Brumbies—one of Australia's top rugby teams—was set to mark the beginning of our grand adventure.

I'm looking forward to a nice cold glass of Riesling. After all that Thai beer, it will be a refreshing change." I grinned as Seb loaded our backpacks into the rental car.

"Oh, Gramps is going to adore you. He spent some time in the forces and was stationed in Hawaii for a while, where he met Gram. He's always had a penchant for all things American. He loves talking about his days stationed overseas and how much he enjoyed the culture. I wouldn't be surprised if he tries to impress you with his knowledge of American sports or jazz music."

"Wait, your grandmother was American? How come you never mentioned it?"

"I suppose she was. Her father was an American who worked with the RAF during the war, so she spent part of her childhood moving between the U.S. and the UK. They eventually were stationed near Birmingham after the war, and over time, Gram lost her American accent."

"You are just full of surprises."

"I've got to keep you on your toes, Miss Silverson," Seb teased, giving me a playful nudge with his shoulder. He flashed me that familiar, cocky grin before turning his gaze back to the dusty road ahead.

The shift from our exotic adventure in Thailand to the rustic charm of Australia's wine country was like stepping into a painting. Our rental car meandered along the winding roads, and the scenery transformed into picturesque rows of grapevines, stretching toward the horizon. The sun dipped low, casting a warm golden glow over the valley. The gates of the Winery emerged, their ornate ironwork reflecting the fading light. As if we had stumbled into a dream.

Seb leaned forward in his seat, a familiar smile playing on his lips. "Welcome to Estrella Vineyards. Gramps pride and joy."

"Your grandpa's winery is named *Star* in Spanish?"

"Yeah, some coincidence, huh? Don't worry, he loves to tell how the name came to him when he was working in the vineyards of Spain as a young man."

"Your gramps sounds like he's had a colorful life."

"You have no idea. He's a bit eccentric, don't let that put you off, everyone else in my family is very normal."

"Apart from you."

"Very funny. Look, that's it." He pointed to a modern yet modest ranch-style home.

I was drawn to the place's simple charm. The house had clean lines with dark, corrugated metal siding and expansive glass windows overlooking the vineyards. Nearby, the wine-making facility stood sleek and understated, with wooden beams blending into the landscape. A stone accent wall by the entrance added a rustic touch, grounding the house in its natural surroundings.

The sign above the tasting room read *Estrella Vineyards* in elegant script, its letters shining against the soft, overcast sky. The sprawling rows of vines stretched out into the distance, framed by the rolling hills and a hint of the mountains beyond. It wasn't grand or opulent, yet it radiated a quiet sophistication, perfectly suited for the Canberra countryside.

We arrived at the house, where Seb's Grandpa Arthur stood tall on the porch, his frame sturdy despite the years. Dressed in worn Wrangler jeans and a bolo tie beneath his collar, he resembled a figure carved from the land, shaped by seasons of hard work and harvest. Though originally from England, there was something about him that reminded me of Grandpa Ellis.

Maybe it was the way the sun had weathered his skin or the quiet strength in his eyes. His presence was seemingly formidable, almost as if the weight of the vineyard rested on his broad shoulders, and it didn't bother him one bit.

Then, he smiled.

A slow, genuine smile that softened the hard lines of his face. The gruff exterior melted away, revealing the heart of a man who'd obviously poured his soul into the land.

"Sebastian, me boy! And this must be Star, eh?" His accent was an eclectic mix of Cockney London, softened by years of living in Australia.

"Hello, Mr. Cahill. It's nice to finally meet you," I replied.

"Mr. Cahill? Nah, call me Gramps, love. Everyone else does," he said, pulling me into a big, hearty hug and planting a sloppy kiss on my cheek. "Now, lemme get a good look at ya," he continued, stepping back to hold me at arm's length, his sharp eyes twinkling with glee.

"I must look awful; we've been traveling for days." I ran my hands down my pant legs, trying to smooth out the wrinkles.

"Nonsense. You look fine. But what're ya doin' with this bloke? Much too good-lookin' for him," he chuckled, his laugh deep and raspy.

"Ha, very funny, Gramps," Seb shot back, rolling his eyes. "Where's Livy?" He engulfed the older man in a huge bear hug.

"Oh, she's off gettin' some feed for the horses," he replied, waving a hand. "Can't keep her away from 'em. Come on in; I bet you're hungry after that long trip, and you're ready for some wine, too?"

"Sounds perfect, Gramps," Seb responded.

"That sounds like Livy pullin' up now. I'll leave you two to get settled in while I give her a hand with the feed," he said. "Dinner is at six sharp, and you know Livy—she likes us lookin' sharp for it, too." He winked, a grin creasing his weathered face. "There are glasses and a bottle of chilled rosé waiting for you in the bunkhouse."

"Thanks, Gramps."

"Good to have you here," he said. The warmth in his voice wrapped around me as he turned to leave.

"This is gonna be interesting," Seb remarked, squeezing my hand gently as he motioned toward Gramps, who ambled off toward the truck, his gait steady and purposeful.

Suddenly, the weight of the ring on my finger felt heavier than ever. Inside, our little charade was about to begin. "Seb, how are we going to pull this off?"

He flashed me a smile. "We'll make it work. Stick with me, angel."

CHAPTER 12
Every Rose Has a Thorn

CANBERRA, AUSTRALIA

DECEMBER, 1999

Starla Silverson
Twenty-Two Years Old

A s we walked to the main house after unpacking, the aroma of roasted meat and herbs welcomed us, hinting at the evening's meal. Soft evening light and the low hum of jazz music from the dining room enveloped us, enhancing the welcoming charm of the house. The dining room embodied farmhouse chic, with sturdy beams overhead and a chandelier casting a warm glow over the long table. Livy sat elegantly at the table, pouring wine from a crystal decanter.

She was the picture of grace in a tailored blouse and long skirt, her silver hair pinned back in a neat chignon.

There was something commanding about her presence, yet also a connection that instantly put me more at ease.

"Sebastian, darling, Starla," Livy greeted us with a warm smile. "Lovely to have you here. I hope you're hungry. The chef's prepared a culinary delight. I hope you like New Zealand Lamb."

"I'm sure we'll love it. Star, meet Olivia." Seb's tone was a little tighter than before. "Livy, this is Star."

She smiled indulgently. "You can call me Livy, dear. Sit and let's get acquainted."

We settled into our seats just as the chef emerged with a roasted lamb and colorful sides of roasted vegetables. The aroma was incredible, however my nerves were dancing too wildly to savor it.

"So," Livy began, pouring us all glasses of wine with a mischievous spark in her eye. "Sebastian mentioned you're engaged."

I felt Seb tense beside me, and the ring on my finger felt heavy.

"Oh, uh, yes," I stammered, glancing at Seb for backup. Livy leaned in. Her blue eyes sparkling. "You must tell us! How did he propose?"

Seb shifted in his seat and shot me a quick, conspiratorial glance. He leaned forward. "It was on Maya beach in Thailand. We were watching the sunset."

"Yes," I jumped in, catching on. "That's in Ko Phi Phi. It was so beautiful. The sky was all shades of pink and orange."

"And then, I got down on one knee, right there on the sand."

I felt the heat rise in my cheeks. "I had no idea it was coming. I thought we were just going for a sunset swim. The sun was setting, and there he was, with a ring."

"How romantic," Livy sighed, her hands clasped together, clearly delighted by the story. "Thailand, a sunset. Sebastian, you've outdone yourself."

Gramps grinned from the other end of the table. "Didn't know ya had it in ya, boy. Ko Phi Phi, eh? I been there a few times myself. Proper magical, that place. Well done, son, well done."

Seb laughed nervously. "I wanted it to be special."

Livy's smile grew. "Well, I'm just glad you two are engaged. You know I wouldn't dream of letting you share a room otherwise."

I nearly choked on my wine, locking eyes with Seb as we struggled to maintain our composure. "Of course," I replied, forcing a tight smile. "We wouldn't dream of it."

Gramps chuckled, shaking his head. "Livy's always been a stickler for that sorta thing. Old-fashioned, she is, but her heart is in the right place."

"Well, someone has to keep standards," Livy said with a playful wink. "Besides, I can start planning an engagement dinner. We'll have to invite the Whites, Aunt Ginny and her family. I'll have to make a list."

Seb cleared his throat, clearly thrown off by that last

comment. "Please don't go through any trouble. We're enjoying being engaged."

"Yes, all my family is in California, and I think it's a bit far for them," I added, trying to come up with an excuse to avoid enduring a fake engagement party.

Livy leaned back in her chair, pleased with herself. "Of course. When the time comes, you know who to call. You'll want a proper wedding, I'm sure."

"Proper, for sure," I said, suppressing a grin.

Seb gave my hand a gentle squeeze under the table. We'd survived the first round. As the conversation drifted away from wedding talk, Seb and I exchanged quick glances, our little performance feeling more natural by the minute. And how right it felt. His hand in mine, the affection of the family around us. Maybe Seb *was* the one. Things seemed to flow naturally between us, once I got used to his sarcastic humor and began giving it back to him. I'd even come to enjoy our flirtatious banter.

The night carried on with plenty of good conversation, delicious food, and some of the best wine I'd ever had. Once the stress of the engagement talk had subsided, I began to relax. Seb's family, despite the old-fashioned quirks, was warm and welcoming, and as the evening unfolded, the tension that had been building all day finally began to melt away.

Gramps regaled us with stories of his younger days, traveling through Southeast Asia and working in the vineyards.

Livy listened with a fond smile, chiming in with her own memories, adding details or teasing Gramps when he exaggerated. Seb squeezed my hand under the table, giving me a soft smile. "See? Not so bad, huh?"

I nodded, smiling back. "Not bad at all."

The dinner stretched into the night, the warm glow of candlelight flickering around us. By the time dessert arrived —a perfectly crafted lemon tart with a delicate, flaky crust and a dusting of powdered sugar—I felt utterly at ease.

As the last of the wine was poured and the plates were cleared away, Livy dabbed the corner of her mouth with her napkin and looked over at Seb. "Well, it's been a lovely evening, you've got a big day tomorrow, Sebastian."

Seb raised an eyebrow with a knowing look. "Yeah, training starts tomorrow."

"You should get some rest," Livy dismissed us from the table, gesturing toward the front door. "No use staying up all night and dragging yourself to training half-asleep. I've had the old Bunkhouse prepared for your stay. It's not anything fancy, but it's clean and cozy."

Gramps leaned back in his chair, a grin spreading across his face. "Don't let her fool you, Livy's been at it, fixin' the place up ever since she got wind you were comin'. The best for me grandson, that's the motto. You can have a proper look in the daylight."

I smiled, taking Seb's hand in mine. "They're right; we should call it a night. You've got a long day ahead of you."

We made our way to the bunkhouse, about fifty yards from the main house, and as soon as we were out of earshot, I slowly exhaled, glancing over at Seb. "That wasn't so bad."

He chuckled softly. "Could've been a lot worse, right? I mean, it seems like she bought the engagement story."

I smiled, a slight twinge twisted in my chest as I reflected on the reality we'd built tonight. It was all pretend, and yet it didn't feel so fake anymore. Shaking off the thought, I squeezed Seb's hand as we reached our accommodation.

The bunkhouse was inviting, with its weathered timber walls and a wide porch, offering a view of the vineyards. Inside, the soft glow of vintage fairy lights draped along the rafters created a warm, inviting atmosphere. A few mismatched quilts adorned what looked to be a brand-new king-sized bed. Rustic wooden furniture filled the space. The air was tinged with the faint scent of polished wood and a hint of lavender from some dried bouquets that Livy had dotted around the place.

"Well, it looks like Livy thought of everything," I said. "Are you ready to hit the hay early? Tomorrow's a big day, and you don't want to be a zombie at practice."

Seb nodded, a playful grin creeping onto his face. "Yeah, bright and early. I might need a bit of loving before I can drift off." He reached his hand out to mine. He hesitated, glancing at the ring on my finger, then back at me. "Thanks for playing along tonight. I know it's a bit silly."

I grinned. "Anytime. Go get your PJ's on, future Rugby star."

He chuckled, giving me a mock salute. "Yes, ma'am."

As we settled in for the night, the weight of the charade caught up with me. The engagement may have been fake, but the feelings stirring within were very real. How much longer could we maintain this charade before the lines between pretense and reality blurred?

BY THE TIME SEB LEFT FOR TRAINING THE NEXT MORNING, the December air had already warmed under the sun. He kissed me on the cheek, the fake engagement ring still on my finger as part of our charade. "Good luck with Gramps; he'll probably put you to work today."

I smiled, feeling a mix of delight and nervousness. "I'll be fine. Go, impress those coaches."

With one last grin, Seb jogged off, leaving a warm tremor in my chest. I stepped outside, the morning air infused with the earthy scent of eucalyptus and rain-soaked soil. In the distance, I spotted Gramps near the vineyards, his broad-brimmed hat casting a shadow over his weathered features.

"Ah, there ya are," Gramps called out, waving me over with a grin. "Hope you're ready to get yer hands dirty." Clad in his usual bolo tie and Wranglers, he stood by the main house, his face crinkling into that familiar smile as I approached. "Ready for yer first day on the job, love?"

"I'm ready," I said, tying my hair back. "What's on the agenda?"

"Well, it's December, so we're just past flowering season. We're keepin' an eye on the fruit set. Makin' sure the berries are comin' in good and proper." His Cockney accent rolled off his tongue like music, still strong despite his years in Australia. "The technical term is Veraison."

"Veraison," I echoed, the word foreign yet intriguing.

"The work ain't glamorous, but it's important. Gotta make sure them vines are thinned out to let the sunlight in. Sunlight's the key this time of year." He handed me a pair of pruning shears and motioned toward the nearest row of vines. "Come on then. I'll show ya how it's done. We're lookin' to do a bit of canopy management, keepin' good airflow to avoid rot. Ain't nothin' worse than losin' a crop to mold."

As we walked through the rows, I took in the sight of the thick, healthy vines with clusters of small green grapes just beginning to form. The air smelled earthy and fresh, a faint hint of sweetness mingling as we moved between the vines.

"See here," Gramps said, crouching to point at a section of the vine. "This bit's growin' too dense. We'll thin it a bit, make room for the grapes to get more light. Go on, give it a go."

I took the shears, feeling their weight in my hands, and carefully snipped away the excess leaves. To my surprise, I felt right at home. The work was oddly satisfying. The summer sun warmed my back, and there was something peaceful about being out in the vineyard, the gentle rustle of the wind through the leaves making it all feel like a sweet, quiet song.

"You're a natural, love," Gramps said, watching me with a proud smile. "You've got the touch. Not everyone does, mind you."

"Thanks," I said, straightening and wiping the sweat from my forehead. "I didn't think I'd enjoy this so much."

Gramps chuckled. "Well, there's somethin' special about workin' the land. You get to see the fruit of yer labor. Every bottle of wine we make, there's a bit of us in there. Family legacy, and all that."

"I can see why you stayed after all these years."

Gramps' expression softened. "Aye, well, I didn't come here by choice, mind. Sometimes life throws you a curve ball and you have to pivot. Lost me first wife back in London, and my dad was runnin' this place alone. Came out to lend a hand, and before I knew it, the vineyard had its hooks in me. Fell in love with it. A few years later, I fell in love with Livy, too."

"I'm glad it all worked out for you, losing a wife had to be hard on you."

"Ain't that the truth." He nodded, his voice steady, infused with the wisdom of years. "Struggling is just part of life. Take these grapes, for instance. The tougher the struggle, the better the wine. When the vines have to fight.

Drought, poor soil, rough conditions. It forces them to channel their energy into the fruit, not the leaves or branches. That's when you get the best flavors. Grapes with real character and depth."

"I've never thought of it like that." I wiped at the sweat forming at my brow.

"Same goes for people, love. A bit of hardship makes a person resilient, more complex. It builds strength, richness, and a fullness that you can't find in the easy times."

I gave a small, appreciative smile, feeling a new respect for the vineyard and the work that went into it. "I'm glad to be part of it."

"Good," Gramps said, clapping me on the shoulder. "You'll learn a lot. And who knows, by the time you're done, you might fancy yerself a winemaker."

I giggled. "Maybe. Let's see how I do with pruning first."

Gramps chuckled, watching as I continued working the vines. The day passed quickly. We continued to talk about wine, family, and life, and with every passing hour, I felt more at ease. There was something about being out here in the fresh air, working with my hands, that made me feel connected. Not to the land, but to Seb's family, and maybe even to my own roots. Grandma and her family had been migrant farm workers, living their lives in tune with the seasons, and I could almost feel the spirit of my ancestors guiding me as I pruned the vines.

As the afternoon began to fade, Gramps called it a day.

"That's enough fer today, love. You did good. We'll get back at it tomorrow."

I wiped my hands on my jeans, feeling surprisingly satisfied with the work. "I can't believe how much I enjoyed this. I didn't think I'd be the vineyard type."

"You never know what suits ya 'til you try. It might not be as exciting as jet-setting around in one of them aeroplanes, yet there's a beauty in this, too. It's all about finding joy in the little things. Come on, let's head back. Chef will have dinner on soon."

As we walked back toward the house, the vineyard behind us bathed in the golden light of late afternoon, I couldn't help feeling like I'd found something, a sense of purpose, of belonging. It wasn't just Seb's world anymore; it was mine, too.

THE WEEKS UNFOLDED LIKE THE SLOW RIPENING OF THE grapes in the vineyard. Steady, deliberate, and full of promise. Each day, I found myself more connected to the rhythm of this place, the quiet harmony of nature, and the satisfaction of working with my hands. Gramps taught me everything. How to care for the vines, how to read the soil, how to listen to the land.

Seb came and went, busy with preseason training, even when he wasn't around, I felt at ease. The vineyard had a way of grounding me, like it had been waiting for me all along.

By the time the vines began to thicken, and the grapes swelled with juice, I had learned to appreciate the subtle beauty in the process. Each step, from pruning, watering and harvesting, was a reminder nothing worth having comes without patience and care. Some afternoons, I took time off from working the vineyard to watch Seb practice.

There was something mesmerizing about the way he moved. So fluid, so focused. I loved watching him. It was as if the pitch was his stage, and he was performing with every ounce of his being.

"You're staring, love," Seb called out, catching me watching him from the sidelines, a playful smirk on his face.

"Can't help it. You're kind of good at this," I shot back.

He winked and returned to the game. Moments later, the world seemed to stop. Seb had taken a hard hit and was on the ground, pain etched across his face, clutching his knee.

"Seb," I screamed, my heart in my throat as I ran to him.

I seemed to be running in slow motion as I sprinted across the field, my anxiety catching in my chest. When I reached Seb, he was still on the ground, his face twisted in agony. He was clutching his knee like it anchored him to the earth.

"Seb!" I knelt beside him, my hands trembling as I reached out to touch his arm. "What happened?"

His face drained of color, a look of anguish etched across his features. "My knee," he grimaced, his voice tight with pain. "It gave out. It's bad, Star."

The medics were rushing over, their footsteps pounding the earth, all I could see was Seb. The confidence, the strength that always radiated from him, was crumbling before my eyes. His career, his future. It all hung in the balance.

I reached for his hand, squeezing it tight, my mind racing with a thousand questions, a thousand fears. This wasn't part of the plan. This wasn't how things were supposed to go.

"Seb, you're going to be okay," I whispered, even as I said the words, doubt gnawed at the edges of my certainty.

His eyes found me, brimming with pain and something else. Fear. The kind of fear that made my stomach twist into knots.

"What if this is it, Star?" he responded, his voice barely audible over the rush of footsteps and frantic chatter around us. What if everything I've worked for is over?"

I opened my mouth to reassure him, to tell him that it would be fine, that we would get through this together. The words wouldn't come. Because in that moment, as the medics lifted him onto the stretcher, and the sirens began to wail in the distance, I realized that I didn't know what was going to happen next.

Then I thought of Lacey and everything she'd been through. I remembered her telling me how, in the darkest moments, all she needed was someone beside her, someone to remind her she wasn't alone.

"I'm here, Seb. Whatever happens, we're in this together."

But as the words left my mouth, a quiet fear crept in, and I found myself bracing for the storm upon us, uncertain if either of us was truly ready for what was coming.

CHAPTER 13
Torn

CANBERRA, AUSTRALIA
JANUARY, 2000

Starla Silverson
Twenty-Two Years Old

Seb's face was all I could see as the medics loaded him into the ambulance. His expression was a haunting mix of pain and fear that clung to me like a shadow. The rest of the day blurred into a series of frantic moments. The rush to the hospital, the sterile waiting room, and the suffocating silence that hung in the air until the doctor finally stepped in with news like a punch to the gut.

"A torn ACL," he said, and the ground beneath me shifted. This wasn't just a temporary setback; it threatened to unravel everything Seb had built. In the days that followed, the house changed, as if a heavy fog had settled over the vineyard. Once filled with laughter and playful banter, it now echoed with an unyielding silence.

Seb's crutches scraped against the hardwood floor, each sounding like a painful reminder of his new reality—a prison of stillness where frustration simmered beneath the surface. "I'm supposed to be out there, not stuck in here," Seb muttered one evening, his words taut with frustration as I adjusted the pillows under his injured leg. I could sense the weight of his dreams crumbling, and it broke my heart.

"This sucks, Seb, but you're more than just a fullback," I said, trying to infuse some hope into the heavy air. "We'll figure this out together." I handed him the painkillers, wishing I could take away his suffering.

"Easy for you to say, Star." His words were sharp, tinged with bitterness, then softened as guilt washed over him. "Sorry, love. It's hard."

"I know it is," I whispered, reaching for his hand, wanting to bridge the growing distance between us. "Let's focus on what you can do, not what you can't. We're in this together."

He squeezed my hand, and for a moment, his eyes flashed with a vulnerability that made my heart ache. "I don't deserve you," he murmured, the crack in his voice echoing the fragility of his spirit."

"You've got me anyway," I said, leaning down to kiss his forehead, feeling the warmth of him beneath my lips. "We'll get through this together."

Gramps, with his weathered wisdom, took it all in stride.

"Ah, I've seen worse, mate," he said one evening, leaning on the porch railing as he watched Seb struggle to move about. "Back in my day, we didn't have all this fancy medicine. Ya had to grit yer teeth. Listen, son, sometimes life deals ya a hand that ain't what ya hoped for. Don't mean ya fold. Maybe it's time to pivot."

Seb sighed, his jaw clenched tightly. "That's the thing, Gramps. The doc doesn't think I'll be able to play at all. Says the injury is too severe. Even with surgery. It's going to take a lot of physical therapy to walk without a limp."

Gramps regarded him with a steady gaze. "Well, I ain't gonna sugarcoat it, mate. That's a bloody hard blow. Life ain't just about what yer doin'. It's about what ya do next."

Seb managed a faint smile, I could see the struggle beneath. His world had always revolved around motion. On the pitch, in the gym, always charging forward. He was stuck, a restless energy bubbling beneath the surface.

As the weeks passed after his surgery, time seemed to drag along with the weight of his injury. The rugby organization sent a physical therapist daily, it was only a band-aid on a wound that ran deep. Our once vibrant ranch house felt muted, its joy eclipsed by the heaviness in Seb's heart. Little by little, I noticed something beginning to shift.

"You ever think about what you'd be doing if you weren't a rugby player?" I asked one night as we sat on the porch, the moonlight spilling over the vineyard, casting everything in a silver glow.

Seb was quiet for a moment, lost in thought as he stared out at the vines. "Not really. Rugby's always been my life."

"Well," I said gently, "You've got time to figure it out."

He chuckled, a hint of bitterness in his smile. "Time? That's all I've got."

I felt a pang of sorrow for both of us. The Seb I had known. Driven, ambitious, always pushing forward. Grappling with a new identity, and it terrified me to see him so lost. Our relationship had shifted, too. It wasn't just about love anymore, but about navigating this unexpected territory together.

As I looked at him, I realized our connection would be tested. How we faced this challenge would not only shape who Seb became, but also define us as a couple. Would we grow together or drift apart? The weight of uncertainty settled heavily in my chest, yet I knew one thing: we had to navigate this storm together.

"How ya feelin', mate?" Gramps appeared, wiping his hands on his jeans as he joined us.

"A bit better," Seb replied, though I could see the weight of his injury still lingering.

"Well, let me tell ya somethin', boy," Gramps said, settlin' into the chair beside Seb. "If there's one thing I've learned, it's that ya got to keep busy. Get outside, find somethin' that lights a fire in ya. This winery saved me, when I thought I was done for. Might just be what saves you, too."

Seb looked at him, something flickering in his eyes. "What are you suggesting?"

Gramps grinned, his eyes twinkling. "Star's been learnin' a lot about winemakin'. Maybe it's time you start, too."

Seb sat there, Gramps' words hanging in the air like the evening mist. I reached for his hand, squeezing it gently. Like the vines, we were growing through the struggle. Finding a new purpose.

Seb took a deep breath, glancing at me with a small smile. "Guess we better start thinking about our next vintage."

I smiled back, feeling a sense of peace wash over me. "Yeah. I think we've got a good one coming."

The weeks that followed stretched on, a subtle shift in the air signaling change. Seb, still on the mend, began spending more time with Gramps in the vineyard. At first, he hobbled alongside him on crutches, then transitioned to a cane, and finally walked unassisted. While frustration lingered, it began to fade as he immersed himself in the winery's daily rhythm. Each morning, Gramps would be waiting at the kitchen table with a strong cup of coffee and a knowing smile. "C'mon, mate, time to get yer hands dirty. The vines don't wait, an' neither should you."

At first, Seb was reluctant. The work was grueling, and his leg remained stiff, making every task feel like a monumental effort. He often found himself frustrated, as simple tasks that once took mere moments now demanded intense concentration as he learned to maneuver with his new limitations.

Eventually I began to notice a change in Seb. He began

to ask questions—about the soil, the grapes, and the fermentation process. His interest was piqued. Soon, he looked forward to joining Gramps in the fields, trimming the vines, checking the irrigation, and even helping with the early stages of the winemaking process.

One afternoon, as we stood together in the vineyard, Seb turned to me, wiping sweat from his brow. "You know, this isn't so bad. I never thought I'd find myself enjoying this kind of work. It's been good for me."

I smiled, feeling a sense of pride swell in my chest. "I knew you'd come around. There's something about being out here, working with the land. It gets under your skin."

Seb nodded, his gaze sweeping across the rows of vines. "I'm starting to get it. It's like rugby in a way. You put in the work, trust the process, and hope for a good result. There's always that element of unpredictability. You can't control everything."

Gramps appeared, holding a pair of pruning shears in his hand. "That's the beauty of it, mate. Every season's different, every vintage has its own story. Ya just gotta be willin' to roll with it, adapt when things go sideways. The best grapes come from the toughest years."

Seb chuckled, the sound more genuine than it had been in weeks. "You've said that a few times now, Gramps."

Gramps grinned, his weathered face lighting up. "Well, it's true, ain't it? This here vineyard's been through droughts, storms, all sorts of hardships. Now it's stronger than ever. Same goes for you, boy. Ya just gotta trust in the process. Might not be playin' rugby again, but that don't mean yer done."

I watched as Seb took in Gramps' words, his gaze softening as he looked out over the vineyard. "Yeah," he said quietly. "I guess you're right."

Seb's spark slowly returned in the coming days. He threw himself into learning the ropes of the winery, spending hours with Gramps in the cellar, tasting the wines, understanding the delicate balance of flavors.

One evening, as we were just cleaning our dinner dishes, Seb turned to me, a small smile pulling at the corners of his mouth. "I could get used to this. Maybe this is what I'm supposed to do."

"Wash dishes?" I teased.

"No, smarty pants. This wine-making business. It's been therapeutic."

I leaned into him, resting my head on his shoulder. "I think you're right. You've found something here, Seb. Something worth sticking around to see."

He wrapped his arm around me, pulling me closer. "Yeah. Maybe we'll make the best vintage yet."

And in that moment, I knew we were becoming stronger, ready to face whatever the future held.

CHAPTER 14
Don't Want to Go to London

CANBERRA, AUSTRALIA
FEBRUARY, 2000

Starla Silverson
Twenty-Two Years Old

Could this really be the future I was meant to have?

As February 15th loomed closer, the weight of my decision pressed heavily on my chest. I found myself caught in a relentless cycle of what-ifs: Should I return to Luxe Aire and dive back into the fast-paced life of a flight attendant, or should I choose to stay here with Seb, basking in the warmth of something genuine? Deep down, I knew I didn't want to go back. Seb's injury had complicated things, and it never felt like the right moment to bring it up. But tonight, over dinner, I was determined to talk to him about it.

This land had become more than just Seb's world; it was mine now too. Each step I took between the rows of vines felt like a step toward an unexpected future—one that fit me better than any life I had imagined.

I used to crave the fast-paced life of a flight attendant— the exhilaration of new places and the thrill of adventure. But working on the vineyard brought a sense of stability. I felt no longing for the long flights, the jet lag, or the endless shuffle through crowded airports. The frantic energy that once defined my days now felt foreign.

No, I was changing. Slowly, like the vines reaching for the light, I was finding my place in this new world. I learned to embrace stillness and appreciate the beauty of nurturing something to fruition. This land, this life, was beginning to feel like home.

But all of that shattered one afternoon as we worked side-by-side on the family vineyard, embracing our new purpose. Suddenly, Seb's cell phone rang, slicing through the moment like a bolt of thunder. He pulled it from his pocket, glancing at the screen. I noticed the change in his expression; the contentment in his eyes was replaced with concern.

"It's Mum," he said, as if that explained everything. He stepped a few paces away to take the call, but even from a distance, I could see the tension in his shoulders growing with every word she spoke.

I tried to focus on the vines, on the life we'd nurtured here together, but my mind kept drifting back to Seb. His voice, usually so steady, edged with frustration. Words like 'revoked' and 'visa' floated over to me, each one landing with heavier weight. He hung up and turned to me, his expression a blend of frustration and resignation.

"Mum says I need to go back to England to sort things out," he said, the weight of his words heavy with defeat. "My work visa has been revoked since I'm not playing rugby anymore. If I want to come back to Australia, I have to apply for a new visa from England."

"That doesn't make any sense," I protested, grasping at any possible solution. "You're working here now. Your grandpa is an Australian citizen, and you're contributing to the family business. We can reapply from here, can't we? Maybe talk to an immigration lawyer? There has to be a way to sort this out without you leaving. I was able to get my working holiday visa without returning to the U.S."

He sighed, running a hand through his hair. "Star, I want to stay, but Mum thinks it's too risky. If I don't leave voluntarily, they could deport me. If that happens, I might not be allowed back for years. We can't fight this from here."

"Mum thinks, Mum says." I heard the bitterness in my voice and cringed, yet I couldn't help it. "What about what I think, Seb? What about us? Isn't it worth making one phone call to a lawyer for advice? It feels like you want to make this big decision without me, and I left everything behind to be here with you. If we're going to make this work, you can't keep calling the shots alone."

He looked at me, eyes filled with conflict. "I want to do

this the right way. I don't want to risk making things worse. We've worked so hard to build something here. If I don't handle this properly, it could all be taken away. I could get deported. I hadn't thought of that. I'd been so focused on my recovery; I forgot about my visa."

I felt a tight knot form in my stomach, a familiar mix of frustration and helplessness. Memories of my parents making decisions for me—forcing me into paths I didn't choose—flashed through my mind. It was like being a child again, standing on the sidelines while everyone else dictated my future. "Seb, you're making me feel like I have no say in this," I said, my voice trembling slightly. "I came all this way, and now it feels like I'm just supposed to sit back and watch you leave. What if you don't come back?"

"Star, please try to understand."

I felt his frustration and my own fear bubbling inside me. "So, you're going to leave? Just like that?"

"It's not like I have a choice," he shot back, the sadness laced in his words impossible to miss. "I'm trying to do the right thing. Come with me."

I stepped back, crossing my arms over my chest like a shield. "I followed you halfway across the world once. I left everything behind for you. And you want me to follow you back to England without making a single phone call?"

He shook his head, a flicker of dread appearing in his eyes. "Can't you just wait here? Keep working at the winery?"

"Stay here? Without you?" My voice cracked, the

vulnerability I'd been trying to hold at bay spilling over. "How long will you be gone? Weeks? Months? And what if things don't work out? What if you can't get a visa?"

"Star, please," he pleaded, reaching out to touch my arm. I pulled away. "I need you to trust me. I'll come back as soon as possible. Wait for me."

"Wait for you?" The words slipped out before I could stop them, my chest tightening as a familiar wave of dread crept in. The air around us grew thick and heavy. My heart pounded as memories surged back. Nights in Hollywood, a young girl staring out the window, waiting for Mom to come home. Missing Dad, missing the life we had. The sound of a key in the door that never came until I was fast asleep. The endless waiting, the broken promises. It all came flooding back.

"Do you even know what you're asking?" My hands shook, panic rising in my throat like a tide I couldn't control. "I can't sit here, wondering if or when you'll come back."

"Please," he said softly, his voice trembling with urgency. "I don't want to lose you over this. You're overreacting."

Overreacting? That word stung, revealing a side of Seb I didn't want to see. It felt dismissive, and I couldn't shake the unease growing within me. Just this morning, I'd felt a surge of hope, eager to discuss my desire to stay in Australia with him. I had envisioned us planning a future together, but now, it seemed as though he wasn't showing me the same consideration.

"I'm not going to stay without you, Seb," I said firmly.

"If you're going back to England, then I'm going back home, too. Back to California."

He looked at me, shock and hurt in his eyes. "What? No, Star, please. This place means so much to you. To us. Don't let this setback ruin everything we've worked for."

"It's already ruined," I said softly, feeling the weight of my words settle between us. "Maybe this was all just a dream. Maybe we were foolish to think we could make this work."

"Don't say that," he pleaded, taking a step toward me. "We can make this work. Please, just trust me."

I shook my head, the tears I'd been holding back finally spilling over. "I can't live my life chasing after you. I need you to put me first, like I've done for you. I don't see that happening."

His face crumpled, pain evident in every line. "So, that's it then? You're just going to run away again?"

His words hurt. "I don't want to go to London," I said, my voice barely steady. "Maybe we need some time apart to figure out what we both really want."

He looked at me for a long moment, his eyes searching for something, anything, that might change my mind. All he found was my resolve.

"If that's what you want," he finally said, his face brimming with resignation.

I nodded, unable to trust my voice anymore. There was nothing left to say.

Seb exhaled slowly, his gaze dropping to the ground. "When are you leaving?"

"I'm booking the next flight back to LAX," I answered. "No point in dragging this out."

His shoulders slumped as the reality settled between us in silence.

"I'm sorry," he said softly as I turned to walk back toward the house. "I never wanted it to end like this."

"Me neither," I whispered, not turning around, knowing if I looked back, I might cave in, and then I'd never be able to leave.

Two days later, I found myself alone in the departure lounge of Sydney Airport, my suitcase by my side and a boarding pass clutched in my hand. The bustling noise of travelers around me felt distant, muted by the numbness that had settled over me. Saying goodbye to Livy and Gramps was hard enough, but the hardest part was saying goodbye to Seb.

I glanced out the large windows, watching as planes taxied and took off into the clear blue sky. It was time to figure out what I wanted for my future.

Part of me wanted to believe that this was a temporary separation. Another part, deeper and more cynical, feared that this was the end of our story. A beautiful chapter closed too soon.

"*Flight 372 to Los Angeles now boarding at Gate 12*," a voice announced over the intercom. I took a deep breath and grabbed my bag, making my way to the gate.

As I boarded the plane, I found my seat and settled in, fastening my seatbelt as the flight attendants moved efficiently through the cabin while preparing for takeoff. I was overcome with memories of the vineyard as the plane taxied down the runway. It was magical, like something from another life, a world I wasn't ready to leave behind.

When the plane lifted into the sky, I opened my eyes to the endless expanse of clouds and sky before me. It was a blank canvas, full of unknowns and possibilities, but as the ground fell away, I couldn't shake the feeling that I was leaving a part of myself behind.

CHAPTER 15
Sometimes She Cries

MONTCLAIR, CA
SPRING, 2000

Starla Silverson
Twenty-Two Years Old

E verything around me felt distant, disconnected. I was a ghost in my own life, unable to touch or feel anything real.

Montclair had always been my safe haven, it felt like a refuge for the lost. I was back where I started: no job, no degree, no boyfriend. I wasn't the same person who had left.

Mom stepped out onto the porch, her footsteps soft against the wet wood. "I brought you some tea," she said gently, placing a steaming mug in front of me.

"Thanks," I mumbled, staring blankly at the rain-soaked yard.

She sat beside me, the quiet sound of the rain filling the

silence between us. "Sweetheart, you've been so quiet since you got back. It's hard, but you don't have to go through this alone. We're here for you. Have you thought of returning to the airlines? Or maybe going back to finish school?"

I nodded, her words felt distant, like everything else. "I don't know what to do, Mom," I responded, my voice sounded small and broken. "I thought Seb and I were building something real. And now it's gone. I don't know what I want anymore. I just need to catch my breath before I decide what to do with the rest of my life."

She reached out and took my hand, her grip firm and reassuring. Even that felt distant, like it was happening to someone else. "You're strong, and you'll find your way again. It's okay to take time to figure things out. You're young, and coming home was the right choice. If this guy is for you, he'll fight for you."

I wanted to believe her, but I was looking up from a deep hole in the ground, one I didn't know how to climb out of. "I feel so stuck. Like I'm spinning my wheels and going nowhere. I keep thinking about all the things I could have done differently, all the ways I might have saved us. It's like I'm suffocating under the weight of it all."

Mom squeezed my hand again, her eyes full of love and concern. "It's okay to feel lost. You've been through a lot, and it's going to take time. You'll get through it, I promise."

I nodded again, her words felt like they were coming from the other side of a thick glass wall. My phone buzzed on the table beside me, and for a moment, I thought about ignoring it. Anything was better than sitting in this oppressive silence, listening to the rain and my own doubts. I reached for the phone, seeing Shannon's name flash across the screen. It had been a while since we talked, since before everything fell apart with Seb.

"Hey, Shannon," I answered, trying to inject some life into my words, but they still sounded flat.

"Starla! I've been trying to reach you! I heard you're back in California. Your mom called. How are you?" Shannon's voice crackled through the line, bright and buzzing, almost too alive against the rain-soaked quiet of my mood. It was like sunshine breaking through a storm when you'd just gotten used to the gray.

"I'm okay," I said, trying to mask the hollowness creeping into my tone.

"Listen," Shannon continued, not missing a beat, "I know things have been rough, and I've got just the thing to snap you out of it. How about a weekend in Vegas? Just you, me, and a whole lot of fun. And guess who's headlining at one of the clubs? Shawn DeLeon. Remember my cousin? He's a DJ and has been dying to reconnect with you. He was bummed when he heard you moved to Australia. Come to Vegas! It'll be like the Three Musketeers back together again."

Vegas. The idea was absurd. How could I think about a place bursting with lights and noise, when I felt so dead inside? Maybe that's why I needed to go. Perhaps Vegas could be the escape I was desperate for, the lifeline to pull me out of this sinking pit.

"Vegas?" I echoed, trying to picture myself there, away from the rain, the cold, and the suffocating familiarity of home.

"Vegas, baby! Come on, Star. It'll be a blast. We can let loose, forget about British whatshisname for a bit, and just have some fun. And who knows? A little flirtation with an old flame might be what you need to get your groove back. I still remember that Shawn was your first kiss."

I glanced at my mom, who was watching me with that gentle, knowing look. She didn't say anything, but her eyes spoke volumes. *It's okay,* they seemed to say. *Go. Live.*

"Maybe," I said, and I could feel my despair lifting just hearing Shannon's cheerfulness. "You know what? Let's do it."

"Atta girl," Shannon's voice was full of encouragement, the kind I didn't know I needed. "Pack your bags, Star. We're going to Vegas."

As I ended the call, a tiny flicker of something stirred within me. Maybe hope, maybe fear. I wasn't sure, it felt better than the emptiness that had surrounded me for days. "I guess I'm going to Vegas."

Mom smiled softly, her eyes warm with understanding. "Sometimes, a little adventure is the best medicine. Be safe and remember. You can come home."

I tried to absorb her words, to believe them, to feel

anything other than this tremendous emptiness settling inside me.

As I went inside to pack, all I could think about was how lost I felt, how far I'd fallen, and how this trip felt like my chance to claw my way back to the surface. Vegas wasn't just a getaway—it might just be a lifeline. And I was grabbing onto it with everything I had left.

CHAPTER 16
Don't Know What You've Got Until it's Gone

LAS VEGAS, NEVADA
SPRING, 2000

Starla Silverson
Twenty-Two Years Old

"Welcome to Sin City, Star!" Shannon shouted over the noise of the bustling Paris Las Vegas Casino.

"The Paris hotel? You didn't mention this is where Shawn was playing."

"Yeah, it just opened last year. Do you like it?" Shannon asked, her eyes sparkling.

"It's perfect," I replied, forcing a smile. But the glitz of the Parisian décor tugged me back to memories I was trying hard to bury—Seb and I wandering the real Paris, his hand warm in mine as we watched the city lights shimmer along the Seine. The memory was so vivid I could almost smell the croissants, feel the cobblestones beneath my feet.

Las Vegas was a neon-soaked jungle, a stark contrast to the calm of my parents' house or the quiet charm of actual Paris. This city buzzed with electric energy, alive with possibility and a touch of reckless abandon. The moment we arrived, a weight started to lift from my shoulders, replaced by the intoxicating sense of freedom that only Vegas could offer.

"Let's make the most of it," I murmured, more to myself than to her. I needed to lose myself in the lights, the music, and the commotion of the Strip.

Later that night, we found ourselves at one of the hottest nightclubs in Vegas. The air at Napoleon's Lounge was thick with the scent of expensive cologne mingling with sweat, while the pulsing beat of the music vibrated through my entire body. Shannon had insisted we dress to impress, and as I caught a glimpse of myself in the mirrored walls, I had to admit—I looked pretty damn good. The dress clung in all the right places, and for the first time in a while, I felt like I was regaining my confidence.

Earlier, we'd had a nice dinner and spent some time at the slots before heading to the club, but as we made our way onto the dance floor, the night felt like it was just beginning.

"Look who's here, babes," Shannon said, gesturing toward the DJ booth.

I followed her gaze, and my heart skipped a beat. There he was. Shawn DeLeon. Even in high school, he'd had that effortless magnetism about him. But here, under the flashing lights, commanding the crowd with his music, he was on a whole new level. He looked even hotter than I remembered, confidence radiating from every pore.

He caught my eye, and for a moment, the entire club seemed to fade away. Shawn's lips curled into a slow, knowing smile, and a shiver of delight ran down my spine.

"I think he still likes you," Shannon teased, giving me a nudge. "Go say hi."

I hesitated for only a second before making my way through the crowd, my heart pounding in time with the music. As I approached the DJ booth, Shawn stepped down, his eyes locked on mine.

"Starla Silverson," he said, a slow smile spreading across his face. "It's been a long time."

"It hasn't been *that* long," I replied, trying to keep my face from flushing, despite the fluttering in my chest.

"It feels like a long time. You look incredible," he said, his gaze sweeping over me in a way that made my pulse race. "You've turned out to be even more stunning than that hot mom of yours."

"I knew it! I knew you had a crush on my mom," I snorted.

"She's not the only one I had a crush on." He wriggled his eyebrows.

"You're not so bad yourself." A blush crept up my neck.

He flashed that same crooked smile that had always driven the girls crazy back in the day. "I'll be done in an hour. How about a late-night snack when I'm finished? We could catch up a bit. I've got a huge suite right here at the casino," he explained.

"Okay, Shannon and I are going to hit the dance floor," I said with a grin. "Come find me when you're done."

A few hours later, Shawn led me to a swanky, private suite in the Paris Casino, the lights of Vegas twinkling far below us. The suite was pure luxury, with floor-to-ceiling windows framing a breathtaking view that I barely noticed.

All I could think about was how close Shawn was, how the air between us crackled with anticipation.

He mixed us each a cocktail, and as he handed me the glass, our fingers brushed. A spark shot up my arm, unexpected and electric. He held my gaze, a slow smile spreading as he raised his glass. "To old friends," he murmured, his voice low, making me wonder when "friends" had started feeling like something more.

"To new beginnings." I replied, clinking my glass against his.

"Think we should order some room service?" he asked.

"Sounds good. Should I ask Shannon if she wants anything?"

"Nah, she said she was heading to bed."

I glanced at my watch, surprised. "It's already two in the morning"

He grinned. "Are you tired? I'm always so wired after a set. I'm kind of a night owl now. Don't feel like you have to stay up. I could walk you to your room if you want."

I shook my head. "No, I'm good. I've done enough sleeping lately."

"Good, because I want to hear everything about Australia."

We talked about my time at the winery, then reminisced about high school, laughing over the 1980s hairstyles and clothes we used to wear. There was an undercurrent to the conversation, a tension neither of us acknowledged but both felt. The way his eyes lingered on my lips, the way I found myself leaning in just a little closer—it all felt inevitable.

And then, without warning, he closed the distance between us, his lips meeting mine in a kiss that was both intense and urgent. I melted into him, all the pent-up emotion, loneliness, and heartache pouring out before I finally pulled back, breathless.

"Shawn, wait. I'm getting over someone. I'm not sure I'm ready for this."

His eyes filled with understanding. "I know. Shannon filled me in. She thought maybe a little fun in Vegas with me might help you out of your funk."

"She said that?" My face flushed. "What is this, a pity fuck?"

"No, not even close. I've liked you for a long time, Star. Always have. How could I not? You're hot as hell, and you're just overthinking things. I want to be with you, and I think you want that too. Am I wrong?"

I hesitated, then shook my head. "We've been friends for so long. I'm not sure we should complicate things."

He smiled, leaning back. "It's all good. Now we'll be friends with benefits. It'll be fun. Heck, we can even play spin the bottle, if it'll make you feel better."

I burst out laughing as I plopped down on the sofa. "You did always have a way of making me feel better."

"If you let me, I'll make you feel really good," he murmured, his fingers gently easing down the waistband of my skirt as his lips brushed against my belly. His warm breath trailed lower, sending goosebumps skittering across my skin.

Before long, we were intertwined on the plush sofa, our drinks long forgotten on the table. For the first time in months, I felt alive again. Truly, deeply alive. But just as Shawn's warm embrace deepened, an image of Seb flashed through my mind—Seb standing in the vineyards, his face crumpling as I told him I was going back to California.

I sprang to my feet, my heart racing. "Shawn, wait. I can't go through with this."

"What's wrong?" Concern filled his eyes.

"I really care about you, I do, but everything feels so rushed. I'm still trying to untangle my feelings for Seb, and this just doesn't feel right. I need some time to sort through it all."

"I understand. Do you want to talk about it?"

"Not really. Do you mind if we just hit the pause button on this?"

"Look, I care about you, and I don't want you to feel rushed. I thought spending time together might get you out of your funk."

"I appreciate that, but maybe I should go back to my room." I felt the tears prickling at the corners of my eyes.

"No, please stay," he murmured, his tone soft. "I promise, I'll be a good boy. Sleep in the spare room if you want. Call Shannon up if it makes you more comfortable."

"She's probably already asleep." I managed a faint smile. "I just don't want things to get... complicated."

"Don't worry," he said, brushing off my concern. "I'll take a cold shower to clear my head. Make yourself comfortable—borrow my clothes, use my toothbrush, whatever you need."

"Thank you, Shawn. I think I'll just go to sleep. I'm exhausted; it's been a rough couple of months."

He nodded, his expression softening. "I get it. And Star? He's a lucky guy if he's captured your heart."

As he disappeared into the bathroom, the room spun gently around me, the alcohol making my head heavy and an ache settling in my heart. I slipped into one of his over-sized T-shirts and climbed into the bed in the spare room. Closing my eyes, I drifted off into the sweet respite of sleep, seeking escape from the memories I couldn't shake and the emptiness lingering within.

DAPPLED SUNLIGHT STREAMED THROUGH THE WINDOWS AS I awoke the next morning. In the kitchenette, Shawn was busy making coffee. I felt a sense of relief that I'd stopped things when I did; the last thing I needed on top of my heartbreak was a guilty conscience.

In the days that followed, Shawn, Shannon, and I became inseparable, just like we had been during all those years ago in Hollywood. We explored Sin City, went to the best pool parties at the swankiest casinos, and lost ourselves in each other's company. Shawn had a way of making me laugh, making me feel desirable, and helping me forget about everything that went wrong. Shannon was her usual supportive self, but eventually, it was time for her to return to work.

"Are you sure you want to stay?" she asked, concern etched on her face. "I'm worried about you getting hurt. Shawn's a bit of a player. I love him. He's my cousin and all, he's not the boyfriend material."

"He's a breath of fresh air. I want to have some fun. I'm not looking for anything serious. We just kissed a bit that one night, but, I think we're safely back in the friend zone."

"Okay babes, you're a big girl. Do whatever you think is best."

"I love you, Shannon." We hugged our goodbyes, and I went back to the hotel to freshen up.

Shawn invited me to stay with him in the spare room of

his suite, and the place quickly became a temporary sanctuary. Every time my phone buzzed with a text or call from Seb, I ignored it. I wasn't ready to face him or let the mess we'd made in Australia penetrate my safe haven.

Seb was relentless. After days of dodging him, I finally reached a point where I could no longer pretend he didn't exist. I perched on the edge of the bed, my cell phone clutched in my hand, his name lighting up the screen like a neon sign. I paused, gathering my thoughts and bracing myself for the conversation I dreaded. With a hesitant swipe, I answered the call.

"Starla," Seb's expression was a mixture of relief and desperation. "I've been trying to reach you. Are you okay?"

"I'm fine," I said, my tone flat.

"I miss you," he responded, his voice heavy with longing. "I know I messed up, but we can fix this. I'll come to California, or you can come to London. We'll figure it out. I'm lost without you."

I squeezed my eyes shut, his words washing over me like a tide I couldn't escape, leaving me yearning for clarity. "Seb, I need time. I can't keep pretending everything's okay while you make all these major decisions without considering me."

"I'm sorry. I'm still learning, we sort of went from no strings into a serious relationship" he admitted, his tone softening. "I've never been in love before."

"Love," I echoed, the word tasting both foreign and familiar on my tongue.

"There, I said it. I *love* you," he repeated.

"Seb, we might as well be from different planets. I mean, I'm from California, and you're from England. It will take more than love to make this work."

"Please, Starla." His voice trembled, and I could hear the desperation. "Don't give up on us."

My tears threatened to spill over, I blinked hard, trying to hold my ground. "I'm not giving up. I'm just trying to figure out what's best for me. It broke my heart when you wouldn't listen to what I had to say. I don't want to be in a relationship where I'm making all the sacrifices. You've got to meet me halfway if this is ever going to work."

"So you're saying there is a chance?"

Silence stretched between us, and I could almost feel the flicker of hope in Seb's voice.

"I'm not sure, Seb, I think I need more time."

"Okay," he finally whispered, his voice barely audible. "Just know, I'm not the kind of guy who gives up easily."

My voice sounded strained as I tried to hold back tears. "Goodbye, Seb," I replied.

"Goodbye, Star."

I ended the call and set the phone down, a strange mix of relief and sorrow washing over me. I wasn't sure what the future held but for now, I needed to be here. In this place, with Shawn. I owed it to myself to see what else was out there. Didn't I?

"Everything okay?" Shawn asked from the other room.

"Yeah," I replied, desperately trying to convince myself it was true. "Everything's fine."

"You know, you don't have to have it all figured out right now," he appeared in the doorframe. "Stay here with me, as long as you need. I only want what's best for you. No pressure."

"I know," I said, a small smile creeping onto my face. "That's one of the things I like about you—no pressure at all."

"Do you think you'll go back to your job with the airlines?" he asked, genuinely curious.

"I'm not sure," I admitted, my voice dropped to a whisper. "It used to be everything I dreamed of. But the vineyards? There was something different there. Something real. I'm thinking about taking some viticulture classes," I paused, glancing at my hands, suddenly heavy with the weight of my indecision. "Jetting across Europe was incredible, but honestly? It was exhausting. I'm beginning to wonder if that's what I want for the rest of my life."

"Like I said, you don't need to decide tonight. Take a break from all your worries. You put so much pressure on yourself to have it all figured out," he said, his eyes soft with understanding.

"You're right. I think it comes from how I was raised," I said, a touch of vulnerability creeping in.

"That makes sense," he replied. "I'll always be here for you—as a friend or something more. This doesn't change that. It doesn't have to be complicated."

"Love always complicates things," I sighed, a hint of frustration in my voice.

"Do you love him?" he asked, his gaze steady.

"I think so," I said, the words tumbling out before I could catch them. "I'm sorry, Shawn. I shouldn't be sitting here in your hotel room talking about another guy. But you've always been so easy to talk to." I hesitated, feeling the weight of the moment settle around us. "Are you sure you don't want me to leave?"

"Of course not," he said, his expression unreadable yet kind. "If you're in love, you should tell him. Don't let me be the reason you hold back."

I smiled and shook my head, affection spreading in my chest. "How did you become so incredible?"

"It comes from learning what *not* to do," he chuckled softly.

"I can relate to that," I said. "We've both been through a lot, and it shapes our decisions."

"That's the understatement of the year," he said, a teasing glint in his eyes.

"Maybe I should get my own hotel room," I suggested, uncertainty creeping in. "I have a lot on my mind, and I don't want to burden you. I'd never want to hurt you."

"We're adults, we can share a hotel together without ripping each other's clothes off."

"You're right." I laughed. "I can't promise anything. Have a good night. I'll see you tomorrow."

As I made my way to the bedroom, warmth from his

fondness touched my heart, but the weight of my looming decision pressed heavily on my chest. "And Shawn, whatever happens, you mean a lot to me."

"I know, sweet girl," he said, lingering as if trying to memorize the moment.

Exhausted, I slipped into my pajamas and collapsed onto the inviting bed. As sleep began to take over, Seb's smiling face flashed in my mind. A reminder that no matter how far I ran, I wasn't over him.

THE FOLLOWING NIGHT, I STOOD IN FRONT OF THE MIRROR, putting on the finishing touches to my makeup. My hand was steady, but my heart? It was a different story. Practically doing somersaults. Shawn had left earlier to set up for his gig at Napoleon's Lounge, and I was planning to join him.

Here, amidst the vibrant madness of Vegas, I could drown out the emotions I'd been avoiding. With Shawn, I didn't have to be the girl nursing a broken heart; I could be the carefree spirit who danced through the night, leaving her worries on the floor. Tonight was all about forgetting, letting go, and losing myself in the music, the vivid lights and the big city.

I slipped into my tiny black dress, which flared above my thighs and accentuated my long, tanned legs. My honey-blonde hair, once perfectly shoulder-length, now grazed my shoulders, having grown out from hours spent soaking up the sun in the vineyards. The sun-kissed strands had light-ened to a warm hue that framed my face invitingly.

As I buckled the strap on my sexy red stilettos—irre-sistible Italian heels I had splurged on during my last layover—a wave of confidence surged through me. I caught my reflection in the mirror and smiled. Even though I didn't feel great inside, I looked fantastic on the outside, ready to step into the night and leave everything behind for a little while.

Or so I thought.

As I strolled through the hotel lobby, the familiar hum of the casino buzzed around me, yet a strange sense of unease tugged at the edges of my mind—something I couldn't quite place. The elevator doors slid open, and I stepped out, my heels clicking against the marble floor as I headed toward the lounge.

As I approached the entrance to Napoleon's Lounge, my steps slowed, my heart caught in my throat at the sight before me. There stood Seb, bathed in neon glow, looking worn and fragile, as if sleep had eluded him for days. But it was his eyes—those deep amber pools that once felt like home—locked on mine, pulling me in.

All the buried emotions I'd tried to ignore came crashing back, flooding my chest with warmth and confusion. Every unsaid word and unacknowledged feeling swirled around us, creating a tension that vibrated in the air, a stark reminder of everything I'd been running from.

"Seb?" I uttered, my voice catching in my throat. "What are you doing here?"

"After our last conversation, I called your mum," he began, his lips pressed tightly together. "I didn't know who else to turn to. I've been a mess since I got back to England. When she told me you were in Vegas with DJ Shawn, I couldn't stay away."

"You flew all that way to find me? Why, Seb? What do you want?" My voice sounded shaky.

He swallowed, stepping closer. "I needed to see you. I was wrong—about everything. I know I hurt you. When my mum called about the visa, I panicked. I wasn't thinking of you. I was selfish and scared. The truth is, I've never stopped loving you, Star."

His confession rippled through me, shattering the defenses I'd spent months building. "*You* were scared?" I echoed, hands trembling as I fought to keep my composure. "Seb, you're the one who decided to go back to England. You were the one person I thought I could always count on, and yet you wouldn't make a single call for me. Those rugby teams have visa lawyers. They could've helped us."

"I'm sorry," he said, his voice breaking. "I've always been the reliable one. When my mum called, I should have handled it better—included you in the decision, instead of facing it alone. I made it worse. I should have fought for us. I'm so sorry."

I crossed my arms, trying to shield myself from the vulnerability threatening to spill out. "And now what? You show up and expect everything to work out?"

He shook his head, eyes filled with regret and longing. "I

know it won't be easy, Star. I had to come. These past few months, I tried. I really tried to let you go, but I can't." He stepped closer, locking his gaze with mine. "For the first time in my life, I'm against something I can't walk away from. Falling out of love with you? It's impossible. And I don't want to fight it anymore. I don't want another day pretending I can live without you."

My heart raced, torn between the love I still felt for him and the pain of his betrayal. "I've been pretending, too."

"We made a mess of things." His gaze softened. "I lost rugby, losing you was worse. Sometimes, you don't realize what you have until it's gone. I've had to rethink everything. I want a fresh start—with you."

"But how? I can't go back to Australia. I don't have it in me anymore. I'm tired, Seb. The trust is broken."

"I have something I want to run by you. I've been looking at vineyards in California. Temecula, to be specific. I've got some money from the rugby settlement, and I can't stop thinking about starting over. With you."

I stared at him, blindsided. "You want to buy a vineyard in California? You want to move to America? What about your grandpa's vineyard?"

"My little brother is almost eighteen, he can help Gramps out. I don't want to keep asking you to follow me. It's my turn to follow you. I want to build a life with you, to put down roots where we can be happy. You thrived at the winery, and honestly? I loved it, too. It felt right. I want to start my own—with you." He bit his lip as our eyes locked.

"A winery? That sounds expensive. How could we afford it?" I was still reeling from the bombshell he'd just dropped.

"We don't have to open a winery. We can buy a few acres of vineyards. Grow the grapes and sell them to the wineries. "What could go wrong?""

I looked away, struggling to process it all. Taking a deep breath, I asked, "And what about Shawn?"

Seb's expression hardened, and I could see the shadows of his pain flicker across his face. "I don't care what you've done with him. I care about you. I love you. It's not easy for me to be here, Star, knowing you've shared your life with someone else while I was back in England, trying to get over you. I should have realized this could happen. You're amazing. I didn't think it would be so soon."

"I'm sorry, Seb. I really thought things were over between us. You know I'm not really like that," I replied.

He paused, his jaw tightening as he wrestled with the hurt that threatened to spill out. "Look, I'm not here to compete with him. I want you to look me in the eye and tell me you don't love me. If that's the case, I'll walk away and let you build a life with *him*, I need to know the truth."

"It's not like that, Seb. Shawn and I aren't together like that," I replied, feeling the weight of his words. "And I can't tell you I don't love you."

He inhaled, his expression a storm of frustration and yearning. "The truth is, I can't imagine my life without you. Even if it feels messy and complicated. I'd rather face that mess with you than walk away again."

The air between us felt charged, a tangled web of love, regret, and a deep longing for what we had once shared. Tears stung my eyes as I looked at him, my heart aching with the weight of his confession. This was Seb, who had always been there until that one moment. The man I had fallen in love with. The one who had broken my heart.

"I don't know if I can do this again. What if you leave me again?"

Seb reached out, gently cupping my face in his hands. His thumb brushing my cheek. "I'm not going anywhere. I've learned my lesson. I panicked and made the worst mistake of my life. I know what I want now. I want us. I want you. Take a chance on me—on us. Let me make this right."

He bit his lip, the gesture making him look undeniably sexy, as if he were holding back something vulnerable. His eyes searched mine, full of sincerity. "Marry me. Tonight. Let's start again. For real this time."

I glanced at the ring still resting on my finger, the fake engagement ring that had become so familiar it felt like an extension of myself. Seb's gaze followed mine, his eyes softening as a wistful smile crept onto his lips, as if he could sense the tangled history wrapped up in that simple piece of jewelry.

"I see you're still wearing my ring." He reached into his pocket and pulled out a small velvet box, his expression shifting to something more serious. "Can I have it back?"

"Why would you want it back?" I closed my hand into a fist. I wasn't sure what he was getting at.

Then he sank slowly to one knee, opening the box to reveal a real princess cut diamond ring. Simple but perfect, a symbol of the future he was offering. "I want to exchange it for this one."

My heart thundered in my chest, every nerve in my body in high alert. I stared at the ring, my mind racing with a thousand thoughts, memories, fears. As I looked into his eyes, I knew the truth I'd been trying to deny. I had never stopped loving him. I'd been running from the one thing that had always felt right.

I felt a cluster of fear in my chest, but also something else—a quiet certainty was breaking through.

"Okay," I finally said. A grin spread across Seb's face, and before I could process what was happening, he pulled me into a deep kiss. Everything around us—the noise of the Strip, the neon lights of Vegas—melted away. It was just the two of us, caught in this moment.

His full lips on mine, strong hands holding me close; for that brief, breathless instant, it felt like all the doubts, all the pain, instantly vanished.

I was home.

As the kiss broke, reality came rushing back. "I need to talk to Shawn. He's been a good friend, and I owe him that."

Seb's smile faltered a bit, confusion glimmering in his eyes. "Do you have feelings for him?"

"It's not like that. He's an old family friend, you have nothing to worry about," I reassured him.

"In that case, take your time," he said gently. "I'll be right here. I'm not going anywhere."

The firmness in his words steadied me, guilt surged through my chest. This was Seb. The man who had flown halfway across the world for me. The one who had always been steady, dependable, the one who had disregarded me was now standing here, fighting for us.

And here I was, hiding away in Vegas, distracting myself with someone who wasn't him. Although it was true, Shawn *was* an old friend, I couldn't ignore the chemistry between us. But when push came to shove, we hadn't crossed that line; our relationship hadn't gone beyond a heavy make-out session. Maybe Shawn's attention and flirtatious nature had been stroking my ego, but deep down, I knew it wasn't enough to fill the void left by Seb.

"I'm sorry, I was avoiding you. I really needed this time to figure things out. I was so confused."

Seb closed the velvet box, his gaze steady on mine. "Whatever you need, Star. I understand, and I'm not mad." His sincerity wrapped around me like a lifeline in the mayhem. This wasn't just a proposal, it was a declaration that everything we'd been through, the trials and the heartaches, had led us here and made it all worth it.

"I'll be right back." I kissed him one last time before turning away, determination surging through my veins as I sprinted toward Shawn's DJ booth, the pulsing beat of the music thrumming in my chest.

"Starla, what is it?" Shawn's voice cut through the noise as I approached.

"It's Seb. He's here. We're getting married," I shouted over the chaotic sounds of the drum and bass he was spinning, lifting my hand to show the beautiful engagement ring.

"Oh my gosh, Star! This is huge! I'm so glad he finally woke up. Congratulations!" Shawn beamed. "How did this happen?"

"I'll fill you in later, just tell me you're happy for me."

"I'm happy for you, Star, of course I am. I know you love him."

I navigated through the writhing crowd of dancers, each pulse of the bass reverberating in my chest. My heart raced as I moved back toward Seb. For the first time in months, I wasn't running from anything—I was running toward something, toward my future.

Each step felt like a declaration, a shedding of the fears that had held me captive for too long. The pandemonium of the club faded into the background as clarity sharpened my focus. I was ready to embrace what lay ahead, ready to fight for what I wanted. And what I wanted was Seb.

I found him waiting in the lobby, as handsome as ever, while the frenetic energy of Las Vegas buzzed around us. The neon glow from the Paris Hotel's Eiffel Tower flickered above, casting a surreal light upon his silhouette. Ironic, really. Here we were, standing beneath a replica of one of the world's most romantic landmarks, surrounded by artificial glamour—and yet, this moment with Seb felt achingly real, raw, and honest. Nothing else mattered beyond us.

We lingered there a moment longer, Vegas flashing and pulsing around us, but all I could see was Seb. My Seb. The man who had crossed oceans to fight for me.

Maybe, just maybe, I was finally ready to fight for him, too.

CHAPTER 17

You're Still the One

LAS VEGAS, NEVADA
SPRING, 2000

Starla Silverson
Twenty-Two Years Old

"I can't believe we're doing this. Erin is going to *kill* me. We swore we'd be each other's bridesmaids," I exclaimed as the neon lights of Las Vegas flashed by the taxi window, each burst of color stoking a whirlwind of emotions.

Seb chuckled, squeezing my hand. "This one's just for us, love. My family's going to want the full deal. Would you marry me again? In Australia?"

I laughed, though my heart danced at the thought of our future together. "I'd marry you a thousand times, Seb. I love you."

"That makes me the happiest man alive." He smiled wide, his excitement contagious. "Look, we're almost there."

As the Chapelle De Paris came into view, my pulse quickened. Its soft, twinkling lights glowed under the night sky, a quiet beacon amidst the Strip's frenzy. Next to the mega casinos and gaudy façades, the tiny white chapel stood out in its simplicity. The contrast struck me—amidst the noise and liveliness of Vegas, this humble chapel felt like an oasis. It was a reminder that love didn't need extravagance to be real. I gripped Seb's hand, my nerves and excitement tangling together.

"Are you ready for this?" his voice was steady despite the rush of sounds outside. His thumb traced comforting circles on my palm, and I leaned into him.

"I am," I said, though a flicker of anxiety tightened in my chest. As much as I wanted him there was still that nagging thought. "But... you haven't even met my parents yet."

Seb grinned but didn't miss the hint of hesitation in my voice. "I've already won them over. Just like I won you."

"What are you talking about?" I asked.

Seb chuckled. "Oh, I had a long talk with your mom before I flew out. How do you think I knew exactly which ring you wanted? I also asked your dad's permission to propose, and they're onboard with this whole thing, angel."

My words caught in my throat. The thought of Seb taking that step—of forging bonds with my family—made my heart swell. "You did what?"

"Honestly, I figured if we're going to dive headfirst into this, we might as well do it right," he said, a mix of seriousness and playfulness dancing in his eyes. "You mean everything to me, Starla. I wanted them to understand how serious I am about us. And I have one more surprise for you."

"What's that?" I asked, my heart fluttering with anticipation as we stepped out of the taxi.

Then, outside the chapel, I spotted two familiar faces beaming with joy. "Mom! Dad! How did you get here so fast?" I rushed toward them, my voice bubbling with disbelief.

"We flew in this morning," Dad said, enveloping me in a massive bear hug that felt like home. "We figured you were going to say yes and didn't want to miss seeing our only daughter get married."

"And this must be Seb?" Mom chimed in, her smile warm and welcoming. "Come here, son. Give me a hug. I'm Twyla, you can call me Mom."

Seb stepped forward, his nervousness evident but replaced by a genuine grin. "It's great to finally meet you both."

Mom pulled him into a quick embrace, a wide smile breaking across her face. "You're one of the lucky ones, you know. Our Starla has a heart of gold."

"Will Mum be alright with you?" Seb asked, a hint of uncertainty in his face.

"Absolutely," she replied, her laughter contagious. "Give me a hug, you're part of our family."

As I watched them, my heart swelled with a warmth I didn't expect. This was everything I had ever wanted. Love, acceptance, and a family that celebrated the wild choices I had made. I glanced at Seb, who met my gaze, his eyes sparkling with joy.

"See?" a soft smile playing on his lips. "This is only the beginning."

With the chapel's charming facade behind us, and my family by our side, a rush of euphoria washed over me. This wasn't just a spontaneous decision. It was a leap into a future promising love, laughter and excitement.

"Let's do this," I said, taking Seb's hand as we walked toward the chapel, the sound of laughter and the scent of blooming roses filling the air. I could feel the universe aligning, like everything that had ever happened led me to this moment.

As we neared the chapel, a gentle glow of ambient light wrapped around the entrance like a quiet promise. My heart raced at the thought of walking out those doors as Seb's wife. Soft light streamed through stained glass windows inside, casting vibrant colors across the room, filling the air with a sacred presence. I squeezed his hand, seeking his reassurance as we stepped forward together.

The chapel was intimate and cozy, adorned with flowers and twinkling lights that gave it a dreamlike quality. A small crowd gathered, a mix of tourists and couples seeking their own moment of magic. The wedding officiant stood at the front, a warm smile on his face as he welcomed us.

"Welcome, are you ready to say your vows?" His enthusiasm rang through the air, and I nodded, my heart pounding in my chest.

Seb stepped closer, his eyes sparkling with affection. "I've never been more ready for anything in my life."

I laughed, the sound echoing off the chapel's walls. "You'd better not back out now."

"Never," he said. "You're the only adventure I want."

As we exchanged vows, a rush of emotions washed over me—joy, exhilaration, and a sweet release from fear. Memories of all the times anxiety had held me back flickered through my mind. Standing here, with Seb by my side, I reveled in the lightness that surrounded me, liberated from the shadows of my past and ready to embrace the future.

When it was time for the rings, Seb slipped a delicate band onto my finger, a perfect fit. "You're mine now. And I'm yours."

"I always wanted to belong somewhere," I murmured. "And with you, I feel like I finally do."

"It's funny how the heart knows where it's meant to be. With you, I've found a home I never knew I was missing."

As the officiant pronounced us husband and wife, exhilaration washed over me like a tidal wave. We kissed, sealing all our promises and hopes for the future.

Once we stepped back, laughter and applause erupted from the people in the room. I beamed, feeling lighter than air as Seb pulled me close. "Ready for the adventure of a lifetime?"

"Always," I replied, my heart was full.

As we exited the chapel, the neon lights of Las Vegas beckoned us into the night, a world full of endless possibilities. We dashed down the sidewalk, hand in hand, laughter spilling from our lips.

I wasn't running anymore; I was stepping boldly into the life I had always dreamed of—a life rich with love, adventure, and the promise of a future that was finally mine. An unwavering strength surged through me, as if every choice I had ever made had led to this instant. This was my beginning, not an escape, but a profound embrace of everything I had yearned for. I was finally ready to chase the horizon of endless possibilities, knowing that this time, I was home.

PART THREE
Starla Wylder

"Maybe the journey isn't so much about becoming anything. Maybe it's about unbecoming everything that isn't really you, so you can be who you were meant to be in the first place."

— Paulo Coelho

CHAPTER 18

She Talks to Angels

TEMECULA, CALIFORNIA
JUNE, 2018

Starla Wylder
Forty Years Old

T he mist glistened over the rolling vineyards lining Rancho California Road, and the earthy scent of the harvest mingled with the crisp morning air. We made our way to Grandma Dawn's 90th birthday celebration, the calm atmosphere of the car tinged with an undercurrent of anticipation I couldn't quite place.

"Mom," Laney broke the quiet, her voice curious and thoughtful, "what was Grandpa Ellis like?"

Her question pulled me from my thoughts, and I glanced at her through the rearview mirror. Her wide, inquisitive blue eyes sparkled with curiosity, and my heart warmed as memories of my grandpa Ellis flooded back. Memories as vivid as the lush green vineyards outside.

"He was a real character," I said, a smile creeping onto my face. "Fun and generous. He had this incredible knack for making everyone feel special, you know? Like the whole world revolved around them."

Laney leaned forward, intrigued. "What's your favorite memory of him?"

I paused, letting the question linger, savoring the memories. "There was this one time he took me to the fair. We rode every ride, even the ones that made me queasy, and he bought me a huge cotton candy. I felt like the luckiest kid alive."

The girls laughed, and my oldest daughter, Brooke added softly, "I wish we could've met him."

"Me too, lovebug," I replied, the comfort of nostalgia wrapping around me like a cozy sweater as we drove toward the mountains.

I couldn't help but chuckle, recalling the man who had been such a bright light in my childhood. "He had this astonishing ability to light up a room. He loved surprising us with gifts, and he always made time for the people he cared about. If he were alive, I'm pretty sure he would have bought you a horse by now."

Laney rang out with joy. "Really? A horse? That would've been so cool!"

I smiled at her reaction. "He loved horses, and he knew

how much little girls do too. He would've done anything to make you happy."

"Would he have gotten me a horse, too?" Brooke asked, her voice laced with the pure hope of a child.

"Absolutely. He would have loved that you're both taking riding lessons."

Excited giggles filled the car, blending with the soft drone of the engine. It was one of those rare, perfect moments where everything seemed to align. Our laughter, the warmth of the sun streaming through the windows, and the feeling of being completely at peace. Beneath it all, a small voice whispered inside, urging me to savor it, as if these moments were fleeting and these girls would grow up with a blink of an eye.

I thought the conversation might end there, but Laney wasn't finished.

"I wish your grandpa could come back," she declared, her tone innocent yet brimming with an unexpected determination that caught me off guard.

A twinge of sadness pulled at my heart, mingling with tenderness as I considered her words. "He's in heaven, sweetheart. I was only ten when he passed," I explained gently. "He's not coming back."

From the backseat, Brooke chimed in with a hint of seriousness, "People don't come back from the dead, Laney. That's just how it is."

Laney was clearly not convinced. "Jesus came back."

She responded with a childlike certainty that made me pause.

I smiled at her innocence, understanding the depth of her belief. "That was a special case," I said softly, wanting to honor her faith. "You should go ahead and pray for whatever is in your heart."

"I will, I'm going to pray every night."

As we continued down the road, the sun shone brightly in the sky, casting long shadows over the vineyards. Inside the car, a quiet warmth lingered, like the last rays of the summer sun.

"We'll get Grandma Twyla first, then head over to Great-Grandma Dawn's. Are you kids ready for a party?" I asked, trying to match their excitement.

"Yeah," they chimed in unison.

"When will Daddy get there?" Brooke, always my little worrier, asked.

"Grandpa Caleb is picking him up at the airport as we speak," I reassured her. "They'll both be at the party later on. Don't you worry."

AFTER PICKING UP MOM, WE CONTINUED OUR JOURNEY along the winding roads of the San Bernardino Mountains. Soon, the sight of Grandma Dawn's cabin nestled among the towering firs and pines enveloped me in a deep sense of comfort. The woods surrounding the cabin were a constant in my life, much like Grandma herself—steady, unchanging, and full of history.

Stepping inside, we were greeted by the cozy glow of the wood-burning fireplace, its crackling flames a reflection of my grandma's fiery spirit. The honeyed wood interior, the scent of pine, and the sight of her framed by the glowing fire made me feel at home.

"Gram, it's almost summer, and you're still running the fireplace?" I asked, raising an eyebrow as she tended to the fire.

"Just to take the chill off. It was brisk this morning," she replied, her voice carrying that quiet strength I'd always admired.

I hugged her, feeling the weight of her ninety years in the embrace and also the unyielding vitality that still radiated. "Happy birthday. Ready to celebrate?"

"There's something we need to do first," she said, her tone hinting at something more.

"You look lovely, Gramcracker. Very 1920s." I smiled at my grandmother's sparkly dress and shoes as she pretended to puff on a vintage cigarette holder.

"It belonged to Aunt Hatt. Dressing like this brings back so many memories. This was my mother's era, you know? Now, come here, dear, I have something for you."

I exchanged a glance with Mom as anticipation filled my chest. Grandma gestured toward a worn-out cardboard box in the corner, curiosity washing over me.

"A gift for *me* on your birthday, Grandma?" I asked,

raising an eyebrow as I opened the box. Inside, I found old letters, journals, and photographs. Pieces of a life well lived.

"Everything you'll need is there," she said, her voice softer but brimming with emotion.

"What do you mean, Grandma?" I asked, my heart racing as I sifted through the memories inside the box.

With a tender smile, she replied, "It's what you need to write the story of my life."

The weight of her words settled on me like a cozy blanket. "Are you sure you're ready to let all of this go? You should be the one to write it, or maybe mom?"

"Your mother and I are too close to this story to tell it the way it deserves," Grandma said, her voice gentle but steady. "But you're the one who can share it truthfully, without all the baggage. It'll be better that way." She extended her hand to me, her touch warm and reassuring. "Now, help me up those stairs. Come along, girls—we've got a party to get to!"

"Yeah!" my daughters chimed in unison.

Later that night, as the party unfolded around us, I reflected on the significance of what Grandma had passed on to me. The box she'd given me held more than just memories—it held stories untold, and could be the key to understanding the woman who had shaped so much of my life.

The party continued around me, but my mind drifted to what lay ahead. What secrets had Grandma kept hidden all these years? Why had she chosen now to reveal them? By the time we returned to my parents' cabin in the woods, I felt ready to tackle everything tucked away in Grandma's box of memories. With my mother by my side, we began the task of uncovering the stories woven into the fabric of our family history.

As we carefully lifted the lid, a musty scent greeted us. A perfect mix of nostalgia and forgotten time. Each item seemed to whisper a story: old letters, yellowed with age and tied with frayed ribbon; photographs of faces I barely recognized; and trinkets that held the weight of memories. My heart raced with anticipation as I unearthed an old journal, its leather cover cracked and worn.

"What do you think this will tell us?" my mother asked, her voice barely above a whisper.

"I don't know," I replied, flipping through the brittle pages. "But I'm ready to find out."

Together, we settled into the cozy living room, the soft glow of the fireplace illuminating our discoveries. With every turn of the page, secrets began to unravel, connecting the past to our present in ways I had never imagined. Each revelation felt like a thread, weaving a tapestry of our family's legacy—one I was eager to understand and carry forward.

"Good morning, dear," Mom said the next morning. We'd stayed up late, surrounded by Grandma Dawn's box of memories. "Want some coffee? I'm sorry I kept you up with my tales from the past."

"Mom, your story and Grandma's story, they're both incredible. I had a hard time sleeping last night after hearing all of it. I can't wait to start writing it down. I had no idea about so much of it. Thanks for sharing this with me," I said, feeling a blend of sadness and understanding.

"That's why I always encouraged you to find yourself and experience some life before settling down with kids. I wanted you to have an adult life before getting married. Not that I ever regretted having you, of course. You are the best thing in my life, and you've honored me with two beautiful granddaughters and a wonderful son-in-law. I admire you so much. You're everything I wished I could have been as a mother."

"You've been an incredible mother. You've raised me to be strong, to persevere, and so much more. I don't know how you did it when you were seventeen."

"I was young and selfish at times," Mom said. "I didn't really know who I was or what I wanted when I had you. I guess we kind of grew up together. Sometimes we lose parts of ourselves, and it takes a journey to find them again. After Grandpa died, I thought moving to Hollywood would help us start fresh, it was a mistake. Then, Lacey was kidnapped, well, it didn't take long for me to realize what I was losing by dissolving my marriage and leaving Montclair. The stability you were losing. That whole experience helped me see things more clearly."

"Then, we returned to Montclair, where everything began to come together again. And you did it. You're a successful songwriter, and you've been teaching those songwriting classes at the college. I'm proud of you, Mom. Is there anything you can't do?" I asked.

"Lots, dear. I'm still a terrible cook." We both laughed.

I rummaged around in Grandma's cardboard box, smiling to myself. "I can't wait to show the girls some of these old pictures."

The atmosphere shifted as I pulled out a slip of paper stuck to the bottom of the cardboard box. "What's this?"

"It looks like a birth certificate," Mom replied. She held her breath in silent anticipation as I examined it, my eyes widening in disbelief.

"Mom, why does this birth certificate say Twilight Lockhart?" The room seemed to spin as the weight of the revelation settled upon me.

"I don't understand," Mom stammered, her gaze shifting between the birth certificate and my eyes.

"And here's another birth certificate. It says Dawn Cameron and it was amended in 1966. What does it mean? Who's Twilight Lockhart? Why would Grandma leave this for us to find this way?"

"I don't know what it all means. We knew some Lock-hearts back in Pomona. This is ever so strange." The room thrummed with unspoken questions.

As a cloud eclipsed the sun, shadows enveloped the room, casting us in a suspenseful gloom. Our gazes intertwined, heavy with the realization that we had stumbled upon a mystery. A key poised to unlock long-sealed doors hidden within the intricate maze of our family's history.

"What does this mean, Mom?" My voice quivered, mirroring the uncertainty hanging in the air.

"We'll go see Grandma right now and get to the bottom of this."

Her look intensified, and I watched her mind race with the implications of the discovery. "Grandma will tell us the truth, Mom. We need to ask her in person. Maybe that's why she was adamant about giving us this box yesterday. She wanted us to find this birth certificate together."

"Get dressed and we'll go see her," Mom agreed.

I squeezed her hand, offering my presence as a comforting anchor in a world of confusion. The truth about our background was cloaked in mystery, like a riddle waiting to be solved. "We'll figure this out together. Maybe there's a simple explanation."

Why had Grandma never mentioned this before?

THE MORNING SUN CLIMBED HIGHER AS WE DROVE TOWARD Grandma Dawn's cabin. The tension within Mom's Subaru was thick with anticipation. We needed answers, and she was the only one who could provide them.

"Do you think Grandma will be surprised we came over so early?" I asked, glancing at Mom as we rounded the last bend in the road.

"She's probably expecting us," Mom replied with a tight smile, her earlier apprehension replaced with determination.

When we arrived, the cabin looked peaceful, nestled among the towering firs and pines. Yet, today, something felt different. The curtains were still drawn, and there was an unsettling stillness settled over the place. We pulled onto the gravel driveway. Maybe Grandma was enjoying a slow morning after a long night of revelry.

"She could be sleeping in," I said, more to myself than to Mom, as we got out of the car.

Mom nodded. "She did do a lot of dancing last night, I hadn't seen her move like that in years. I didn't know she still had it in her."

We made our way toward the steps, the sound of gravel crunching beneath our feet. I reached the door first and knocked, not wanting to startle her.

"Grandma? It's us. Starla and Mom. We want to talk." I called out, half expecting to hear her cheerful voice beckoning us inside.

There was only silence.

"Maybe she didn't hear you," Mom suggested, stepping up beside me. "She could be in the back, or maybe in a deep sleep."

I knocked again, a little louder this time. "Grandma? We need to talk."

Still nothing.

The quiet was beginning to feel strange, yet not alarming. After all, she could be in the shower somewhere she couldn't hear us knocking.

"I'll try the door," Mom said, reaching for the handle. It was locked, which was unusual for Grandma during the day.

Mom hesitated for a moment, then raised an eyebrow. "I guess we should use the spare key she keeps hidden."

With practiced ease, Mom approached the pot of yellow roses by the porch and retrieved a key hidden beneath. The door creaked open, and we stepped inside, greeted by the familiar scent of pine—warm, inviting, and perfectly in place.

"Gram, are you here?" I called out.

There was no answer.

Mom and I exchanged a quick glance, and her brows furrowed. "Let's check the bedroom."

We moved down the hallway, our steps light on the wooden floor. As we reached the bedroom door, Mom pushed it open, expecting to find Grandma lost in a good book, concentrating so hard she didn't hear us knocking.

Instead, we found her lying peacefully in bed, the quilt pulled up to her chin. She looked as if she was merely resting, her face serene, almost as though she were lost in a pleasant dream.

"Grandma?" I said, stepping closer. There was no movement, no stirring at the sound of our arrival.

Mom moved to the bedside, with a small smile on her face. "Looks like she's having a lazy morning," she whispered, reaching out to touch her shoulder gently. "Mom, we're here. We've got some questions for you—" She stopped suddenly, her hand freezing in place.

The realization struck us both at once, like a cold wave, leaving us momentarily stunned. The stillness in the room, the unnatural quiet—it wasn't just sleep. My words caught in my throat as I watched Mom's face crumble, her hand slipping from Grandma's shoulder.

"Mom, no," I choked out, my voice filled with disbelief. Mom's hand dropped to her side, and she collapsed onto the bed. Her body wracked with silent sobs.

"She's gone, Starla," she managed to say, her words barely audible through her tears.

"No, no, no," I shouted, shaking my head as I stumbled back against the wall, the truth hitting me like a freight train. The woman who had been the rock of our family, our matriarch, was gone. Just like that, without a chance for goodbye, without the answers we had come searching for.

I felt the floor drop out from beneath me as the room seemed to spin. This wasn't how it was supposed to happen. We were supposed to come over, have a cup of coffee, and Gram was supposed to answer all our questions.

"Why now?" I managed to choke out, my words thick with tears. "Why, when we still need her so much?"

Mom didn't answer, couldn't answer. She hugged me. "She always said she wanted to go in her sleep like this, like her brother John."

The room, once a place of comfort and warmth, now felt cold and empty. The loss was staggering. My grandmother, the woman who had been my anchor, my guide, was gone. The person who had always been there, whose wisdom and love had shaped so much of who I was, had left me without warning.

I knelt beside her bed, my hands trembling as I reached out to touch her one last time, feeling the coolness of her skin beneath my fingers. Tears blurred my vision, spilling down my cheeks as I whispered a broken goodbye, my shoulders shook with the weight of all the things I would never get to say.

Memories of our time together flashed before me. Her stories, her bigger-than-life laugh, the way she always knew just what to say to make everything better. There would be no more stories, no more laughter.

Only silence.

The unanswered questions and unresolved mysteries hung over us. How could we uncover the truth now, piecing together fragments of a story left unfinished? The thought of moving forward without her felt impossible. As I sat there, my tears soaking into the quilt she tucked around herself, I sensed this was only the beginning.

The secrets and truths felt insignificant compared to the void of her absence. As I held her hand one last time, the weight of the moment settled deep within me. I realized I had to be strong. Not just for myself, but for my mother, who had lost something even more precious today.

With a heavy heart, I gently pulled the quilt over her face, a final act of love, and turned to face the future. A future unknown, but one I knew we would face together.

CHAPTER 19

Losing A Whole Year

TEMECULA, CALIFORNIA
DECEMBER, 2018

Starla Wylder
Forty-One Years Old

On Christmas morning, I forced myself to wear a cheerful face, determined to inject some holiday spirit into my family. Standing at the counter, I mashed potatoes with more vigor than necessary, hoping to shake off the heaviness clinging to me like a thick fog. The air was rich with the aroma of butter and cream, mingling with the nostalgic scent of pine from the intensely decorated tree in the corner.

The rhythmic sound of the masher against the bowl echoed in the kitchen, a reminder of the comforting routines we once shared. After the exhausting tasks of funeral planning, sorting through Grandma's belongings, and months of grief, the holidays had arrived in full force, marking our first Christmas without Grandma Dawn. Each twinkling light and joyful decoration felt like a cruel reminder of her absence, amplifying the ache in my chest.

"Thanks for hosting dinner today. I just wasn't feeling up to it." Mom whisked away at a boiling pot of giblets.

"We should decide who's taking on Christmas and who's stuck with Thanksgiving from now on. It feels so different without her."

"It doesn't matter who hosts, as long as we're together," she replied.

Just then, I heard a car door slam outside.

"Merry Christmas! Where is everyone?" Aunt Rory called as she passed the front window, her son and husband right behind her, arms full of wrapped gifts.

"We're in the kitchen," I shouted back, hearing Seb open the front door for our guests. "Lacey and her family should be here soon."

"Did you find Grandma's recipe?" Rory asked as she entered, her auburn hair styled in feathery spikes, her smoky eye makeup hinting at the vibrant woman she once was.

"No, but I made it with her enough times, I think I have it down," Mom replied, smiling despite the bittersweetness in the air.

"So who else is coming?" Rory grabbed a pickle off the relish platter Laney and Brooke were helping prepare.

"Erin and her family, Susan and Daniel, Lacey and her crew will be here soon," Mom said, her tone tinged with a wistful note. "Meanwhile, the brothers are all gathering in Redlands. It feels like everyone's carving out their own little lives."

We could all sense the shift in our family dynamic, like branches of a tree spreading out, each with its own direction. It left me grappling with the feeling our tight-knit moments were becoming fewer and farther between.

"I guess that's what happens when the matriarch passes," Rory added, her voice laced with understanding.

"Maybe we can all get together for Easter?" I suggested, hoping to spark some continuity in our family traditions.

"Let's not worry about it right now," Mom replied, her smile softening the weight of her words. "Let's just focus on today."

As more guests trickled in, the kitchen buzzed with hugs and laughter, enveloping us in a warm cocoon of the holiday season. Three generations of Cameron women worked side by side, each stirring, chopping, and seasoning, carrying on a tradition as timeless as Christmas itself.

In the other room, the men tackled the gifts needing assembling, the faint sounds of the football game playing in the background mingled with the Christmas playlist I had playing gently in the background.

As we prepared the Christmas dinner, our chatter drifted between the mundane and the meaningful, the savory aroma of turkey wafted through the kitchen. It wrapped around us like a warm hug, there was an unmistakable hint of sadness in the air. Grandma had always been the heartbeat of these gatherings, her laughter echoing in every corner, making her absence sting just a little more.

"Gram would've loved this," Lacey said, her voice catching slightly as she gently rocked her first grandchild in her arms. After years of working through her trauma from Mexico, it was heartwarming to see her thriving as a school counselor, building a family of her own.

"No one made Christmas like your mom did," Dad chimed in from his spot next to the fireplace. "She had a way of making every meal so special."

"It's one of the many ways she showed her love," I added.

Christmas dinner was a lively affair, with laughter ringing through the dining room and the clinking of glasses blending with the mouthwatering scents of roasted turkey and spiced cranberry sauce. Family members jostled for the best seats, while kids zoomed around. Their excited chatter filled every cranny.

Even though we all missed Grandma Dawn, it felt like we'd made an unspoken pact to keep that longing tucked away in the kitchen, a poignant whisper that couldn't quite reach the dining table. As we gathered around, we leaned into the joy of the moment, savoring the embrace of togetherness. Stories flowed like wine, and the room buzzed with the comfort of familiar faces, as if we were stitching new memories into the fabric of our holiday traditions.

Amid the clatter of dishes and shared smiles, I felt we were honoring her memory in our own way. We filled the space with love and laughter, weaving together a new chapter that was uniquely ours.

Once we filled our bellies it was time to move into the living room to open gifts. Seb stepped forward, placing two small, wrapped packages in front of Mom and me.

"Happy Christmas," he said softly, his British accent warming the cold evening air. "I know this year has been different. I think you both need this."

Mom glanced down at the gift in her hands, brow furrowed. "Seb, you didn't have to."

"I did," he interrupted gently. "Open them together."

I exchanged a glance with Mom and slowly unwrapped the paper. Inside was an envelope with two tickets nestled within. "Seattle?"

Brooke and Laney looked over, curiosity dancing in their eyes. "What's going on?"

"It's Daddy's surprise," I said, holding the tickets up. "He thinks we need a trip to Seattle."

Erin chimed in, her eyes lighting up. "A getaway sounds perfect right now. I always say there's nothing like a little trip to get the juices flowing. Right, dear?"

In a twist none of us saw coming, Erin had been happily married to her high school crush, Brandon, for over ten years. It was funny how life works out. After all our talks about meeting new people while flying, her soulmate turned out to be just a stone's throw away, growing up right down the street in Montclair. He'd popped up on one of her flights, and just like that, the rest was history. She juggled her career as a flight attendant with family life like it was second nature.

"I know it was exactly what I needed," Brandon said, his fingers gently brushing a lock of hair from Erin's face. The affection in his eyes reminded me that love often finds you when you least expect it, sometimes in the most ordinary of places.

Mom scanned the room, taking in the faces of our family, and a soft smile broke through her tears. "Maybe it's just what we need. Grandma would've wanted us to keep going, to be happy."

Seb's eyes softened with a small smile. "I know you've always wanted to take the train from LA to Seattle. From there, I've hired a driver to take you both to Neah Bay. I booked flights back for your return—figured you'd want to get home quickly after meeting with Talie."

Mom's breath hitched as she looked at him, surprise mixing with something closer to fear. "Oh, I don't know. Do you think it's a good idea to go stirring up the past?"

His gaze was steady. "You've waited long enough, Twyla. It's time to go. To find the answers you deserve."

My heart raced. "You think we should confront Talie?"

"I do," he replied, his voice firm. "It's important you do it in person. She was your grandma's closest friend. She'll likely to open up if you catch her off guard."

"I agree," Erin chimed in. "Look, we all know about this mystery birth certificate. In a family like this, it was hard to keep a bombshell like that quiet. Everyone knows and has an opinion on it. This could be the only way to find out the truth." Erin didn't mince her words.

"I don't know if I'm ready." Mom's hands trembled as she held the tickets, tears welling in her eyes. She twisted her wedding ring, taking slow, deep breaths.

"You are." Dad placed a gentle hand on her shoulder. "I know you're scared, but this has been weighing on you for months. You need to do this. Your mom must have wanted you to find out. Otherwise, why would she have left that birth certificate for you?"

"It could have been a mistake," I countered, uncertainty flooding back.

"There are no mistakes," Seb said firmly. "And I think this will be good for both of you. A change of scenery, some mother daughter bonding time. I'll take care of the kids and you two go have an adventure."

"Susan," Mom said, turning to her sister. "You don't remember Mom ever having a boyfriend, do you?"

Susan's brow knitted in thought. "Oh, I remember when Mom and Dad separated. It felt like there was fighting all the time. Grandma Jensen even came down to help, I was a little kid back then, so it's a bit of a blur. Eventually they made up, and having Dad back felt like such a relief. You know, in the end, it doesn't matter what your birth certificate says. Ellis was your father, in all the ways that mattered. We all knew you were his favorite."

"I know, sis. It's just something that's been bothering me. Mom passed without explaining what happened." Her voice trailed off, the weight of unsaid words hanging in the air.

"We've got your back, sis, no matter what you uncover. This doesn't change a thing for us. If this is something you need to explore, you've got all our support," Rory chimed in, her tone reassuring.

I glanced between the three sisters, each a unique piece of our family puzzle. Mom, petite with delicate hands and sun-kissed hair, exuded effortless elegance. In stark contrast, Susan and Rory were more ruggedly built, rich red hair framing broad faces. They were all attractive women, but Mom looked more delicate with her tiny waist and waifish build. It was a funny sight, really; the Camerons were known for their fiery hair and height, while Mom, with her heart-shaped face and golden locks, resembled a sunflower in a field of wildflowers.

Mom's gaze met mine, searching for reassurance. After a long moment, she nodded, a small, trembling smile breaking through. "Okay," she said, her tone steadier. "We can go during Spring Break."

Seb's relief shone in his dark amber eyes. His shoulders relaxed as he let out a breath he seemed to have been holding. "Good. It's time, Twyla. Time to put the past to rest."

As I stood there, the thought of confronting Talie sent a flicker of hope sparking to life in my chest. Seb was right. We couldn't keep running from this. Maybe Talie was the missing piece we needed.

My once stoic, stiff-upper-lipped Brit had transformed into a man who wore his heart on his sleeve. As he sat across from me, I caught glimpses of the man I fell in love with. The former rugby player was still so full of energy. His emotions flowed more easily now, and he had become less guarded, more open. I reflected on how much he changed over the years.

"I think this trip will provide the closure you've been looking for," he said.

A flicker of hope ignited within me. "I've always wanted to visit Neah Bay. The way Gram spoke about it made me feel like I've already been there. This is exactly what we need to reconnect with her." I looked at my handsome husband, gratitude spilling over. "Thank you, Seb. You have no idea how much this means."

I had recently begun working on Grandma's life story but hadn't quite found my flow, with too many feelings swirling around. Now, I was on the verge of visiting the places she'd known as a child during the Great Depression, and the thought filled me with a mix of excitement and purpose. This journey could be the key to unlocking her memories and, in turn, resolving the mystery behind Mom's birth certificate. It was going to be incredible.

Visiting Neah Bay would be more than a pilgrimage. It would be an opportunity to ensure the stories she had entrusted to me were preserved with the care they deserved.

By walking in her footsteps, by seeing the world through

her eyes, I knew I could tackle the monumental task of chronicling our family history. In doing so, I hoped to bring her story to life—not only for the pages of a book, but for myself. It would keep her with me, even in her absence, and, hopefully, provide the answers my mother needed to hear.

GRADUALLY, THE DAYS BRIGHTENED. THE SHARP LOSS BEGAN to soften into a quieter ache. Still there, yet no longer all consuming. I missed Grandma dearly, yet a new purpose had emerged, something to look forward to.

The months passed, and soon we found ourselves boarding the train to Seattle. The journey was breathtaking, a parade of dramatic landscapes set against an undercurrent of tension.

The train rocked gently as it headed north, the rhythmic clatter of wheels on tracks providing a comforting backdrop. I gazed out the window, watching the dramatic Pacific Northwest landscape rush by. Towering firs reached toward the sky, their evergreen needles mingling with the bursts of white from blooming dogwoods that dotted the scenery like confetti.

Mom and I reminisced about her summers spent in Oklahoma, the wistfulness of those memories wrapping around us like an old familiar friend. As the mist clung to the window and the sun peeked through the clouds, it felt as though we were skirting the real reason for our journey, with unspoken thoughts lingering between us, echoing like the fading sound of the train's whistle.

The hours passed slowly as I began to read Grandma's journals while Mom listened quietly, her gaze often drifting out the window as if searching for answers in the shifting landscape. Each page I turned revealed snippets of Grandma's life—her hopes, her heartaches, and the dreams that had shaped our family. I could almost hear her voice in the words, a soft whisper intertwining with the rhythm of the train.

Eventually, we arrived in Seattle, where a driver awaited us, just as promised. A tall, dark-haired man with chiseled features and intense eyes stood by the curb. There was a quiet confidence about him, with a hunting knife clipped to his belt, hinting at a rugged edge beneath his calm demeanor. He nodded politely as we approached, exuding an air of quiet professionalism.

"Justin, right?" I asked, glancing at him.

"Yeah," he replied, his voice steady. "You must be Starla and Twyla. Nice to meet you." He gestured toward the car. "It's a long way to Neah Bay; we'd better get going."

I smiled softly, appreciating his no-nonsense approach to things.

Justin didn't pry into our reasons for making this trip, simply allowed us the space we needed as he loaded our bags into the back of his car. I felt a sense of comfort in his strong presence.

As we navigated the winding roads toward Neah Bay,

Justin began to share snippets of local history and stories about the area. His deep, knowledgeable voice transformed what could have been a long and arduous drive into a captivating, guided journey through time.

"Back in the old days, the people would have used crude log bridges to cross these rivers and streams, nowadays the journey is much quicker, but it still takes about four hours from Seattle, that's without traffic," he explained.

The past enveloped us like a warm embrace, deepening our connection to the land our ancestors once walked. Each of Justin's stories resonated within me, linking the present to the echoes of those who came before. I could almost sense Grandma's presence, as if the soil whispered her name and the trees held her secrets. The beauty of the towering mountains and vast, shimmering waters felt infused with her spirit.

As I took notes for Grandma's biography, the landscape unfolded around me, offering a glimpse into the wild woods of Washington from her youth. Dogwoods swayed in the breeze, framed by rugged mountains and dense forests where the wind whispered secrets from the past.

"How much further is it?" I asked, my curiosity tinged with anticipation.

"We should be close to Neah Bay soon," Justin replied.

The afternoon stretched into an endless day as we traveled for the better part of an hour. The road continued to twist and turn, and at one point, I must have dozed off.

When I awoke, I realized we were one of the only cars on the road. The further we drove from Seattle, the fewer cars we encountered, as urban highways transformed into two-lane roads winding through lush forests and rolling hills. Each mile felt like a step deeper into a forgotten world, where the whispers of nature replaced the city's noise.

We passed small towns and hidden coves, catching occasional glimpses of the vast expanse of the Pacific Ocean. As evening approached, we arrived at our destination.

When we rounded the final bend, Neah Bay revealed itself in all its rugged glory—crashing waves, rocky cliffs, and the fresh scent of saltwater filling the air. A sense of awe washed over me as I took in the thick forests surrounding the sparkling turquoise waters of the Pacific. The reservation exuded an enchanting allure.

"Welcome to Neah Bay," Justin said, shifting in his driver's seat as he took in the view.

I was struck by the untamed splendor of the place, where lush green forests whispered ancient tales, and the people thrived in harmony with nature. Yet harsh realities loomed in the form of towering cliffs and icy waters. I could see how dangerous fishing here could be, testing the bravery of anyone daring to seek the sea's bounty.

As we climbed out of the car and I took in the untamed beauty surrounding us, I couldn't help but feel a little disoriented. "It's so remote. I was expecting it to be more built up by now."

"Neah Bay is as remote as it gets," he explained with a touch of pride. "The town is small. There's only one grocery store serving the whole community, and a couple of restaurants open during the tourist season. Life here is simple, centered around the natural rhythms of the land and the sea."

"It's beautiful." Mom took my hand in hers. "Where will we stay?"

"I thought you might want to get acclimated to your surroundings before I take you to your accommodations. The Hobuck Beach Resort might be small, but it's close to the ocean and has everything you'll need. Your husband has arranged everything. You're welcome to use this car; I have my own room at the resort, and I'll be here to drive you back to the airport when you're ready."

"Thank you, Justin. However did my husband find you?" I asked, feeling grateful for our impromptu guide.

Justin chuckled. "On Google, where else? I take city folks out on fishing expeditions. Your husband mentioned this is a different kind of fishing trip." He winked.

"You hit the nail on the head," I said, smiling. "We're fishing for answers."

Justin gave a small, understanding nod, recognizing the weight of our mission. "Would you like to stretch your legs before I take you to the resort?"

"That would be great," I replied, glancing over at Mom. "I need to pick up a few things from the market. Are you coming, Mom?"

She looked taken aback, as if the reality of where we were had finally hit her. I caught a flicker of the young girl she once was, the one who had grown up on the stories of this place and was now being confronted with its stark reality.

"Sure," she said. "I could use some air."

We stepped out into the cool, salty breeze and made our way to the small market Justin had pointed out. The store was quaint, the kind of place where everyone knew each other by name. Shelves were stocked with the essentials, and as we moved through the aisles, I noticed how the locals greeted each other, their exchanges both familiar and genuine.

As we gathered the few items we needed, a sense of anticipation washed over me. There was something comforting about this simple market, a reminder life moved at a slower pace here. It didn't seem as if things had changed much in the last hundred years.

Once we had everything, we headed back to the car, where Justin was waiting. He drove us to the resort, a cozy lodge nestled near the coastline, surrounded by towering trees and the distant sound of crashing waves. The cabin he led us to was inviting, with rustic wooden beams and a fireplace crackling softly in the corner.

"This is perfect," I said as we settled in. For the first time in days, I felt a sense of peace.

Mom moved to the window, looking out at the darkening sky. "It's beautiful here."

I joined her, placing a hand on her shoulder. "We'll find the answers we're looking for tomorrow, Mom. Let's just rest."

"Tomorrow," she echoed, as if trying to convince herself.

CHAPTER 20
The Barber's Daughter

NEAH BAY, WASHINGTON

SPRING, 2019

Starla Wylder

Forty-One Years Old

The next morning, we woke up to the majestic beauty of the Pacific Northwest. It felt isolated, as if we had stepped back in time. By the time we arrived at Talie's modest home, my heart was pounding in my chest, each beat echoing in my ears like a drum.

"Are you ready for this?" I asked mom as she hesitated at the door, her hand trembling as she reached up to knock. I could see the fear in her eyes, the uncertainty that plagued her since we found the birth certificate now fully realized.

"It's now or never." She took a deep breath before she knocked on the door.

"It's going to be okay," I uttered. "We'll get through this."

She exhaled slowly before rapping gently on the door. The sound echoed in the stillness of the morning, each knock like a thunderclap.

After a moment, the door creaked open, revealing Talie. Though small in stature, she seemed to fill the room with an effortless grace. Her silver hair framed her face like a halo, highlighting the deep lines reflecting a life richly lived. But, it was her eyes that held me captive—mysterious and piercing, they seemed to reach the depths of my soul.

A guarded expression flickered across her face as her gaze moved between us. I hadn't seen Talie in years. She looked more fragile than I remembered, yet the strength in her demeanor was as formidable as ever, a quiet storm simmering beneath the surface.

"This is a pleasant surprise," she greeted us, her voice calm but cautious. "I was so sorry to hear about Dawn. She was my closest friend."

"And you were hers." I enveloped the smaller woman in a hug.

"Talie," Mom began, her resolve wavering slightly. "We need to talk. About my mother. About everything."

Talie's eyes darkened as she hesitated, then stepped aside, motioning for us to come in. The living room was small and cozy, brimming with old photographs and mementos that spoke of a life rich with history.

"I knew this day would come. Please, sit," Talie said, her voice softer, almost kind. "Would you like some tea?"

"No, we just had breakfast." Mom and I sat down on the worn sofa, our nerves thrumming with anticipation. Talie moved slowly, over to a small cabinet. She opened it, revealing a stack of letters and a small velvet box. She held the letters out to Mom, her expression reflecting both love and regret.

"Dawn asked me to keep these safe," Talie said, her words tinged with sadness. "She said if you ever came up here asking questions, well, she wanted you to have them when the time was right. If you came all the way up to Neah Bay, then you deserved the truth."

Mom took the items with trembling hands, her eyes wide with fear and curiosity. She looked at me, then back at the box and the letters, her breath catching in her throat.

"What truth, Talie?" I asked, my voice a whisper.

Talie looked at us both, the sorrow in her eyes seemed to stretch back decades. "The truth about your father, your real father. And who you really are."

Mom's hands shook as she slowly opened the letter, the paper crinkling softly in the quiet room. I could see her eyes scanning the words, her expression shifting from confusion to shock to something much deeper. Something that looked like heartbreak.

"Oh, my God, Mom!" My heart pounded as I leaned closer, desperate to see what the letter said. But before I could make out the words, her eyes welled up with tears, and she covered her mouth with her hand, her whole body shaking.

Dear Twyla,

If you're reading this, it means I never found the gumption to tell you the truth myself, and I've likely moved on from this world. Please don't be sorrowful. I had a wonderful life filled with love, laughter, and yes, a few secrets tucked away. I may not have shown it enough, but I loved you deeply.

What I'm about to share doesn't change who you are, Twyla. Ellis loved you as his own, and he was your dad through and through. I regret that your real father, James, was never a part of your life. I lacked the strength to face the storms that would have surely come from telling the truth, so I did what I thought was best for our family. Looking back, I see that it might not have been what was best for you.

Sometimes, seeing your face stirred old pains—not because of anything you did, but because it was like peering into the past. You bear a striking resemblance to James Lockhart, a special man I first met back in Oklahoma, five years my junior. He had a way of waltzing back into my life just when I needed him most, as if he'd been sent from above at a time when I felt so alone.

You've been married a good while now, so you know that every relationship has its trials. Ellis and I certainly had our share of rocky times. During one of those difficult periods, James returned to my life. Imagine my surprise when I stumbled upon my old friend's barber shop right down the street from us! At that time, Ellis wasn't treating me right, and I thought our marriage was at an end. James helped me gather the pieces, and we shared a summer of love. When Ellis found out, he came rushing back into my life, and I chose to mend things with him and reunite our family, but I was already pregnant with you. It was the hardest time of my life.

I left this letter with Talie because if you were determined enough to make the trek to Neah Bay, then you deserved to hear the truth from someone who lived it alongside me in a place that shaped my life. Neah Bay is a special place and I only wish I could have laid eyes on it one last time.

I'm sorry I didn't have the strength to share this with you face-to-face. If your heart leads you to seek out your Lockhart family, know that you have my blessing. They are good folks, and if you're curious about them, I understand completely.

This doesn't change who you are, Twyla. It just adds another piece to the amazing woman you've become. I love you more than words can say, and I'll always be looking out for you.

With all my love,
Mom

"It's true," Mom whispered, barely able to speak. "Everything. It's all true."

"It's going to be okay, Mom," I reassured her, squeezing her hand as I watched her world unravel before my eyes. She had loved and missed Ellis Cameron so deeply, and she was faced with the devastating truth they weren't genetically related.

What would this revelation do to my mother?

"I'm okay, really," she said, her voice trembling slightly. "I guess I've had my suspicions, I couldn't bring myself to face them. I mean, I'm the only blonde in a sea of redheads. I should have realized the truth."

"Don't forget this," Talie said softly, breaking the silence as she motioned to the small velvet jewelry box. Her eyes met mine with a mixture of sadness and understanding, a silent acknowledgment of the weight of this moment.

Mom slowly opened the box, revealing a delicate ruby-and-gold ring nestled inside. Inscribed on the band was a single word, "Always."

Tears welled up in my eyes as I looked at the ring, speechless. It felt like a symbol of a love story never fully told, a promise never fulfilled.

Talie's voice broke the silence, her tone gentle and firm. "They were going to be married. You know, when Ellis came roaring back, the kids all wanted their daddy, and your grandma had to make some tough decisions."

Mom stared at the ring, tears glistening in her eyes. "It's like a piece of the puzzle finally fits."

I watched her, my heart aching for the hurt she must be feeling, the unanswered questions she'd kept buried. Holding this small token of a past love, it was as though she could finally begin to heal, to reconcile the woman she had always known herself to be with the truth she now faced.

"Mom," I said gently, "maybe it's time we go back to the cabin and rest for a bit. This is a lot to take in."

She nodded, still staring at the ring, her thumb brushing over the inscription. "You're right. I think I might lay down for a bit."

"Thank you, Auntie. It would make Gram happy to know we were here together."

"Of course, dear," Talie replied, her voice gentle but wise with years. "It was such a hard time for her, and I was right there with her. When Ellis came back, there was terrible fighting between the men. She really thought they were going to kill each other. That choice she made wasn't easy, but your grandma did what she thought was best for her family. Once she made up her mind, she was so strong. Right or wrong, she stood by it—and I see that same strength in both of you."

Talie paused, placing a gentle hand on my mother's shoulder, her eyes teeming with understanding. "You've got his eyes and you've got her strength. Remember, real power isn't always about holding on, it's about your ability to adapt, to find peace even when times are tough, and keep moving forward, even when the path is unclear."

"Thank you, Talie," Mom enveloped her in one of her

huge bear hugs before we made the short trek back to our cabin.

WHEN WE STEPPED INTO THE CABIN, A QUIET SOLITUDE surrounded us, broken only by the soft rustling of leaves outside. I built a fire in the old stone hearth, watching the flames catch and flicker, bringing a warm glow to the room. The day's revelations weighed heavily on us, but as Mom and I sank into the worn leather sofa, the warmth of the fire and the quiet of the cabin began to soften the edges of our pain, bringing a hint of peace to the storm still stirring within.

Mom stared into the fire, lost in thought, while I waited beside her, searching for the right moment to break the silence. Finally, she sighed and turned to me, weariness and determination reflecting in her eyes. 'Star, there's something I need to tell you—something I've suspected ever since we found that birth certificate." I leaned closer, sensing whatever she was about to share would change everything.

"You remember my friend Penny from middle school?" she asked.

"Of course. You used to talk about her all the time."

"Penny's father was James Lockhart. I think he might be my real father."

My heart skipped a beat as I processed her words. "Wait, the same James Lockhart?"

"I think so. How many James Lockharts could there be who are also barbers?" she asked, her voice quivering slightly. "It all makes sense now—the way the families always acted awkward around each other, how they never wanted me and Penny to go to each other's houses. And then, one day, out of the blue, they just up and moved away. I never knew why, until now."

She paused, her gaze distant, as if she were seeing those memories in a new light. "Penny is my half-sister."

"You need to call her," I said, the words settling between us with a weight I hadn't expected. I reached for her hand, giving it a reassuring squeeze, steadying her as the realization landed, it was time to take the next step. "Do you know how to reach her?" I asked.

Mom nodded, her resolve hardening. "Her family must still be around, and Lockhart isn't exactly a common name. Finding a number shouldn't be too hard."

We ran a quick search on my iPhone, our hearts pounding with anticipation. We found a listing for a Penny Lockhart in California. Mom dialed the number, her breath hitching as it rang on the other end.

"Hello?" a female answered the phone.

"Penny?" Mom said, her voice was barely above a whisper. "It's Twyla. Twyla Cameron."

There was a long pause at the other end of the line, and for a moment, I thought the call might drop. Then, Penny's words broke through, thick with emotion.

"Twyla. I never thought I'd hear from you again," she

said, her words heavy with the weight of years gone by. "It's been so long."

"It has." Mom's voice cracked slightly. "I need to talk to you. I found out something—do you know what I mean?"

Another pause followed, then Penny sighed, "Not really."

"I think you know exactly what I mean."

"What do you know?" She let out a heavy sigh.

"I want you to tell me the truth," Mom pressed, her tone urgent.

"I think I'm your sister," she finally squeaked out. "My dad admitted it one night when he was drinking. He got all emotional and said he'd been in love with your mom. It was just before he married my mom."

"Yes," Mom gasped, tears welling in her eyes. "I just found out, and I didn't know who else to turn to."

There was a heavy silence, the air thick with unspoken truths. Finally, Penny spoke again, her voice trembling. "I'm sorry, Twyla. Dad made me promise never to tell you or contact you. He said it would be too disruptive to your life. There's something else you need to know. Dad's not well."

"What? He's still alive?"

"Yes." Penny interrupted gently. "He's not well, Twyla. He's living with me, and I don't know how much longer he has left. If you want to see him, if you want to meet him, I don't think you should wait too long."

Tears streamed down Mom's face as she processed the

news. "I don't know what to say. I never thought I'd get the chance."

"I'm sorry to tell you this now," Penny said, her words full of compassion. "I think you need to meet him before it's too late. There are things he might want to say to you."

Mom nodded again, even though Penny couldn't see her. "Thank you for telling me. I only wish I could have found you sooner."

"I did look for you. I even went to see your mom once on Harvard Street," Penny replied, her voice softening.

"What did she say?"

"At first, she pretended she didn't know Dad. Then, she gave me a picture of you and begged me not to reach out. She said it was too late, it would upset you too much. I didn't want to go against their wishes. I should have been stronger," she admitted.

"If it were the other way around, I would have found you, nothing would have stopped me," my mom said softly, her eyes glistening with unshed tears. "We've lost so much time already. I can't believe he's still alive. It's just a lot to process. When can I come meet my dad?"

"Come anytime you're ready, but hurry."

When the call ended, Mom sat in stunned silence, the phone still clutched in her hand. I wrapped my arms around her, holding her close, as the weight of this revelation settled over us like a heavy blanket. The existence of a father she never knew—James Lockhart—was like a spark igniting a deep, buried yearning.

"We're going to meet him, your birth father, and we'll do it together," I said firmly, trying to sound calm despite the trembling of my heart.

"I have a living father," she declared, astonishment lacing her words. "I can't believe I have a dad again. I want to meet him. Can we move our flight up? I don't want to wait."

The prospect of a meeting with James Lockhart was not just about reconnecting. It was a chance for Mom to get the answers to her questions about her own identity. The family saga we were part of, steeped in secrets and long-lost connections, was about to unfold in a way that might reshape our lives.

As I held her, I thought about our family's journey. Marked by resilience and the weight of history. This discovery was a chance for healing, for both of us. We needed to face the truth together, and I was determined to help her find closure and new beginnings.

"Of course, Mom, I'll take care of everything."

And as we sat there, embracing each other in the quiet of the cabin, I recognized our journey was far from over. We finally had a chance to understand the secret Grandma Dawn had been keeping for nearly sixty years.

CHAPTER 21

Take me to the Ocean

SAN DIMAS, CALIFORNIA
SPRING, 2019

Starla Wylder
Forty-One Years Old

The sun hung low in the sky as we pulled into the parking lot at Puddingstone Lake. The landscape was peaceful, almost surreal, as if it knew the gravity of the moment about to unfold. My heart pounded in my chest, a mix of anticipation and anxiety, as I looked at Mom. She was staring out at the lake, her hands clenched in her lap.

Penny had called, her tone a blend of anticipation and worry. "He wants to meet you," she said, "but he has one request. He wants to meet at Puddingstone Lake. That place means a lot to him, but…" She hesitated, choosing her words carefully. "I'm not sure he can make the trip. It's his last wish, and I don't want to take that away from him."

Here we were, parked at the edge of the lake, waiting to meet my grandfather for the first time. I glanced at Mom again, and she turned to look at me, her eyes wide with a mix of emotions.

"You ready?" I asked, reaching over to squeeze her hand.

She tilted her head, I could see the uncertainty in her eyes. "As ready as I'll ever be," she responded, her voice barely audible. Penny's car pulled up beside us, and my heart skipped a beat. This was it.

Penny got out first, walking around to help James from the car. He was frail, his body bent with age and illness, there was a spark in his eyes that spoke of determination. He was hooked up to oxygen, his breaths labored, when he looked up and saw us, he smiled, warm enough to make my heartache.

Mom and I got out of the car, and I watched as Penny helped James into his wheelchair. He wobbled, but Penny steadied him, her face a mask of worry and love.

"Dad," Penny said softly. "This is Twyla. And this is Starla, your granddaughter."

James looked at us, his green eyes the same vibrant shade as my mother's and mine, shining with unshed tears, a mix of longing and regret. He was a handsome man, his skin almost translucent, carrying a quiet strength that seemed to anchor him. His white hair framed a face etched by time, every line a memory of both joy and sorrow. He took a deep breath and leaned forward, hope flickering across his face as he turned to Mom. In that moment, decades of separation seemed to dissolve, leaving only the undeniable pull of a bond that had always been there, waiting to be rediscovered.

For a heartbeat, time stood still.

"Hi, Dad," her voice broke as the words left her lips. James reached out with a trembling hand, cupping her face as if she were something fragile, something precious.

"Twyla, oh Twyla" he breathed, his expression infused with wonder. "I loved your mother."

Tears welled up in Mom's eyes, and she nodded, her own hand coming up to cover his. "It's okay Dad, I understand. She left me a letter explaining everything, she loved you too."

Seeing them together was like watching my mom being born. It was as if everything she had ever been, everything she had ever questioned about herself, was finally finding a place, finding a reason. The way he held her face reminded me of when Seb held our newborn baby for the first time. How his eyes had sparkled with awe and an overwhelming sense of love.

Penny gave us each a big bear hug then turned to her dad. She looked hesitant, torn between staying and giving us space. "I'll leave you three alone. I'll come back in a couple hours to pick him up. Call me, if you need anything."

James smiled softly, not taking his eyes off my mom. "Thank you."

Penny gave one last, tight-lipped smile before turning and walking back to her car. I could tell it was hard for her to leave. What was she thinking as she drove away, leaving us standing at the edge of the lake—a family reuniting after years of separation? This woman, who from behind looked exactly like my mother, moved like my mother, and sounded like my mother. It was mind-boggling.

James let out a deep sigh, interrupting my thoughts, as if the weight of the world had been lifted off his shoulders. "This place is where Dawn and I had our first date. We came here and sat by the water, talking for hours. It was the beginning of everything."

A lump formed in my throat as I imagined them. Younger and in love, sitting by this very lake, unaware of the future that would unfold, the paths their lives would take. Mom guided James's wheelchair over to a nearby bench, where she and I sat down beside him, the quiet of the lake surrounding us. For a while, none of us spoke, content just to be in each other's presence, letting reality sink in.

"Twyla," he said, "I'm so sorry for not being there for you. I wish I could go back and do things differently, but I can't. All I can do is tell you how much I love you, how proud I am of the woman you've become. I followed your career, you know? I loved the song you wrote."

Mom's tears flowed freely, and she leaned into him,

resting her head on his shoulder. "I'm glad I got to meet you. That I get to have this time with you."

His eyes watered as he pressed a kiss to the top of her head. "And I'm so grateful you're here. You and Starla. I've dreamed of this moment for so long."

We sat there for what felt like hours, talking, sharing stories, and laughing through our tears. James told us about his life, about the choices he made and the regrets he'd carried with him. And Mom shared her own stories, filling in the gaps of a life he had never been a part of.

James took a deep, labored breath. "There's one more thing I want to do. Starla, would you and your mom take me for a drive to the ocean? I've been cooped up at home for too long," he said, a small smile playing on his lips. "I think a nice long drive would do me good."

I hesitated, glancing at Mom, but she nodded. "Of course, Grandpa. Let me call Penny and let her know."

The drive to Crystal Cove was serene, the air heavy with the scent of salt. In the backseat, James sat with his eyes closed, a contented smile playing on his lips as he inhaled the briny breeze.

When we arrived, Mom and I helped him out of the car and into his wheelchair. We pushed him down the board-walk, the sound of the waves crashing against the shore filling the air. James closed his eyes, inhaling as if he were trying to take in as much of the ocean as he could.

"This is where I used to come when I needed to think,"

he said, his words barely audible over the sound of the waves. "It's always brought me comfort."

We sat with him by the shore as the sun sank into the horizon, painting the sky in shades of pink and orange. It was a simple moment, but it felt like everything—like the past, the present, and the future were all coming together in this one place, in this one moment.

"Thank you," he said, his face filled with emotion. "For being here with me. For giving me this. This was the perfect day."

Mom squeezed his hand, tears streaming down her face. "Thank you for loving my mom and for being there for her when she needed a shoulder to lean on."

We stayed there until the stars began to appear in the sky, the three of us connected by something deeper than blood—by love, by forgiveness, and by the understanding that life is full of twists and turns, and it's never too late to find your way back to where you belong.

THE FOLLOWING MORNING, I AWOKE TO THE PHONE RINGING, cutting through the stillness of the morning. I hesitated for a moment before answering, the familiar name on the screen sending a jolt of anticipation through me.

"Penny," I said, trying to keep my voice steady.

"Hey, it's me." Her voice trembled slightly, as if she were

standing on the edge of something heavy. "I have some news about Grandpa."

I leaned against the kitchen counter, bracing myself. "Is he okay?"

There was a pause, too long and too weighted. "He passed away last night. In his sleep. It was sudden, but... not unexpected."

The words hit me like a punch to the gut, and I felt the world around me blur for a moment. "Oh, Penny. We didn't even get to really know him."

"I'm so sorry. He was so grateful for that time you spent together, you know? It hurts, I think he had been holding on to meet you both."

"I could see that." I fought to hold back my tears, trying to be strong for this stranger—my aunt—who had just lost her father.

"We honor him by being a family. Or at least trying to be one, he would have wanted that."

I took a deep breath, nodding even though she couldn't see me. "You're right. Have you called my mom?

"I wanted to let you know first, I was going to call her next."

"I'll let my mom know. I should be the one to tell her."

"I understand. Come over to the house later, if you're comfortable. The family is gathering, and they are all excited to meet you. You have a lot of cousins who live nearby."

"That will be nice. I wish it was under better circumstances."

"Me too, I wish that more than anything."

As I cradled the phone, I felt the ache in my chest—a mix of gratitude for the moments we shared and a deep sorrow for all that was lost.

CHAPTER 22
Father's Eyes
RANCHO CUCAMONGA, CALIFORNIA
SPRING, 2019

Starla Wylder
Forty-One Years Old

Weeks drifted by, each day a slow march through a thick fog of grief that seemed to settle over us anew. Just when I thought I'd found my footing in the shifting rhythms of our lives, something would inevitably come along to throw everything off balance again. Then, suddenly, the sharp ring of the phone cut through the quiet, yanking me back into the moment.

It was Penny's husband, Rick, his voice strained and urgent. "Starla, I don't know who else to call. Penny's not herself. She won't eat, won't talk. It's like she's given up. I think she needs you and your mom. Maybe seeing you both will help her snap out of this."

My heart sank at the thought of Penny's pain, the sister my mother had only just found, now lost in sorrow. "We'll be there."

As we drove to Rancho Cucamonga, the gravity of the situation settled heavily in the car. I reached across the small SUV to hold my mom's hand. "Thank you for coming with me today. I know this hasn't been easy."

"It's been a lot, when Rick called, I knew we had to try to help," she replied, her grip reassuring.

"It's so strange. Meeting a new grandfather and having a new aunt. Do you think we can ever be a real family?"

"I truly hope so. There's been too much lost time," Mom said steadily.

We arrived at Rick and Penny's house, anxiety coiling in my stomach. Rick opened the door, looking pale and exhausted. "She's really struggling. I don't know what to do."

Mom and I exchanged a glance, bracing ourselves for the emotional storm that awaited us inside. This wasn't only about family ties anymore; it was about reaching out to a woman drowning in grief.

"Thank God you're here. I've tried everything, nothing seems to reach her. She's in bed. Would you like to come see her?" Rick asked.

Mom's expression was determined as she followed Rick down the hallway. The house was quiet, too quiet, and the stillness was heightened by the grief in the air. When we entered the room, my heart broke at the sight before us.

Penny was lying in her bed, her eyes staring blankly at the ceiling, her body curled into a tight ball under the covers. She looked like a shadow of the vibrant woman I'd met not so long ago. Her skin pale, her hair limp, her cheeks hollowed out from days without food. It was as if the grief had consumed her, leaving nothing but a shell behind.

Mom moved first, sitting on the edge of the bed and taking Penny's hand in hers. "Penny? It's Twyla. I'm here. We're here."

There was no response, no flicker of recognition in Penny's eyes. She laid there, lost in her own world of despair.

"Penny," I knelt by the bed, gently massaging her feet. "It's Starla. We've come to see you."

Still, there was nothing. Penny was a million miles away, trapped in the depths of her sorrow. I looked up at Mom, my eyes pleading for guidance, for something that could bring her back to us. Mom's jaw tightened with resolve. "Rick," she said, turning to him with a steely gaze. "What's her favorite food?"

"Uh, Mexican," he replied, his voice trembling. "She loves the chicken tortilla soup from that little place on the corner."

"Good." Mom nodded, standing as she grabbed her phone. "I'll order something. Starla, stay here with her. Keep talking."

I observed her calm determination as she dialed. I turned back to Penny, rubbing slow circles on her arm, hoping the touch would anchor her.

I helped her dress, each motion slow and gentle, like she was waking from a long sleep. She drifted into the bathroom, freshened up, then returned, tentative yet present.

"You didn't have to come," she murmured, embarrassed.

"We're here because we want to be. Let's head to the front room—the food should be here soon."

Just as we made it to the living room, a knock at the door brought us back to reality. The delivery driver handed over warm bags, and Mom paid and accepted them with a quiet, "Thank you," setting them down with steady hands, even though everything else felt shaky.

"Penny," I said, nodding toward the table. "Lunch is here. Come eat with us."

The air filled with the familiar scent of chicken tortilla soup, cutting through the heavy quiet between us. I handed Penny a bowl and spoon as she settled onto the sofa. "Think you can take a little bite?"

Penny took a small, hesitant bite, and then another. I could see the struggle in her eyes, the war between her grief and the part of her that wanted to fight.

We sat there together, coaxing her to eat, to drink, to take small steps back into the world of living. Slowly, she began to gain color in her cheeks. Her eyes grew less vacant, and the weight of her sorrow seemed to lift enough for her to breathe again. Penny's voice was hoarse, barely above a whisper, but it was there. "I can't believe Rick called you."

"Of course he did. We're family. We're going to be there for each other," Mom replied.

"I'm sorry," she choked out, tears spilling down her cheeks. "I'm so sorry."

Mom reached out, wrapping her arms around Penny and holding her tight. "You have nothing to be sorry for."

Penny shook her head, sobs wracking her frail body. "I was so scared," she confessed, her words tumbling out in a rush. "I was afraid it would be too much for him to handle if I went against his wishes. And then, when he got sick. I didn't know what to do, and he's gone. You'll never get to know him."

I reached for her hand, squeezing it gently. "Penny, you did what you thought was best. None of this is your fault."

She looked up at me, her eyes red and swollen. "I should have found you sooner. That day, when you called, he told me he knew he was dying, and all he wanted was to spend one day with you, even if it killed him. One perfect day."

Mom's breath hitched, and she tightened her grip. "Oh Penny."

Penny pulled back slightly, her eyes searching Mom's face. "I wish I could have been a true sister to you. I want to be an aunt to Starla and the girls. We've lost so much time."

I squeezed Penny's hand, my heart swelling with a mix of relief, sadness, and hope. "We're not going anywhere."

Epilogue

NEAH BAY, WASHINGTON

SPRING, 2022

Starla Wylder
Forty-Four Years Old

"I'm so glad to be back in Neah Bay," I said, walking towards Talie and Erin. The crisp March wind tugged at my hair, carrying the scent of salt and pine. "Thanks for inviting us."

"Your grandma would be so happy you're here," she said. "I am, too." Talie responded.

"It's nice to have the reservation opened up after all that COVID business," Erin chimed in, her eyes sparkling in the sunlight. "This ceremony was supposed to happen two years ago, but they decided to postpone the event until after the pandemic. I'm so glad I could come up for this."

We walked along the pebbled shore, where the waves

kissed the land with a rhythmic grace, echoing the silent pulse of the Makah drums in the background. My heart swelled as I looked at my daughters, Brooke and Laney, each a living reflection of the women who came before us. Brooke possessed a quiet grace that reminded me of my grandmother's sister, Franny. In contrast, Laney was all fire and spirit, much like Grandma Dawn.

As we approached the gathering, the importance of this day settled over us. Today, we were here to honor the fiftieth anniversary of the Ozette Archaeological Site's rediscovery.

Neah Bay was a refuge for my ancestors during the Great Depression, a place where the Makah tribe generously welcomed them. This ceremony centered around the opening of a time capsule from the late 1930s, buried during President Franklin D. Roosevelt's visit, and served as a poignant reminder of the ties that bound us to this land and to one another.

Laney's anticipation shone through as she leaned in for a closer look, her eyes wide with curiosity. Beside her, Brooke tried to maintain her usual composure, I caught the flicker of excitement in her gaze as well.

"Be careful, Brooke," Talie's grandson, Kole, said as she stumbled on the uneven ground. His hand shot out to steady her, and a blush crept across her cheeks as she flashed him a shy smile. He didn't let go. His hand enveloped hers as they turned their attention back to the ceremony.

The officials pried open the time capsule, the sound of metal giving way echoed across the gathered crowd. As the lid lifted, treasures from a bygone era were revealed: black-and-white photographs of Roosevelt, handwritten letters full of hope, and intricate Makah carvings, each item a thread in the rich tapestry of our shared history.

An elder from the Makah tribe carefully unveiled the next artifact. It was a Raggedy Ann doll, its fabric worn and its yarn hair still a lustrous, unruly red. He held it up, and a collective breath seemed to be drawn by the crowd.

"Look at this," the elder said, his voice carrying across the silence. He handed the doll to his companion, who carefully examined the faded tag attached to its foot. "Property of Dawn Jensen."

"It's great-grandma's," Brooke uttered, awe filled her eyes. Talie's grandson leaned in closer to her, his grip on her hand tightening slightly.

"It's more than a doll. It's like a connection to your past, to your family. Kinda cool, right?"

Brooke looked up at him, her shyness melting into a smile that spoke of something deeper beginning to take root between them.

The older man and Talie shared a glance, their expressions warm and approving as they observed the two young people in this fragile moment. Talie sat in a place of honor, a living link to history, the only tribal member present who had been alive when the capsule was buried. It was a moment thick with significance, a reminder of how the past intertwined with the present.

After the artifacts were repacked, the ceremony began to

wind down. Laney, Brooke and Talie's grandson stayed close. I noticed the two older kids still had their hands intertwined, as the crowd slowly dispersed. It seemed as if something new was beginning.

I stood in quiet reflection by the shore when, out of the corner of my eye, I saw the unmistakable arch of a whale's back breaking the water's surface. I turned in time to see a pod of gray whales frolicking in the sparkling waters of Neah Bay. Some were large, likely mothers, and others were smaller, their playful calves dancing alongside them.

"It's like they're dancing, Mama," Laney called out, her laughter bubbling over as she watched the whales.

"Yes, they are," I replied, a smile spreading across my face, filled with awe and reverence. "Like us, they're part of this story. Part of these tides of history and future we've come to celebrate today."

The sight of the whales felt like a gift from the sea itself. It was a vivid reminder of the deep connection the Makah has with nature, and of the cycles of life that guide us all.

"I know it was a long trip up to Neah Bay, but this," I said, turning to my daughters and Seb, who had joined us at the shore, "is what makes this whole trip worth it. Seeing these whales together, right here where our family history started. It's like Grandma Dawn is reminding us how connected we are to this place and to each other."

Seb draped his arm around me, his gaze following the whales as they continued their dance. "She's here with us," he said softly. "In the wind, in the waves. In everything."

I nodded, feeling the truth of his words in the depth of my soul. Standing there, with my family by my side, I felt the legacy of my grandmother, the strength of the Makah, and the promise of new generations within my heart. Here in Neah Bay, our stories, our histories, and our futures were forever intertwined, like the enduring tides of the mighty Pacific.

As the whales splashed and played, their joy rippling across the water, I felt the connection between the generations of my family. Everything my grandmother and her family had done to survive during those lean years set a foundation for those who came after them, as my actions and teachings would guide my daughters' lives.

We are all connected.

This journey—this trilogy of love, loss, and discovery— was not only a story of the past, but of the future. As we stood there, watching the whales continue their dance, I knew our family's story would go on, carried forward by the tides of time and the women who came after us.

Authors Note

In 2023, as I neared the end of writing *Every Night Has a Dawn*, a longing pulled at me—a call to Neah Bay, a place deeply woven into my family's history. To understand my grand-mother's life fully, I needed to walk the same paths she once walked. Standing on those shores, surrounded by the familiar scents of salt and red cedar trees, I hoped to capture the essence of her world.

On those shores, I aimed to infuse my novel with the vividness and depth only a personal visit could provide. Once we arrived, I was captivated by the turquoise waters and lush rainforests, where untouched beauty bridged me to the past. Immersing myself in this landscape honored the woman who weathered nearly a century of change, inspiring me in so many ways.

Our first stop was the Makah Cultural Research Center and Museum, where a winter storm had unearthed artifacts buried for centuries. We marveled at intricately woven baskets and dog-hair blankets, remnants of the Ozette archaeological dig. Later that week, my cousin harvested razor clams and recreated my grandmother's century-old fritter recipe, a dish I'd heard about but never tasted. It was as delicious as I'd imagined.

Our next stop was Cape Flattery, where we hiked through the rainforest to reach stunning cliffside views of the Pacific. From the trail's end, we could see the Cape Flattery Lighthouse in the distance, built in 1854—a rare connection to my grandmother's time and the gritty depths of the Depression, when she and her family forged a legacy of resilience and resourcefulness. Their sacrifices paved the way for future generations, including my own.

The highlight of the trip was an unexpected sight: gray whales gracefully swimming in the cold waters, sharing the same peace my grandmother's family once found here. As I navigate an ever-changing world with my daughters, I see the torch my ancestors passed on shining brightly—a beacon of perseverance, courage, and hope that I strive to instill in them every day.

Though this trilogy is a work of fiction, its essence is rooted in pivotal moments from my life. I began writing my debut novel in 2018, drawing inspiration from these key events and weaving a family saga of dynamics, personal growth, and the enduring power of love.

The first spark for this trilogy ignited during the summer of 2017, when my vibrant ninety-year-old grandmother defied the odds and survived a heart attack. Despite the distance between my home in Temecula and Grandma's place, I made frequent visits, cherishing every moment together.

Our bond has always been unique, particularly because I'm the only daughter of one of her daughters. While I have other female cousins from her sons, there's a special magic passed down through the maternal line. From mothers to daughters, we tend to be the keepers of family traditions.

Living across the street from Grandma during my childhood deepened our connection, as I cherished her infectious laughter and the stories she shared about her experiences during the Great Depression and World War II. At times, I wondered if some tales were exaggerated for my benefit, but I later discovered they were not.

One day, shortly after her heart attack, Grandma asked me to locate a box at the top of her closet, brimming with notes, old photographs, and letters. She entrusted me with her dream of writing a novel about her life in Washington State. Fueled by her encouragement, I began writing and shared the first two chapters with her before she slipped away into the great eternal.

Life works in mysterious ways.

A few months before Grandma passed, I received an Ancestry DNA kit from my husband for my birthday. Eager to uncover my heritage, I was shocked when the results revealed a family secret: my mother's biological father wasn't the man who raised her, but the town barber, still alive.

Meeting him and witnessing his emotional reunion with my mother was bittersweet, especially when he passed away just six weeks later, followed soon by Grandma. These revelations reignited my need to write as I tried to process the strong mix of emotions my mother and I were experiencing.

While the first installment of this trilogy honors my grandmother's beautiful spirit, the second novel pays tribute to my extraordinary mother. It explores her sacrifices and resilience as a teen mother, detailing her family's struggles when my uncle was drafted into the Vietnam War. A shadow that shaped her young life.

The book in your hands is also inspired by true events I've experienced, including growing up in the nineties, my time as a flight attendant, falling in love, an around-the-world journey I took in my early twenties, and the kidnapping of my beautiful cousin Stacey in 1990. I've woven these experiences into a fictional narrative that explores resilience, love, and the enduring spirit of family. This story is more than just fiction—it's a reflection of my own journey. I hope you enjoy reading it as much as I've enjoyed bringing it to life.

This leads me to an exciting prequel, *Captive Before Dawn*, set a hundred years before *Every Night Has a Dawn*. This novel takes inspiration from the harrowing experiences of another ancestor, named Captivity, whose mother was abducted by Native Americans in the late 1700s. These real-life events influenced parts of James Fenimore Cooper's *The Last of the Mohicans*. If you're a fan of historical dramas like *1883*, this story will be a must-read. Make sure to check my website ***www.RachelValencourt.com*** and join my newsletter to be notified of its impending release date.

Acknowledgments

First, I must express my deepest gratitude to my husband—my best friend, soulmate, and the love of my life. Who would have thought that catching that wedding bouquet would alter my life forever. Your unwavering belief in me and endless support have shaped the astounding life we've built together. This book wouldn't exist without your inspiration and encouragement.

To my incredible daughters, whose kind hearts and brilliant futures light up my world—I'm so excited to see all that you'll achieve. You inspire me every single day, and I hope my journey shows you that with a touch of passion, a dash of persistence, and a whole lot of faith, your dreams are always within reach.

I owe immense thanks to my parents, who believed in me even when my dreams seemed far out of reach. Your love, feedback, and sacrifices as young parents have been invaluable. I love you both more than words can express.

A big shoutout to my writing coach, Dori Harrell—our

hours spent on Zoom at the start of this journey sharpened not only my skills but my understanding of the craft.

Thank you to my fabulous editors, proofreaders, and typesetter—many of whom are talented authors themselves: Anne Leslie Tuttle, Dawn Baca, Jenna O'Malley, Amanda Collier, Jodi Fodor, and Cindy Roper.

To my wonderful readers and street team—you are the driving force behind this book's success. Your enthusiasm, reviews, and support mean the world to me. I'm beyond grateful for each of you.

Thank you to my Grandmother June—entrusting me with your life's notes and stories has been a gift. This book, and so much of who I am, is a tribute to you. I miss you every single day.

Writing this book was a challenge, but it was also a journey of personal growth, driven by something much bigger than myself. I'm incredibly thankful to my family for your constant love and support, which has been vital in shaping this narrative.

Most importantly, I thank my Heavenly Father for creating me, sustaining me, and loving me, flaws and all.

With all my love and gratitude,

Rachel Valencourt

Cover Design

Lilly Dormishev

Editors

Ann Leslie Tuttle, Jenna O'Malley, Jodi Fodor,
Amanda Collier, Cindy Roper

Format Designer

Dawn Baca

Images

Section and Scene Breaks—Golden Border
Ornament (*Edited*) by Yodafunkyo from Pixabay
Pixabay.com/users/yodafunkyo-9881052/
Pixabay.com/illustrations/golden-border-ornament-design-
4203142/
Chapters— Tattoo Style Flower @ Freepik *Freepik.-*
com/free-vector/old-school-tattoo-style-flower-
bouquet_18305679.htm

Recipe

GRANDMA'S SCONES

Ingredients:

- 2 cups all-purpose flour (spooned and leveled)
- 1/3 cup granulated sugar
- 1 tablespoon baking powder
- 1/2 teaspoon salt
- 6 tablespoons cold unsalted butter, cubed into small pieces (must be cold; freeze for 10 minutes and then grate it with a cheese grater)
- 1/2 cup heavy whipping cream, plus more for brushing the tops
- 1 large egg
- 1 teaspoon pure vanilla extract
- Optional raisins, sultanas or dried fruit of your choice.

How to Make Scones:

1. Set your oven to 400°F. Line a large baking sheet with parchment paper or a silicone baking mat.
2. In a large bowl, whisk together the flour, sugar, baking powder, and salt.
3. Use a cheese grater to grate the cold, cubed butter into the dry ingredients. Mix until the mixture resembles small pea-sized crumbs.
4. In a separate bowl, whisk together the heavy whipping cream, egg, and vanilla extract.

5. Pour the wet ingredients into the dry ingredients and stir until almost fully absorbed. Mixture might be slightly crumbly.

6. On a floured surface, roll the dough into a ball and then flatten it into a circle about 7 inches in diameter. Cut the dough into 8 equal pieces and place them on the prepared baking sheet.

7. Chill (*Optional*): For extra flaky scones, pop the baking sheet in the freezer for 5 to 10 minutes.

8. Lightly whip some heavy cream and brush it over the tops of the scones. If desired, sprinkle coarse sugar on top instead of using the glaze.

9. Bake the scones for 18 to 22 minutes, or until they are fully baked and the tops are golden brown.

10. Cool: Remove the scones from the oven and let them cool to room temperature.

Enjoy your freshly baked scones!

Song List

Most chapter titles in this book are inspired by songs that have touched me at various points in my life. Music has always shaped my emotions and memories, and these titles capture the moods and themes woven into the story. Consider it my tribute to the artists and moments that have made a lasting impact on me.

- **One Day** – Song by Matisyahu (2009)
- **Girls Just Want to Have Fun** – Cyndi Lauper (1983)
- **Policy of Truth** – Depeche Mode (1990)
- **All I Wanna Do** – Sheryl Crow (1994)
- **Don't Want to Miss a Thing** – Aerosmith (1998)
- **Here I Go Again** – Whitesnake (1982)
- **My Kind of Scene** – Powderfinger (2000)
- **How's It Going To Be** – Third Eye Blind (1997)
- **Every Morning** – Sugar Ray (1999)
- **Ocean Eyes** – Billie Eilish (2016)
- **Every Rose Has It's Thorn** – Poison (1988)
- **Torn** – Natalie Imbruglia (1997)
- **Don't Want to Go to London** – Third Eye Blind (1997)
- **Sometimes She Cries** – Warrant (1989)
- **Don't Know What You've Got Until It's Gone** – Cinderella (1988)
- **You're Still The One** – Shania Twain (2007)
- **She Talks to Angels** – The Black Crowes (1990)
- **Losing A Whole Year** – Third Eye Blind (1997)
- **Take Me to the Ocean** – The Movement (2008)
- **My Father's Eyes** – Eric Clapton (1998)

About the Author

Rachel Valencourt is a storyteller at heart and an author by trade. After trading her flight attendant wings for a keyboard, she found a newfound freedom that reshaped her life. With a passion for crafting stories that resonate, she weaves her travel experiences and love for twisty romances into epic family sagas filled with cozy nostalgia and a hint of historical drama.

Her debut novel, *Every Night Has a Dawn*, was honored as a finalist in the American Writing Awards and won the Regal

Summit Award for Historical Fiction. Her second book, *Twilight's Hidden Truth*, recently earned both the Literary Titan and the BookFest Awards for Coming-of-Age Fiction, reinforcing the power her words hold to connect with readers.

Rachel now lives in sunny San Diego County with her British husband, two teenage daughters, and their spirited six-toed cat, Saffy. When she's not writing, she's often exploring new beaches or enjoying a quiet coffee, dreaming up her next adventure.

She shares her writing journey—and the occasional travel mishap—on her blog, where she connects with fellow book lovers and wanderers.

On most social platforms, you'll find her as @RachelValencourt, always eager to hear from readers.

Join Rachel's list to stay updated on the latest news and discover upcoming release dates.
http://eepurl.com/im5WFQ

Drop by her website to check out her latest blog post.
www.rachelvalencourt.com

Social Media Links:

facebook.com/RachelValencourt

x.com/rachelvalencourt

instagram.com/rachelvalencourt

amazon.com/stores/author/B0CK63T7X1

bookbub.com/authors/rachel-valencourt

goodreads.com/rachelvalencourt

Also by Rachel Valencourt

THE WINDS OF CHANGE TRILOGY

Every Night Has A Dawn

Twilight's Hidden Truth

Twilight's Brightest Star